"Listen, about last night..."

As Joe said the words he recognized this was the first time they'd been alone since the kiss the day before. He was acutely aware of it and Hannah seemed just as uncomfortable.

Hannah's gaze flew to his face. "I know, it was a mistake. It was stupid—"

"It wasn't a mistake," he said before he could edit himself. "That wasn't what I was going to say."

"Oh." She was silent for a beat or two. "What were you going to say?"

"Go out with me?"

"But—"

"But what?" He took a step closer.

She looked straight into his eyes. In an instant all the heat from last night was there between them. And the only thing he wanted was a repeat of what they'd done the last time they were alone.

Dear Reader,

I am absolutely honored (and thrilled to bits) to be able to congratulate Harlequin on its 60th anniversary—and from within the pages of a Harlequin book, no less! Harlequin Books holds a very special place in my heart because it was through them that I first discovered my love of romance novels. Both my grandmothers had a stack of Harlequin books, and I couldn't get enough of them as I was growing up.

When I first started writing, someone suggested I should write for Harlequin and I can remember the utter shock I felt. It simply hadn't occurred to me that I could be a part of something I adored so much. Now, several years after having my first book published, I still pinch myself every time I see my name on the cover of a book, and I think about both my grandmothers and thank them all over again for introducing me to the world of romance.

I hope you enjoy *Home for the Holidays.* I got so much out of writing Joe and Hannah's journey to finding each other and understanding what family means. I love to hear from readers, so please drop me a line at sarah@sarahmayberry.com if you feel the urge.

Until next time,

Sarah Mayberry

Home for the Holidays
Sarah Mayberry

TORONTO • NEW YORK • LONDON
AMSTERDAM • PARIS • SYDNEY • HAMBURG
STOCKHOLM • ATHENS • TOKYO • MILAN • MADRID
PRAGUE • WARSAW • BUDAPEST • AUCKLAND

Recycling programs
for this product may
not exist in your area.

ISBN-13: 978-0-373-71599-2

HOME FOR THE HOLIDAYS

Copyright © 2009 by Small Cow Productions Pty Ltd.

www.eHarlequin.com

Printed in U.S.A.

ABOUT THE AUTHOR

Sarah Mayberry is an Australian by birth and a gypsy by career. At present she's living in Auckland, New Zealand, but that's set to change soon. Stay tuned! When she's not writing, she loves reading, cooking and hanging with her friends. Oh, and shoe shopping. Never forget the shoe shopping....

Books by Sarah Mayberry

HARLEQUIN SUPERROMANCE
1551—A NATURAL FATHER

HARLEQUIN BLAZE
380—BURNING UP
404—BELOW THE BELT
425—AMOROUS LIAISONS
464—SHE'S GOT IT BAD

Thanks to *Neighbours* for inspiring this story.

Thanks to Claire and Helen for their wise advice
and thoughts on children.

And thanks, as always, to Chris.
You rock, in every possible way.

And last, but never, ever least, to Wanda.
She knows why.

CHAPTER ONE

"DADDY, DO YOU THINK MOMMY will be able to find us in our new house?"

Joe Lawson paused a moment before answering his daughter's question. Ruby stared at him from her bed, her small, angular face anxious.

"I'll bet Mommy can find us no matter where we are," he said.

"That's what Grandma always says, but I'm not so sure. Melbourne is a long way from Sydney. It took us ages to drive here."

As he struggled to find an answer, Ruby sighed heavily and tugged the covers closer to her chin.

"I guess I'd better go to sleep. School tomorrow. I need to be fresh."

She rolled over onto her side and closed her eyes, apparently completely at peace now that she'd voiced her deeper metaphysical concerns.

The joys of being ten years old. If only he could dismiss her question as easily. Not for the first time, he wondered if he'd done the right thing moving the kids away from everything that was familiar to them so that they could be closer to the support his mother could provide.

Be honest. At least with yourself.

The truth was, he'd been more than happy to abandon the family home.

Pulling Ruby's door shut behind him, he walked up the hall to check on Ben. As he had suspected, Ben was out for the count, his bedroom light still on. Joe watched him for a long moment, noting how thin Ben had become over the past few months thanks to a growth spurt. Soon, his thirteen-year-old son would be able to look Joe in the eye. He tugged the duvet up over Ben's shoulders, flicked the light off then returned to the living room.

Boxes were still piled against the walls, filled with DVDs, books and God only knows what else, since he'd paid professionals to pack the contents of their former home. The kitchen was equally disastrous. In fact, the kids' rooms were the only spaces that were even close to being livable.

He stared at the boxes. He hated moving. Always had. Beth had claimed he was the worst packer in the Southern Hemisphere and always supervised him ruthlessly to ensure he was working up to her standards whenever they moved. He was pretty sure Ben had been conceived the afternoon they were packing to leave the small apartment they'd bought when they married. After a day of being dictated to, he'd rebelled against Beth's bossiness and seduced her on the kitchen floor. She'd been laughing and protesting right up to the moment when he'd tugged her bra down and started kissing her breasts.

He shied away from the memory, as he had from all the other memories that had surfaced during the day. It was impossible not to think about her, though, when he was unpacking the life they'd shared together. The dinner set they'd chosen when they were married. The kids' finger paintings from preschool she'd saved. Even the damned side-by-side fridge reminded him of how excited she'd been the day it was delivered.

It had been two years. Everyone said time was the great healer—so why did he still burn with anger and grief when he thought about his dead wife?

He forced himself to cross the room and slit the tape on the top carton. The boxes weren't going to unpack themselves. He peered inside. Books. Good. Books he could handle.

He'd stacked half the contents onto the shelves of the built-in entertainment unit when he found the photo frame. It had been wrapped in several layers of tissue paper, but he recognized it by feel because of its chunky shape. Beth had made it herself as part of a framing workshop and even though it was just the slightest bit off center, it had always held pride of place on the mantel.

He folded the tissue back and stared at the photo inside the frame. They'd been on a family picnic and Beth had asked a passerby to take the shot. The kids were much younger—Ben eight or so, Ruby only five—and Beth's blond hair was long, well past her shoulders.

He stared into her face. Sometimes he forgot how beautiful she'd been. How could that be when he still missed her like crazy?

His head came up as the low, throbbing rumble of an engine cut through the quiet of the house. A motorbike. A really noisy one. He waited for it to pass by, but the rumble grew louder and louder. Just when it seemed as though the bike was about to race through the living room, it stopped.

Unless he missed his guess, the owner of the world's noisiest motorcycle was also his new neighbor. Which meant he could look forward to the roar of a badly tuned engine cutting into his peace morning, noon and night.

"Great."

There ought to be a rule when a person bought a new

house: full disclosure. The vendors should have to reveal everything about the house and the neighbors so there weren't any nasty surprises on moving day. Leaky roofs, yapping dogs, motorcycle gang neighbors, Peeping Toms.

It seemed unnaturally quiet after the racket of the bike. He put the frame to one side. He'd find a place for it later. He reached for more books, then tensed as the motorbike started up again. He gritted his teeth, waiting for the bike to roar off into the night. It didn't. Instead, the engine revved again and again, the sound so loud he guessed the guy must be parked inside his garage, the roller door open, the sound amplified by the space.

Over and over the bike revved and Joe grew more and more tense. His kids were asleep, but they wouldn't stay that way for long if this kept up. Surely the moron next door must have some idea that this was a residential neighborhood, a quiet middle-class suburb full of quiet, middle-class people who liked a little peace at the end of the day? Surely—

"For Pete's sake!"

He slammed the box shut. He was barefoot, but he didn't bother putting shoes on, simply threw open the front door and headed next door. As he'd guessed, the garage was open, light spilling out into the night. A motorbike stood propped on its stand toward the rear of the garage. A man squatted beside it, his back to Joe as he worked on something near the exhaust pipe.

Joe stopped on the threshold as he registered the guy's leather pants and long hair and the Harley-Davidson jacket thrown over the rusty frame of a second bike. It was every bit as bad as he'd suspected—he'd moved in next to a long-haired redneck. No doubt Joe had noisy, boozy parties, visits from the cops and loud domestic arguments to look forward to in the future.

Fantastic. Just what he goddamn needed.

"Hey, buddy, you want to keep it down?" he yelled over the roar of the bike.

The guy didn't even lift his head from whatever he was doing. Joe took a step closer.

"Mate!" he yelled. "You want to shut that thing off?"

Still nothing. Joe's temper began to burn. He didn't consider himself a short-fuse kind of guy, but he was tired and unpacking all the old stuff was tough and he needed this added aggravation like a hole in the head.

He strode forward and reached over the guy's shoulder for the ignition key. One twist and the bike fell silent. The guy jerked in surprise, then shot to his feet and spun around.

Joe took an involuntary step backward as he realized that he'd miscalculated somehow. The leather jacket, the pants, the bike. He'd just assumed...

But he'd been wrong. Because his new neighbor was a *she,* not a he.

Her chin came up as she stared at him.

"Who the hell are you?"

She was tall—almost his height—with brown eyes and long, wavy brown hair.

He frowned. "I'm sorry. I thought... I called out but you couldn't hear me over the engine. I came to ask you to keep the noise down. My kids are asleep."

She blinked at him, then he saw comprehension dawn in her face.

"You're the guy who bought the Steveway place," she said.

"Yeah."

She tucked a strand of hair behind her ear. His gaze dropped to her breasts, then her waist. She had a good figure. Long legs, full breasts.

He looked away. He didn't care what kind of figure she had.

"I didn't realize you'd moved in," she said. "The Steveways were happy for me to work on my bike anytime."

"Then they must have been deaf."

He knew he sounded like a cantankerous old man but he couldn't seem to help himself. Her being a woman had thrown him off balance, one too many curveballs on what had already been a trying day.

"It isn't usually this noisy," she said. "There's a problem with the muffler."

"Maybe you should leave it to the experts to fix, then."

Her eyes narrowed. "Thanks for the advice. I know just what to do with it."

He'd pissed her off. Seemed only fair, since she'd roused him out of his home with her racket.

"So you'll pack it in for the night?"

"Like I said, I didn't know you'd moved in."

She put her hands on her hips and her T-shirt stretched over her breasts. Again he pulled his gaze away.

"Thanks, I appreciate the consideration," he said flatly.

He turned away.

"Welcome to the neighborhood," she called after him as he walked down the drive. She sounded about as sincere as he had when he'd thanked her.

He stopped in his tracks when he reached the privacy of his own driveway, a frown on his face, aware that he'd overreacted and not sure why. He stood there for a long moment, breathing in the cool night air. Then he shook off his unease and returned to his sleeping children.

WHAT A JERK.

Hannah Napier pushed her hair off her forehead then grimaced when she remembered her hands were greasy.

She wiped her hands on a rag then hit the button to close the roller door. She'd wanted to get to the bottom of the noisy muffler tonight, but it could wait until tomorrow. The last thing she needed was Mr. High and Mighty on the doorstep again with his attitude and impatience.

She'd met some chauvinistic assholes in her time, but her new neighbor was going to take some beating. The way he'd spoken to her like she was one of his kids. The way he'd dismissed her with a quick once-over of his very blue eyes.

He'd almost given her a heart attack, sneaking up on her the way he had. She'd turned around and seen six foot plus of solid man standing over her and almost wet her pants. And not in a good way.

Not that he was unattractive. He had short, dark hair, and his face was deeply tanned. His shoulders were broad, his belly flat. Not bad, if your taste ran to bad-tempered, bossy men. She put him at mid- to late thirties, then she remembered the deep lines that bracketed his mouth and the hardness in his blue eyes and upped her estimate to early forties. He'd been around the block a time a two, her new neighbor. Probably managed to piss off everyone he met along the way, too.

So much for her mother's hopes that the new owner of number twenty-four would be nice. Hannah grabbed her jacket and flicked off the lights as she used the connecting door to enter the house. Her work boots sounded loud on the tiled kitchen floor as she crossed to the fridge.

"Is that you, love?" her mother, Robyn, called from the living room.

"Yeah, Mom."

"Your dinner's in the fridge. And there's dessert, too, if you want it."

Hannah sighed. No matter how many times she told her mom not to cook for her, inevitably she came home to find a meal in the fridge, neatly covered with cling wrap. When she'd moved in with her mother six months ago, she'd done so on the basis that she wouldn't be a burden. She should have known that her mother would fight tooth and nail to defend her right to wash Hannah's dirty laundry and cook her meals. It was what her mother had always done, and it had been foolish to even think that things would be different because Hannah was twenty-eight now and had been living independently for nearly six years.

"Did you notice the lights on next door? The new neighbors have moved in."

"Yeah, I noticed." Hard not to when her new neighbor had just read her the riot act.

Hannah took the plate of chicken and salad to the living room and sat next to her mom.

"This looks great, Mom. Thanks."

Her mother dismissed her gratitude with the wave of a hand and leaned forward, her brown eyes dancing.

"So, don't you want to know?"

"Know what?"

"What he's like. The new neighbor. And you'll note I say *he*," her mother said.

"I don't need to know. I just met him."

"Really?" Her mother almost leaped off the couch. "How? Did he come over and introduce himself?"

"He was pissed about the noise, actually. Came over to give me a piece of his mind."

"That doesn't sound like a very promising start."

Hannah bit into a chicken leg, shrugging a shoulder. "Who cares? He's a dick," she said around a mouthful of food.

"Hannah! I thought he seemed very nice when I popped in earlier. His mother was helping him unpack, you know, and there was no sign of a wife."

Hannah scooped up a spoonful of potato salad. She could feel her mother watching her, waiting for Hannah's reaction. She concentrated on her plate, hoping her mother would get the hint.

"You didn't think he was good-looking?" her mother asked after a long pause.

Hannah put down her fork. "Mom. Give it up."

"All I want to know is if you think he's attractive."

She wanted a lot more than that but Hannah decided the best way to defuse this conversation was to answer the question and move on.

"I thought he was sad looking, if you must know. I thought he was about the saddest-looking man I've ever met," Hannah said. Those lines by his mouth, those hard blue eyes. All that anger bubbling just below the surface.

"Oh. Do you think?"

Hannah shook her head in frustration. "It doesn't matter, Mom. He could be Brad bloody Pitt and I wouldn't be interested. You know that."

Her mother eyed her steadily, her face creased with concern. "Don't be like this, sweetheart."

Hannah stood. There was no way she could eat the rest of her meal. She certainly couldn't endure another heart-to-heart with her mother.

"I need a shower. Thanks for cooking."

She scraped the remainder of her dinner into the garbage, rinsed her plate and slid it into the dishwasher. She spent ten minutes in the shower, washing and conditioning her hair and shaving under her arms. All the while, she reviewed the work she had tomorrow, prioritizing things on her to-do list. Anything to avoid thinking about what her mother had been suggesting.

As if she was going to start dating again. What a joke.

A towel wrapped turban style around her hair and another around her torso, she made her way to her bedroom. She stopped in her tracks when she saw the long white box on her bed. A receipt was taped to the front of it, along with a note from her mother.

> H, the dry cleaners called again today. They said if you didn't pick your dress up soon they'd consider it un-claimed goods and sell it. I knew you wouldn't want that.
> Mom.

Hannah circled the box as though it was a wild animal. Even though she told herself she didn't want to look, that it didn't matter to her anymore, that it was all in the past, she reached out and slowly folded back the lid.

Intricate crystal beading sparkled in the overhead light. Her gaze ran over the shaped bodice, the pleating at the waist. The white silk skirt shimmered and she couldn't resist running a hand over it. She could remember the first time she'd seen the dress, the way it had felt sliding over her body when she put it on—cool and slippery and perfect. As though it had been made for her.

Anger rose in a hot flash. She shoved the box so hard it slid off the other side of the bed. She'd paid a small fortune to have it packed in acid-free tissue, but she didn't want it in her room. It was too pathetic—a wedding dress that had never been worn. Too, too sad.

She had a sudden vision of herself taking the box out into the yard, dousing it with gas and setting it on fire. All that pristine silk would burn bright and long. It would be good watching it all go up in smoke. Cleansing.

Almost, she was tempted, but she knew her mom would

freak. Not to mention that it would be a huge waste of money. If she put the dress on eBay, there was a fair chance she could make back some of her money on the damned thing. After all, it had never been worn. That had to be a selling point, right?

She took a deep breath, then rounded the bed to pick up the box. The truth was, she didn't have the luxury of burning her wedding dress. Every dollar she could scrape together got her closer to her goal of being debt-free. And once she was debt-free, she could start planning for her around-Australia trip and get out of here once and for all. Leave it all behind her—the wedding-that-never-was, Lucas, Kelly, all of it.

She laid the box on the floor in the corner and sat on the end of her bed. More than anything she wanted to be gone. If she could close her eyes and make it so right now, she would. She wanted the road unrolling before her and the wind in her hair and nothing holding her back. She certainly didn't want to be sitting in her old bedroom, surrounded by her teenage memorabilia, living this life of quiet endurance and survival.

For a dangerous moment, tears threatened.

She stood and reached for the freshly washed jeans her mother had left folded in a pile on the end of the bed. Three minutes later she was fully dressed and tugging her work boots back on. Her hair was wet, but she didn't care. She could hear the television in the living room as she crossed the kitchen, but she didn't bother telling her mom she was going out. She would only want to know why, and Hannah wasn't up to fabricating an excuse for bailing again so soon after coming home.

In the garage, she tugged her jacket and helmet on then hit the button to raise the roller door. She was about to start the bike when she remembered the fun police next door.

She swore under her breath. For a moment she was tempted to start the bike anyway, then she recalled what he'd said about his kids sleeping. She rolled the bike down the drive and down the street, resenting every step. When she reached the corner, she slung her leg over the saddle. The engine started with a dull roar. She pushed down the visor on her helmet, leaned forward and opened the throttle.

She had no idea where she was going. As long as it wasn't here, she figured it would be good enough.

CHAPTER TWO

"I DON'T WANT TO GO to school. Why can't I stay here with you and help you unpack?"

Ruby's face was beseeching as she looked at Joe across the breakfast table. He'd had a poor night's sleep and a headache building in the back of his skull but he did his best to give his daughter the reassurance she needed.

"I know starting a new school is scary, but once the first day is over you'll be fine."

"I don't want to go." Ruby pushed away her half-finished bowl of cereal.

She looked so small and defenseless sitting there. He stood and circled the table, squatting beside her chair.

"It's going to be okay, I promise," he said. He put his arms around her and pulled her close. She smelled of strawberries and talcum powder and she felt about as substantial as a baby bird in his arms. She burrowed her face against his chest, rubbing her cheek against his shirt.

"I want to stay with you," she said, her arms clinging to him.

He laid his cheek against her head and remembered the fierce, adventurous little girl she'd been only a couple of years ago.

"I'm not going anywhere," he said, drawing back so he could look into her face. She stared at him unblinkingly. "I promise I'll be waiting at the school gate the moment you step out the door at three o'clock."

She didn't say a word, but a small frown wrinkled her forehead.

"How about this? We'll make pizzas for dinner, from scratch like the old days," he said. "That way you've got something to look forward to all day."

Mastering the art of making pizza dough had been his one culinary achievement, and every Thursday night it had been a family tradition for Beth to put her feet up while he made the bases and the kids took charge of the toppings.

Ruby was silent for a long moment. Just when he was beginning to think he'd made a mistake suggesting they revive the tradition, Ruby smiled.

"Can I have three types of cheese on mine?"

Joe smoothed a hand over her fine blond hair, tucking a strand behind her ear. "Deal," he said.

"Okay, then I guess I can go to school."

Joe looked up as Ben entered the kitchen, his backpack already on his shoulders.

"Can I have some money for lunch?" Ben asked, hands dug into his pockets. His gaze shifted around the kitchen, not settling on anything.

"Have you had breakfast yet?" Joe asked.

"Yes."

Joe hadn't noticed a bowl or plate in the sink, but he had no reason to think his son was lying.

"I thought we could pick up some sandwiches from the coffee shop on the way to school," Joe said.

He planned to get to the supermarket sometime this afternoon so he could make their lunches from here on in, but today he was winging it.

Ben frowned. "I don't want to be dropped off."

"Well, tough. It's your first day. I want to make sure you

know where you're going." Joe said it with a smile but Ben's frown deepened.

"I already know where to go. I'm not stupid. I can work it out for myself."

"I know you can, but it won't be the end of the world to have a bit of help on your first day."

Ben pushed away from the counter, hands fisted by his sides. "I don't need help. I don't want it."

Joe stared at his son. Where had this sudden rush of anger come from? "Mate—"

"I'm walking to school," Ben said defiantly.

He stalked from the room. Joe sighed. Ruby was watching him expectantly.

"You should go after him," she advised.

"Thank you, Miss Bossy Boots, I was about to do that."

She grinned as he moved past her and into the hallway. He pulled up short when he saw Ben wasn't in his room. He checked out the window and, sure enough, Ben was on his way down the driveway.

Joe exited the house and took the porch steps two at a time. "Ben!"

His son had reached the street and he paused, turning toward the house. He looked half afraid, half determined.

"What about a compromise? I'll drop you off up the block and you can walk the rest of the way on your own. How does that sound?" Joe suggested.

Ben shrugged, his mouth a tight line. Joe studied him, trying to understand what was going on. Was this simple first-day nerves? A reaction to the move?

"Is there something wrong, matey? Something on your mind?" he asked.

Ben screwed up his face in utter rejection of the idea. "No! Why would there be?"

Joe ran a hand through his hair. "It's just we've had a lot happening lately. Selling the house, saying goodbye to everyone, moving."

Ben shrugged. "So?"

Joe watched him for a beat, but Ben simply stared back, his face blank.

"Okay. Come inside while I get your sister ready," Joe said.

He managed to get them both to school on time without further incident but his gut was churning as he pulled away from Ruby's school.

This is my fault. I shouldn't have moved them. I should have taken Mom up on her offer to sell her place here and move to Sydney.

His hands tightened on the steering wheel. It wasn't as though he could undo the move. They were here now, they'd all have to make the best of it.

He checked his watch. If he hustled, there was just enough time for him to check out a few car dealerships before he was due at his lawyer's office. He'd bought their current sedan to replace the car Beth had been killed in, but for some time now he'd been thinking about getting something bigger. An SUV, or a wagon, maybe. Something that could absorb all of the kids' paraphernalia and still have room to spare.

He was taking a shortcut through the local Elsternwick shopping district on his way to the commercial strip along the Nepean Highway when he passed a shiny black SUV on the side of the road. He slowed when he saw the big For Sale sign in the back window. It was parked in front of an automotive garage and Joe hesitated a moment before pulling to the curb. Why the hell not, after all? Might as well see what the private market was offering before he hit the big car lots.

The SUV was a Mazda, only two years old with shiny alloy wheels. He did a lap of the car, peering in the window, checking out the panels. It was in good condition and a sign resting on the dashboard claimed that the car had been serviced since new at the garage and came with full records.

Joe turned toward the open bay of the workshop. A blue sedan was up on the hoist inside, a red coupe parked beside it. A middle-aged guy in grease-stained overalls was frowning at the underbelly of the sedan. Tinny radio music bled out into the street. The workshop floor was spotlessly clean, the walls freshly whitewashed. A promising start.

"Hey," Joe said, walking forward. "Have you got five minutes to talk me through the Mazda out the front?"

The man shook his head. "No point talking to me, mate. You need Hannah. She's the manager." He jerked his head toward the other car and for the first time Joe noted a pair of legs sticking out from beneath the front of the coupe.

Right. A female mechanic. Apparently it was his week for finding women where he least expected them. In motor-cycle leathers, beneath cars.

He moved closer to the coupe and squatted to make himself heard over the radio. "Excuse me. Any chance you could take me over the Mazda? I'm in the market for an SUV."

"Sure. Give me a sec to tighten this sump plug… There we go."

No sooner had she spoken than the mechanic slid out from beneath the car. He tensed. It was the woman from last night, the noisy biker with the attitude. She was smiling, but the smile froze on her face when she saw him. He wondered if his own surprise was as obvious.

There was a long moment of taut silence.

"Well, are you going to say it or am I?" she finally said. She was still on her back on the mechanics' trolley. He hadn't noticed last night, but she had incredibly plump lips, the bottom lip rounded and full. Her sun-streaked brown hair was pulled back into a high ponytail, leaving her smooth cheekbones and small chin to speak for themselves. He'd noticed her curves last night, but it hit him suddenly that she was a very attractive woman.

"I guess it's up to me, then," she said. Her tone was heavy with irony when she next spoke. "We really have to stop meeting like this."

Because she'd caught him off balance again, his first instinct was to retreat. He stood, sliding his hands into the front pockets of his jeans.

"I wanted to look at the car," he said stiffly.

She wiped her hands down the legs of her coveralls and pushed herself to her feet. He'd forgotten how tall she was. It was one of the reasons he'd been so startled to realize she was a woman last night—she'd been looking him almost squarely in the eye when she'd straightened and her face had been inches from his until he'd taken a step backward.

Now, she held his eye as she offered her hand.

"Hannah Napier," she said coolly.

Joe stared at her hand a second before taking it. "Joe Lawson."

Her hand was warm, her fingers firm. Her mouth quirked up into a lopsided, wry smile.

"Look at that—almost civilized."

She turned toward the parking lot and started walking. Of its own accord, his gaze dropped to check out her body. More specifically, her ass. It was pure instinct, imbedded in him since puberty, and as soon as he registered what he was doing he looked away—but not before he'd noticed she had a full, sweetly curved backside.

"It's two years old, one owner since new. I don't normally

do this but he's a good friend and I wanted to help him out," Hannah said.

Joe lengthened his stride to come abreast of her as they neared the car. "Why's he selling?"

"Scored an overseas job. It's a good car. Bit greedy with gas, but safe, solid. You've got kids, right? There are built-in anchors for car seats."

He didn't bother telling her his kids were well out of car seats. No point extending this encounter any longer than it needed to be.

"What's he asking?"

"Thirty. It's forty-five new, so it's a good deal. Full leather upholstery, six-stacker CD. Cruise control, tiptronic transmission…" She glanced at him to check he was paying attention and his gaze got caught on the line of her cheek-bone.

"Is this the model with the turbocharger?" he asked.

"Yep. It's got it all. Like I said, it's a good deal."

She lifted a hand to smooth it down the length of her pony tail and the neckline of her coverall gaped. He caught a glimpse of shadowy cleavage and white lace.

He took a step backward, frowning. He'd seen more than enough here.

"Right. Thanks for your time. I've really only started looking but I'll keep this in mind," he said politely.

She looked surprised. "You don't want to take it for a test drive, see how it handles?"

He made a big deal out of checking his watch. "I've got an appointment I don't want to be late for."

"Well, we're open till five if you want to come back later."

He nodded, already drawing his car keys from his pocket. Her eyes narrowed and she propped a hand on her hip.

"Be honest. You're not coming back, are you?" she asked.

He frowned.

"Right. Let me guess—you don't trust me," she said, contempt in every line of her body. "What could a woman possibly know about cars, right? What was it you said last night? *Leave it to the experts?* Was that it?"

She was bristling with aggression, her chin high. As he'd thought when he first set eyes on her, she was trouble with a capital *T*.

"Like I said, I've just started looking."

A muscle flickered in her jaw, then she swung back toward the car. As though he hadn't announced he needed to leave, she started talking.

"Tires have got another two years in them, depending on the kind of mileage you do. Suspension is independent, double-wishbone at the back. Brakes are discs all round, and it's fitted with ABS. It's a six cylinder, and with the turbocharger you're looking at zero to one hundred in about 9.8 seconds."

She moved to the front of the car. He remained where he was, arms crossed over his chest. She stopped and looked at him, defiance shining in her eyes.

Stubborn. And a pain in the ass to boot.

"Not real good at taking no for an answer, are you?" he said.

Something flickered in her eyes, then her face went utterly blank.

"You'd be surprised." She shifted her attention to the car for a second, then back to him. "You won't find a better car for the money."

It was possible she was right, of course.

"I'll think about it," he said again. He dipped his head in acknowledgment and walked toward his car. He could feel her watching him all the way, the awareness like a prickle on the back of his neck. Yet when he got to his car and glanced over his shoulder she had already disappeared into the workshop.

Right.

He gave himself a mental shake. He needed to get going if he still wanted to check out the commercial car lots before meeting his lawyer. Then there was the grocery shopping to do, and the last of the unpacking—all before the kids were out of school at three.

He started the car and threw it into gear. As he had last night, he pushed his encounter with Hannah Napier out of his mind. She was nothing to him, the barest blip on his radar. Less.

Still, he glanced back one last time before he drove away, but Hannah was nowhere in sight.

HANNAH WAS SUPPOSED to catch up with her friend Mikey for dinner after work, but he canceled on her at the last minute, leaving her at loose ends. She figured she'd head home instead and put in some hours fixing the muffler on the bike—quietly, of course. No doubt Joe Lawson would come after her with an elephant gun or a lynch mob if she dared disturb his peace again.

The memory of his dismissive attitude over the car had risen up to bite her on the ass all day. How she hated narrow-minded men like him. She'd seen it over and over—the cautious look in their eyes, the doubt as they listened to her tell them what was wrong with their cars. As though having breasts made her less qualified to understand the workings of the internal combustion engine. Please.

She was hungry and more than ready for a shower when she rode into the street. She stopped short of pulling into her mother's garage, however, her attention caught by the car sitting in Joe Lawson's driveway—a Mazda SUV, same model as the one she'd shown him today, dark navy instead of black. She switched off her bike and kicked the stand out before dismounting. She tugged her helmet off as she walked the distance from her mother's front yard to inspect the car. So much for *I've just started looking*. She'd been absolutely right—he hadn't been able to bring himself to buy a car from her.

She narrowed her eyes as she surveyed the rear of the SUV, then dropped into a squat to peer under the wheel arch. She did a slow lap, squatting once again when she reached the left rear wheel arch, craning her neck to confirm her suspicion.

"I assume you won't be billing me for the inspection?"

She started, then glanced over her shoulder. Joe Lawson stood there, one eyebrow raised. Her gaze dropped to his bare feet. No wonder she hadn't heard him sneak up on her.

"Did you get a warranty on this thing?" she asked, standing and jerking a thumb toward the car.

He crossed his arms over his chest but didn't say a word.

"I'm only asking because you're going to need it. This car's been in an accident," she said.

He glanced toward the Mazda. "It's been fully inspected by the automotive association."

"Which just confirms my opinion of those idiots." She gestured toward the wheel arch. "Take a look yourself. Something big ran into the back of this thing, ripped the chassis open. It's been welded back together, but you can see the repair if you look closely. And the shock absorbers are all new. No one puts new shocks on a two-year-old car unless they have to."

His hands dropped to his sides. He looked annoyed. Then, as though he couldn't help himself, he knelt beside the car and craned his neck to see under the wheel well. She knelt beside him and leaned in to point out the line of the weld.

"They've driven around a bit to dirty it up some, but you can still see it there."

"Shit," he said, so low she almost didn't hear him.

He was so close his shoulder brushed hers when he shifted his weight. She stilled, then stood, dusting her hands down her jeans.

"It's not going to fall apart or anything, but you'll probably have issues with panel fit and rattles. Once a car's bent out of whack, it's almost impossible for them to get it straight again even when they put it on the rack."

He stood. "I suppose I should thank you for sharing your expertise," he said grudgingly. She could tell it hurt.

"That's very gracious of you," she said dryly.

He crossed his arms over his chest again and widened his stance, as though he needed to brace himself for what came next.

"Thank you," he said more sincerely. "I really do appreciate the heads-up."

She smiled. She couldn't help herself. He was so damned truculent, like a surly teenage boy being forced to apologize. "Don't mention it. It was my pleasure."

He raised an eyebrow and she shrugged a shoulder as if to say, "Hey, what did you expect?"

"You should take it back," she said, turning to look at the car one last time. "Most of those big dealerships have cooling-off clauses in their contracts. Tell them you don't appreciate being ripped off and make them give your money back."

His chin lifted a little—not much, but enough to tell her that there was no way he was taking the car back. Not now that she'd told him to.

She could almost admire him for his dedication to his own point of view. Almost.

"Suit yourself," she said.

"Oh, don't worry, I will," he said. He beeped the car open, then reached into the back and collected a grocery bag. For the first time she noticed the long, curling scar that ran from the base of his left thumb, around the back of his hand and up his strongly muscled forearm to disappear beneath the pushed-up sleeve of his sweater. Where on earth did a man get a scar like that?

It hadn't occurred to her before to wonder what he did for a living, or why he'd moved into the neighborhood, but suddenly both questions were on the tip of her tongue. She bit down on them. As though he was going to answer anything she asked him when she'd made him look like a fool. She might not be an expert on men, but she knew that much.

He shut the back of the car with a firm click. The grocery bag rustled in his hand. She realized she was hovering for no good reason whatsoever.

"Anyway," she said.

"Yeah."

"See you around."

He didn't bother responding. She could imagine what he was thinking, though: *not if I can help it.*

He headed toward his house. She watched his shoulders rock from side to side with his long stride, then her gaze dropped to his butt. His jeans were faded and soft and they molded his ass faithfully. It was a good ass, too. Firm-looking, round. Quintessentially male.

Hannah registered what she was doing and swiveled on her heel. Who cared if he had a nice ass? It was attached to the rest of him, and that was arrogant and pigheaded and not-so-nice.

Still, she'd more than put him in his place tonight. He might have won this morning's skirmish, but tonight's battle was definitely hers.

Grinning, she headed into the house. Score: one all.

She was still smiling when she pushed open the connecting door from the garage and entered the kitchen. She could hear voices and guessed her mother was already in front of the TV, watching her soaps. Hannah rounded the corner, ready to regale her with the story of her two encounters with Joe Lawson.

"Hey, Mom, guess what just—" The rest of the words died in her throat when she saw who was with her mother. "What are you doing here?"

Her sister stood abruptly and smoothed a hand down her skirt.

"I was just going," Kelly said. She was very pale and her hands were shaking.

Hannah felt sick. She hadn't seen Kelly in months, not since the last confrontation when her sister had begged Hannah to forgive her, to understand, and Hannah had told her she couldn't.

Kelly started gathering her bag and coat.

"Hold on a minute," their mother said. She put a hand on Kelly's arm. Hannah looked at it, then at her mother. "Kelly is visiting me, that's what she's doing here. She's my daughter, too, Hannah, and I need to see her and know how she's doing, just as I need to know how you're doing."

Bile burned at the back of Hannah's throat. How long had this been going on? How long had her mother been comforting her sister behind her back? Didn't Kelly have enough attention and love and adoration in her life?

Without a word, Hannah turned and started for her bedroom.

"Hannah." It was Kelly, her voice high with tension.

Hannah kept walking. She had nothing to say to her sister. Nothing that hadn't been said before, anyway.

"I came to talk about the apartment. We both feel really bad about you taking a loss on the sale. Please let us make it up to you," her sister called after her.

Hannah shoved her door closed, the echo of the slam loud in the small room. Arms folded over her chest, hands gripping her elbows, she crossed to the window and glared out at the backyard.

She couldn't believe her mother had been offering comfort to the enemy, and she couldn't believe her sister was still trying to foot the bill for the sale of the apartment she'd once owned with Lucas. It had been Hannah's place, hers and Lucas's. *Their* home, not her sister's. Kelly had had nothing to do with picking the decor, choosing the furniture, deciding which part of town they wanted to live in. Hannah was damned if she was going to let her sister reimburse her for her losses because she and Lucas had been forced to sell in a bad market. Kelly had stolen Lucas, stolen the dreams Hannah had had for her future with the man she loved. But Kelly couldn't take this one small thing away from Hannah: if it killed her, Hannah would pay off her share of the remainder of the mortgage, no matter what. Just to prove to herself and the world that it had happened, that it had mattered. That for a whole year and a half, Lucas Hall had been hers and not her sister's.

There was a tap on the door. Hannah tightened her grip on her elbows. If her sister dared to walk through the door…

"Hannah, it's me," her mother called.

"I don't want to talk."

"Fine, but you can still listen."

The door opened and her mother entered. Her expression was determined. "I think you should seriously think about your sister's offer."

Hannah made a disgusted noise. "Surprise, surprise."

Her mother held up a hand. "Listen for a minute, will you? You've been planning this trip around Australia for months. Years, really, since you put it off when you first met Lucas. If you take up your sister's offer, you can go now. I know that's what you want, what will make you happy. Why not do it?"

"Because I won't let her buy her way out of her guilt," Hannah said. Her sister had always made more money than Hannah in her high-end IT job. Kelly's yearly bonuses alone were sometimes triple Hannah's salary as a mechanic. Even with the global financial downturn Kelly was still hauling it in hand over fist.

"I don't think that's why she wants to do it. She wants you to be happy," her mother said.

"Then she shouldn't have stolen my fiancé."

"Would you really want to be married to a man who was in love with another woman? Do you think your sister should have stepped aside and let that happen, Hannah?"

"It should never have even been an issue. She's my sister and he was my fiancé. The thought should never even have entered her head."

"Or his head. But it did. Sometimes you can't stop yourself from falling in love with someone, sweetheart."

"Bullshit! I don't want to hear this, Mom. And I'm not taking her money. It was *my* apartment. Mine and Lucas's. I'll pay for my fair share of what's left of the mortgage. She can't take that away from me."

Her mother shook her head. "My God, you always were a stubborn one."

"Yeah, that's me—stupid, loyal, stubborn old Hannah." Her voice broke on the last word and her mother stepped forward, hand extended. Hannah jerked away from her. She was angry with her mother, unfairly or not. Kelly had hurt her, betrayed her utterly. It felt like a further betrayal to learn that her mother had been seeing her sister all these months behind Hannah's back.

"I need to work on my bike," Hannah said.

CHAPTER THREE

HANNAH DIDN'T STOP WALKING until she was safely in the garage, breathing in the smell of damp concrete and engine grease. She sank onto her upright tool chest, pressing her hands to her face. For a moment she was so angry and sad she could barely breathe.

I'm so sick of this. I'm so sick of feeling this way.

The problem was, she didn't know what to do with her anger. She'd thought that not seeing Kelly or Lucas for all these months would have made a difference, taken some of the heat out of her feelings. But she'd only had to look into her sister's perfectly made-up face to feel it all surging back. That, and seeing the pity in her mother's eyes...

Of course, her mother wasn't the only one who felt sorry for poor, jilted Hannah. It had practically become a national pastime once the wedding had been canceled. Their family, all of her and Lucas's friends, the neighbors, her customers—they'd all offered their condolences and shaken their heads. After all, it wasn't every day that a tomboyish older sister was cast aside for her younger, more glamorous, more beautiful sister. It was a classic tale of woe and everyone could relate. And more than anything—perhaps even more than the pain of betrayal and loss—Hannah resented being cast as a victim. It wasn't until her life had crashed around her ears that she'd understood how much pride she took in her independence and her unusual vocation and her own unique, take-no-prisoners view of the world. And now, thanks to Kelly and Lucas, she was simply poor Hannah, victim. Object of pity and sympathy.

And right now she was acting exactly like a victim, wallowing in her own messy emotional soup. No wonder her mother felt sorry for her.

Hannah surged to her feet and crossed to her bike. There was still an hour or so of daylight left and she might as well use it while she attempted to fix the muffler. Seizing the handlebars, she rocked the bike off its stand and pushed it down the driveway. After propping it on its stand again, she went back for her toolbox.

She deliberately focused on what she was doing, on what she needed to do next as she worked, and slowly she calmed. Later, she would apologize to her mother. Hannah knew she hadn't exactly been a dream to live with the past six months, and although she burned every time she thought about her mother listening sympathetically to her sister, she knew it was her mother's right to do what she thought was best. And Hannah was the first person to admit she was hardly unbiased in this situation.

Her stomach rumbled with hunger but she wasn't ready to go in yet. Instead, she grabbed a beer from the bar fridge she kept in the garage and palmed a handful of peanuts from the jar on the workbench. She'd downed half the beer when she became aware that someone was watching her.

She glanced across into a pair of big, intent blue eyes.

"What's wrong with it?" the little girl asked, toes hanging over the edge of the curb as she hovered near the bike.

Hannah had never been very good at guessing kids' ages, but the girl was small and skinny with a delicate, pointed face and Hannah figured she must be about eight or nine. Her very blond hair was caught up on either side of her head in pigtails, and her top featured lots of sparkles and stars in various colors of pink. When she clasped her hands in front of her tummy, Hannah saw her nails were painted with glitter polish.

"There's a hole in the muffler. I'm about to patch it," Hannah said.

"What's a muffler?" the little girl asked, taking a step closer.

Hannah pointed to the round tube at the head of the exhaust pipe. "It's this part here, in front of the exhaust pipe."

"What does it do when it's not broken?" She took another step.

Hannah could see the girl was aching to touch the shiny red finish on the gas tank and she nodded encouragingly. "It's okay, you can touch it."

"It's so shiny," the little girl said, glitter-tipped fingernails gliding over the paint.

"The muffler is supposed to stop the engine from sounding so loud," Hannah said, answering the girl's earlier question. She tapped the motor. "When the bike is going, there's a whole lot of noisy stuff going on in here, and the sound has to escape somewhere. The muffler is supposed to turn the volume down."

"But yours has got a hole in it. Is that why it was so noisy last night?"

Hannah shifted guiltily. It didn't take a rocket scientist to work out that this was one of Joe Lawson's kids. She had his blue eyes, for starters. And there was something about the way she held her head... Which meant he'd been right last night—Hannah *had* woken his kids when she'd been fooling around in the garage.

"I'm sorry about that. I didn't realize you guys had moved in yet," Hannah said.

"It's okay. I didn't mind." The little girl thrust her hand forward. "I'm Ruby Lawson, by the way."

Hannah suppressed a smile. She held up her own hand, displaying the grease on it.

"I'm dirty, sorry. But I'm Hannah," she said.

"I don't care about dirt," Ruby said, and before Hannah could stop her she'd reached out and grasped Hannah's hand, her small fingers wrapping around Hannah's larger ones.

"Pleased to meet you," Ruby said solemnly.

It was impossible for Hannah to hide her smile then. "Pleased to meet you, too, Ruby."

Ruby smiled back, then looked at the bike. "Can I help you fix it?"

Hannah flicked a glance at Ruby's sparkly top and purple pants. She didn't exactly strike Hannah as the tomboy type. Still, Hannah wasn't about to discourage her—she'd been laughed at and sent on her way too many times when she was a curious kid to hand out the same treatment to another little girl.

"Sure. You can pass me tools when I need them, if you'd like."

"Okay. You might have to tell me which one is which, though."

"Deal," Hannah said.

They worked side by side for a while. Ruby was a fast learner, quickly working out how to tell what size the various spanners and wrenches were by checking the little markings on their sides. She took great delight in slapping each requested tool into Hannah's hand with vigor. Hannah figured the kid must have seen more than her fair share of medical dramas on TV over the years.

"My dad used to work with tools like this," Ruby said as they were refitting the patched muffler.

Despite herself, Hannah's curiosity pricked up its ears. "So your dad is a mechanic, is he?" It couldn't hurt to know a bit more about the man. He did live next door, after all. Might as well know what she was up against.

"My dad is an oilman. He works on the offshore rigs," Ruby said proudly. "He's done every job there is."

Hannah didn't know much about oil work, but she was pretty sure that offshore postings meant the person was away a lot. "You must miss him when he's working, huh?"

She knew she was being nosy, but she couldn't seem to help herself.

"He's been working in an office since Mommy died, and now he's going to be a businessman."

Hannah froze for a second.

A dead wife. It went a long way to explaining the look in Joe's eyes.

Suddenly she felt as though she'd invaded her new neighbor's privacy. She was almost one hundred percent certain that he would hate for her to know about his sad personal life.

"You know what? I think we're about done," she said. She stepped back from the bike and Ruby did the same, copying Hannah's hands-on-hips posture.

"Do we start up the motor now, see if it works?" Ruby asked. Her eyes were wide with excitement when she looked at Hannah.

"Absolutely. You want to do the honors?"

Ruby's eyes went even wider. "Really?"

Hannah simply handed over the keys. Ruby vibrated with anticipation as she stood on tiptoes and slid the key into the ignition. With an encouraging nod from Hannah, Ruby twisted the key and the bike roared to life. Ruby gave a little squeal and jumped backward. Hannah laughed, then immediately bit her lip when Ruby gave her a reproachful look.

"It just took me by surprise, that's all," the little girl said.

"I know. It startles me all the time, too," Hannah said.

Ruby cocked her head to one side. "Is it fixed? It still sounds very loud."

She was right; the bike was still too noisy. Ideally, the bike needed a new muffler, but Hannah couldn't justify the expense when she was still paying off the personal loan she'd had to take out to cover what was left of the mortgage after they'd sold the apartment.

"Well, it's not perfect, but it's going to have to do for now," Hannah said. She reached out and switched the bike off again.

"Can we go for a ride?"

Hannah smiled. She'd been waiting for that one. "I don't think your dad would appreciate us doing that."

"He wouldn't mind."

"Hmm. I'm not so sure about that."

Ruby pressed her hands together and gave Hannah a limpid-eyed beseeching look. "Pretty please?"

As pitiful pleas went, it was very effective. Hannah wondered if Ruby had practiced in the mirror. "Sorry, sweetheart. You can have a sit on it, though, if you'd like."

Ruby considered for a moment. "I guess that would be okay," she said grudgingly.

Hannah wiped her hands on her jeans and helped boost Ruby onto the saddle. Ruby's legs barely straddled the seat and she wobbled and clutched at the handlebars, a worried frown on her face.

"Hang on a minute," Hannah said. She slung a leg over the bike so that she was sitting behind Ruby, holding the little girl's hips with her hands. "Is that better?"

"Yes. Can I rev the engine?"

"Sure, why not?"

Hannah twisted the ignition key and the bike rumbled to life beneath them. Ruby giggled.

"It's all bouncy," she said.

Hannah laughed. She vaguely registered the sound of a door slamming shut in the background as she leaned forward to twist the throttle.

"See? You grip this and twist it slowly forward. But not too much—you don't want to push it too hard."

Ruby reached out, fingers spread wide.

"What the hell do you think you're doing?"

Hannah nearly fell off the bike as Joe stalked across the sidewalk, his expression livid.

"Are you out of your freaking mind?" he demanded. He grasped Ruby around the waist, plucking her from the bike as though she weighed less than a feather.

"No, Daddy. Hannah was just going to let me rev the engine," Ruby protested.

Joe set her on the ground and put a hand on her shoulder. "I want you to go inside."

"No! We weren't doing anything wrong. We were just sitting there," Ruby insisted.

Hannah could see the little girl was getting herself worked up. She could also see that Joe was in no mood to listen to reason. She met Ruby's gaze.

"It's okay, sweetie," she said reassuringly. "You do what your daddy says."

The small exchange only made Joe angrier. He forcibly turned Ruby around. "Inside, now!" he barked.

Ruby's bottom lip stuck out and her eyes filled with tears but fear won out over valor. Hannah didn't blame her—Joe Lawson in full-blooded fury was a pretty damned intimidating sight. With one last glance over her shoulder, Ruby raced toward the house.

Joe waited until his daughter was well out of hearing before turning on Hannah. "What kind of a reckless idiot takes a kid for a ride on a motorbike without a helmet? You want to answer me that?"

"You're overreacting. If you calmed down for one second—"

"Don't tell me to be calm, lady." He shoved a finger in her face. "You had no right to risk my daughter's life. Did you even stop to think—" He broke off, unable to articulate his fury.

Hannah held his gaze, pride demanding that she not waver for a second in the face of his misplaced righteousness.

"Are you finished?" she asked calmly. "Any more insults you want to throw at me?"

He gave her a scathing head to toe. "Stay away from my daughter." He turned on his heel and strode toward his house.

Hannah let out the breath she'd been holding.

Wow. That had been exactly what she hadn't needed—a big, shitty cherry on top of an already shitty day.

She started gathering her tools and was dismayed to see her hands were shaking. She squeezed her hands into fists, willing them to steady. She hadn't done a single thing wrong. She refused to let him get to her.

When she opened her hands again, the shaking was barely discernible.

Good. That was the way it should be. Back straight, she wheeled her bike into the garage.

JOE PAUSED OUTSIDE Ruby's bedroom door to take a deep breath and consciously relax his shoulders. His blood was still pounding in his head, but Ruby didn't deserve his anger. She was just a kid, going with the flow. It wasn't her fault that Hannah Napier was reckless and irresponsible.

He lifted his hand and rapped on the door.

"Rubes, it's me," he called.

She didn't say anything but he pushed the door open anyway. She was stretched out on her bed, her face buried in her pillow.

"I'm sorry for yelling at you like that," he said as he crossed to the bed and sat beside her. He laid his hand on her shoulder. He could feel the agitated heat coming off her body. "I didn't mean to frighten you."

Hell, he was the one who'd been frightened. Seeing his little girl perched on the bike like that, realizing what Ruby had been up to while he'd been kneading pizza dough in the kitchen… He'd seen red. If Hannah Napier had been a man, for sure he would have grabbed her by the scruff of the neck and shaken her till her teeth rattled. Luckily for her, she'd been protected by her gender. Just. For a few seconds there, it had been a close-run thing.

"What happened wasn't your fault, okay?" he said. He stroked Ruby's rigid back. "But I need you to promise that you will never, ever go for a ride on a motorbike again without talking to me, okay?"

Ruby lifted her head and he could see she'd been crying. "No!"

He frowned. "I know they look like a lot of fun, but they're dangerous, sweetheart. There's a whole bunch of special equipment you should be wearing before you even think of riding one of those things."

His voice caught as he imagined what could have happened to her if something had gone wrong. Ruby was so small, so bloody fragile….

"No, Daddy, you've got it all wrong. Hannah didn't take me for a ride and now you yelled at her and she'll never let me help her again."

Joe frowned. "Ruby, I saw you on the bike. I know you're only trying to protect your new friend—"

"She didn't take me for a ride! I asked her to but she said no. Then she said I could sit on the bike if I wanted to and she was really nice and lifted me up and held me when I thought I was going to fall," Ruby said in an urgent rush.

Joe stared at his daughter. Ruby held his gaze unflinchingly, her blue eyes drenched with tears. The tight, uncomfortable feeling in his gut told him his daughter was speaking the truth.

Damn.

He closed his eyes for a long moment as he reviewed his reaction through the filter of this new information. Over-the-top? Just a little.

"Hannah's going to hate me now," Ruby said miserably.

Not half as much as she hates me.

"I'm sure she doesn't hate you, Rubes. You didn't do anything wrong. I was the one who made the mistake."

"I tried to tell you, but you wouldn't listen. I asked and asked Hannah to take me for a ride, but she said you wouldn't like it. I even said you wouldn't mind, but she said she thought you would."

Just in case he didn't feel enough of a heel already.

"Yeah. The thing was, Rube, I saw you sitting up there, and the bike was running, and it looked like you guys had come back from a spin around the block."

Dear God, could he sound any more defensive?

Ruby gave him a level look. "You should have listened when I tried to explain."

"You're right. I should have. And next time, I promise I will."

Ruby sniffed loudly, then knuckled her eyes dry. "It's okay. I forgive you," she said magnanimously.

"Thank you."

"But we should go next door right now and apologize to Hannah," Ruby said. She was already wriggling toward the edge of the bed and she looked at Joe expectantly.

He nodded. "That's a good idea."

Even though it was going to make him squirm.

"Oh, I know what we should do!" Ruby grabbed the front of his sweater she was so excited. "We should invite Hannah over for pizza! She won't be able to stay angry with us if we make her pizza."

Want to bet?

"It's a lovely idea, Rubes, but I think we might leave the pizza for another night. Hannah probably doesn't want to have dinner with us just now."

"Then we should take her one for her to eat on her own. I'll make it for her and we'll take it over together and explain how you got it wrong and how you're sorry for yelling at her."

For a moment Joe was tempted to agree to the idea, but he knew that taking Ruby with him was the coward's way out of the hole he'd dug for himself. There was no way Hannah would give him the verbal smackdown he deserved with his daughter standing beside him.

"I tell you what. Why don't you make a pizza for Hannah, and I'll take it over to her on my own and apologize?" he said.

Ruby studied him. "Don't be embarrassed because you made a mistake, Daddy. You only got upset because you love me. I know that."

Joe smiled. Maybe he *should* take his daughter with him, after all. There wasn't a jury in the land that would convict him with her on his side.

He tugged on one of her pigtails. "How did you get to be so wise?"

Ruby smiled and shrugged. "Just lucky, I guess."

They went to the kitchen to create a pizza especially for Hannah. Ruby insisted on putting every single topping available on it, since they didn't know what Hannah liked or didn't like.

"This way, she can pick off the bits she doesn't want," Ruby reasoned. "But if the bits aren't there in the first place, she can't put them back on."

Ben had a bit to say about his sister's logic, but finally Joe had a pizza in his hand and a speech roughed out in his mind.

He'd apologize straight up, not offer any excuses. And when she let fly at him, he'd take it. The way she'd taken it when he dished it out to her.

He felt like a kid going to the principal's office as he walked up the front steps to Hannah's house. Gritting his teeth, he rang the doorbell.

There was a rattle of a door chain being removed, then Mrs. Napier opened the door.

"Oh, hello, Joe. How are you doing? How did the big move go?" Robyn said, a welcoming smile on her face.

"I'm good, thanks. And the move was pretty smooth, all things considered."

"Did you want to come in? Or were you after something? Goodness, is that a pizza?"

"Um, yes, it is. I was actually wondering if I could have a quick word with Hannah?"

Robyn's smile widened. "Of course you can. Why don't you come in and I'll go grab her?"

Joe stepped into the foyer as Robyn disappeared up the hallway. He glanced around as he waited, taking in the fussy wallpaper and antique hat stand in the front hall. Interesting. Not the kind of furnishings he'd imagined a woman like Hannah favoring.

There was a family portrait hanging next to it, a photograph of Robyn and two young girls. He moved closer and recognized the oldest girl as Hannah. He guessed she must have been about twelve or thirteen when it was taken. Her hair was cut short and she wore jeans and a football sweater. She had her arm wrapped protectively around her younger sister and there was a challenge in her eyes as she smiled down the barrel of the camera.

Full of attitude, even at thirteen. It figured.

A door closed somewhere in the house and Joe turned away from the photograph just as Hannah entered the foyer wearing a pale green satin bathrobe. Her hair was wrapped in a towel and she had her arms crossed defensively over her chest as she stopped in front of him. She glanced at the pizza and arched an eyebrow.

"It's for you. Ruby made it," he said awkwardly.

She looked different without her coverall or biker gear. Softer. More vulnerable.

"To say thank you for the motorbike ride I didn't take her on, I assume?" Hannah asked coolly.

He squared his shoulders. "Yeah, about that. I owe you an apology. I jumped to conclusions. I should have let you explain before I barged in."

"Yep, you should have."

He shifted his weight. He hadn't expected her to make it easy for him, but he couldn't remember the last time he'd felt this uncomfortable. "I can't remember exactly what I said, but I was out of line and I'm sorry."

"Let me see if I can refresh your memory. *Reckless idiot*, I think you called me."

He winced. "I'm sorry."

She eyed him for a moment, then her gaze dropped to the pizza. "Ruby made this for me—is that what you said?"

"Yes. It's a Ruby superspecial with the works. Home-made base and everything."

She held out her hand and he passed the pizza over. Now that her arms weren't crossed over her chest, he could see the outline of her breasts against her robe. The soft shape of her nipples was clearly visible beneath the silk, and he realized that she must be naked beneath it.

For a moment he got caught on the thought, his mind filling with images of soft skin and even softer curves.

Where the hell did that come from?

He shoved his hands into his pockets. Then he cleared his throat. "Before I go, I wanted to thank you for taking the time to talk with Ruby. I know she probably got in the way. It was kind of you to let her help."

Hannah gave him a scathing look. "It wasn't kind. She's a good kid. Smart, funny. A minor miracle, considering who her father is. But I won't hold that against her."

She stepped forward and opened the front door. "Tell Ruby thank you for the pizza," she said.

His audience was over. He stepped over the threshold and turned to face her. "I will. And I just want to say again—"

The door closed in his face. He blinked, then slowly turned away. Despite everything, a reluctant smile curved his mouth.

Hannah Napier was a handful. He'd got that much right about her.

And despite that, he wanted her.

The realization killed his smile. He hadn't felt a thing for another woman since Beth died, yet for some crazy reason every time he looked at his new neighbor he found himself thinking things he had no business thinking.

It's only sex. You haven't touched a woman in two years. You're only human.

All true, but somehow not enough to ease the tight feeling in his gut. He didn't want to be attracted to another woman. He wasn't over Beth yet, not by a long shot.

CHAPTER FOUR

THE FOLLOWING AFTERNOON, Hannah pushed through the double doors to The Watering Hole, the local pub and her favorite after-work hangout. It was the kind of pub that used to dominate the suburbs of Melbourne before slot machines were introduced—scuffed and dented around the edges, friendly vibe, no pretense about it. She loved the cream and burgundy tiles behind the bar and the dusty memorabilia hanging on the walls.

Her mate Bugsy raised a hairy arm in greeting when he saw her. "Napier. Took your time."

She smiled. She didn't know what she would have done without her biker buddies over the past few months. Bugsy and Grunter and the rest had quietly circled the wagons when the wedding fell through. No one had said a word, but she knew they'd felt for her and she'd appreciated their silent support.

She slid onto a stool beside Bugsy and accepted the beer he pushed toward her. "Cheers," she said, raising her glass.

"Straight back at you."

She took a long pull from her beer. There was nothing better after a long day at work. She rested her elbow on the counter and smiled at Bugsy. "Gonna let me whip your ass on the pool table?" she asked.

"You can try, little girl."

She laughed. Then she caught sight of a man out of the corner of her eye and did a double take.

Joe Lawson.

Man. Was it too much to ask for her to have a moment's reprieve from the guy? She felt as though he'd invaded her life since he'd moved in.

He was talking to Mandy, The Watering Hole's longest-serving waitress. Hannah hoped she was giving him directions to someplace far away. Hannah had come here to relax and she was pretty damn sure she wasn't going to be able to do that with him sitting across the bar.

He glanced up and caught her staring. His expression didn't change but his shoulders shifted. For a moment they stared at each other, then his focus returned to Mandy.

"What's wrong?" Bugsy asked.

"Nothing," she said. She took another mouthful of beer. "Let's go play pool."

She slid off the stool and grabbed her jacket with one hand, her beer with the other. Bugsy led the way to the seen-better-days pool table in the back corner, but she couldn't help glancing over her shoulder as she followed him, just to check on where her nemesis was. She almost walked into the cigarette machine when she saw Mandy ushering Joe behind the bar. What the hell…?

Mandy was gesturing toward the spirits lined up on the shelves behind the bar. Joe nodded, asked a question. Mandy turned and pointed to the beer taps along the front edge of the counter.

"You coming or what?" Bugsy called from behind her.

Hannah tore her gaze away and walked the final few steps to join him.

Why was Joe Lawson being invited behind the bar? If she

didn't know any better, she'd think Mandy was giving him an orientation tour.

Shit. What if he'd taken a job at The Watering Hole? It was possible, after all. He was new to the area, and Ruby had said he'd retired from the rigs. He must need to work. Still, this was the one place she could relax and not worry about anything, the one place where she felt utterly comfortable. She didn't want to have to run the gauntlet of her surly neighbor every time she wanted a beer and a game of pool.

Hannah was distracted as Bugsy set up the table then flipped a coin to see who would break. She kept glancing across to the bar to check what Joe was doing. Sure enough, he'd started pulling beers for customers.

"Bloody hell."

Bugsy broke and started sinking balls. Hannah tried to concentrate, but she was too thrown to really follow the game. When Mandy sailed past with a tray full of empty glasses, Hannah called after her.

"Mandy. You got a minute?" she asked.

The older woman paused and smiled at Hannah. "Sure. You guys want another round?"

"We're all right for now, thanks. I was just curious about the new guy."

Mandy rolled her eyes and fanned herself with her free hand. "I know, isn't he gorgeous? Talk about dumb luck, huh? When Arnie told me the news I was sure it was going to suck big-time, but now that I've met Joe I've got to say, I'm definitely coming around."

Hannah frowned, confused, but Mandy just kept talking.

"And the great thing is, the way he's talking, Joe's not going to change anything. He's definitely not going to put in slot machines or try to turn the place into one of those slick yuppy hangouts, thank God. So even though it'll be sad saying goodbye to Arnie after all these years, I think I can live with it."

Hannah blinked as she deciphered Mandy's ramblings. "He's *bought* the place?" Hannah hoped against hope that she'd gotten it wrong.

"Yeah. Didn't you see the notice?" Mandy pointed to a handwritten note stuck near the till. "Sale was finalized yesterday, but apparently they've been negotiating for over a month."

Hannah swallowed the four-letter word on the tip of her tongue. "Well. How about that."

Mandy wiggled her eyebrows suggestively one last time before moving off. Hannah tried to come to terms with what she'd just learned.

Joe Lawson, arrogant, judgmental neighbor extraordinaire, had purchased the one place left on earth where she felt like a normal human being. What were the odds?

She was seized with the sudden urge to march across the bar and demand he undo the sale, that he choose some other pub to invest in. This was her home away from home. She'd already lost the apartment she and Lucas had lived in, the future they'd planned. She'd narrowed her life to working hard and paying off her debts so she could escape. The Watering Hole had been her solace.

And now Joe Bloody Lawson had taken that away from her, too.

She should walk out the door and never come back. She didn't like him, he didn't like her. He made her uncomfortable. There were plenty of other places she could play pool and drink beer with her mates. But leaving felt like admitting defeat. Even if he owned the place now, she'd been here first. She'd been coming here for years, for Pete's sake. There was no way she was going to let him run her out of town, so to speak.

"Your shot," Bugsy said.

Hannah dragged her gaze away from where Joe was pouring shots for a group of university students. Jaw set, she took up her cue. Lining up a ball, she took her shot. The ball sped straight into the pocket with a satisfying thwack.

"Aw, man," Bugsy complained as she started to clean up the table.

She wouldn't back off. She would come here after work two or three times a week, same as she always had. Joe was nothing to her. Less than nothing.

Absolutely.

TWO WEEKS LATER, Joe let himself into the house to find his mother dozing on the couch. He tried to be quiet but she started to wakefulness as he entered the room.

"Joe! You scared me."

"Sorry. I tried to be quiet."

She sat up and ran her hands over her hair.

"My goodness, it's after eleven. I didn't mean to fall asleep, but television was dreadful tonight. All that horrible reality TV just celebrates the absolute worst in humanity. What happened to good old-fashioned dramas like *Dallas* and *Dynasty?*"

"Joan Collins got old and J.R. got sick," he said. He dropped his keys onto the coffee table and stretched out his back. "How were the kids? Did Ben get through his homework okay?"

Joe had been making a point of being home when the kids got in from school most days, only heading into the pub after they'd had their dinner. His long-term plan was to hire a night manager, but his mother had been good enough to cover the evenings while he learned the ropes at The Watering Hole in these early weeks. Tonight, however, he'd had to delegate all child care to his mother while he dealt with a staff crisis. Not a big deal, but annoying given that the whole point of buying the business had been to offer his kids a more stable home life.

"He told me he did it. I'm not sure what that means anymore," his mother said.

He ran a hand over his hair. He knew exactly what she meant. Ben had become increasingly incommunicative lately. He spent a lot of time alone in his room listening to his iPod or playing on his handheld game, and no matter what Joe said or did he couldn't get more than a shrug and a handful of words from his son.

"Have you had that talk with him yet?" his mother asked.

"Yes. He said school is fine, he's making friends. He likes the new house. I couldn't get anything more out of him." He sat on the couch beside her. "I should have stuck it out in Sydney."

"Maybe, but you're here now. And once Ben and Ruby settle, things will even out, you'll find new rhythms and routines."

"I guess."

"How's the pub going?"

"Good. Still getting used to being on my feet most of the day." He gave her a tired smile. "Got soft over the past few years, being a desk jockey."

He'd given up his work on the offshore oil rigs when Beth died and taken a desk job so he could be around for the kids. It had been more than enough to prove to him that suit-and-tie stuff was not for him. Hence the purchase of the pub. It had always been Beth's dream that they buy their own place and run it as a family.

"You look tired," his mother said, her eyes concerned.

"I'm okay."

"I know it must be hard. You and Beth always planned on doing this together."

He shrugged. He had to do something with his life now that he could no longer do the rig work he loved. He'd decided to go ahead with Beth's dream because he hadn't had one of his own and she'd always said that when he gave up offshore work he'd go stir-crazy if he tried to take on a nine-to-five job. The past two years had more than proven her right.

Just for a moment he allowed himself to wonder what she'd think of The Watering Hole. He hoped she'd like its old-fashioned wooden bar and beat-up floor, the scratched and scarred tables and chairs and the chalkboards dating back to the 1930s. She'd always talked about buying a traditional place, a pub where families could get a reasonably priced meal and where the locals came to spend time with each other. No slot machines, no loud bands to scare people off. A neighborhood place.

His mother stood and started collecting her things. "I'd better get going. I'll see you around dinnertime tomorrow, okay?"

He looked at her. "I appreciate this. You know that, right?" He'd never been great with words, but he hoped she understood how much he valued everything she'd done for him and his kids.

"I do. And you don't have to keep thanking me. Ben and Ruby keep me young." She squeezed his hand and stood on her toes to kiss his cheek. "Get some sleep."

He walked her to her car and waited until she'd rounded the corner before turning back to the house. He glanced at the Napier place as he walked up the front path. The light was on in the garage, illumination leaking out around the edges of the roller door. He could hear the radio playing. Hannah was obviously in there, tinkering away at something. He didn't need to check his watch to know it was late, well past eleven. What the hell did she have to do in there that couldn't wait until morning?

Over the past two weeks he'd watched her at The Watering Hole. He hadn't wanted to, but he'd been unable to help himself. The moment she walked in the door she exerted a gravitational pull on his senses that he found impossible to ignore. She came in twice, maybe three times a week. She had a beer, sometimes two, played a couple of games of pool with her biker friends, then she left. She never got drunk, never flirted, never let the guys win to make them feel good about themselves. Watching her interact with them, he was almost certain she wasn't sleeping with any of them. Although why that was any of his business he had no idea.

She'd let Ruby help her twice since his knee-jerk reaction. Both times Ruby came home with greasy fingernails and clothes and conversation peppered with lots of "Hannah saids." Through his daughter he'd learned that Hannah was restoring an old Triumph Thunderbird, that she planned to take off on a round-Australia road trip as soon as she had enough money saved, and that Hannah couldn't stand Brussels sprouts, turnips or radishes.

He couldn't work her out. She was gorgeous, yet she spent most of her time alone, up to her elbows in oil and grease. He'd finally discovered that her mother owned the house next door and that Hannah was living with her, and not the other way around. Yet Hannah didn't strike him as the kind of person who would cling to her mother's apron strings.

She was a mystery. One that his mind kept mulling over, again and again.

He climbed the steps to the house, shutting out thoughts

of his provocative neighbor along with the cool night air as he closed the front door. He had no business speculating about her, just as he had no business fantasizing about what she looked like naked or how her skin would feel against his own. It was a dead end, and he didn't have time or energy to waste on dead ends.

He locked the door then did his nightly check on the kids before heading to bed. Ben's door was closed, but Joe eased it open and stepped into the room. His son looked much younger than his thirteen years when he was sleeping, his face more rounded, his chin less determined. Joe backed out silently then made his way to Ruby's room. Her door was ajar and he swung it open quietly. Unlike her brother, Ruby was twisted in her quilt, one hand flung up near her head on the pillow. He crossed to the bed to untangle her and frowned when he saw the damp patch on her pillow. Her eyelashes were spiky with moisture, her cheeks flushed. She'd been crying, had cried herself to sleep, in fact. That was a blow to his solar plexus. It was one thing for him to be around while his daughter cried, to be able to comfort her and talk to her, but it was another thing entirely to know she'd been huddled in her bed, crying her misery into her pillow all on her own.

He wanted to wake her and reassure her and make her world right again. Instead he crouched beside the bed and smoothed the hair from her forehead. She looked more and more like Beth every day. She was going to be beautiful like her, too.

Because there was nothing else for him to do, he straightened her quilt, making sure she was warm enough. His fingers encountered something where the bed met the wall and he pulled out a crumpled ball of paper. He waited until he was in the hallway and the door was closed before smoothing the page. It was a flyer, sent home from Ruby's school.

Elsternwick Primary School invites entries for its annual Mother and Daughter Fashion Parade. All funds raised will go toward the new gymnasium...

Joe swore under his breath and let his hand drop to his side. No wonder she'd been crying.

"Damn."

Life was going to be full of moments like these for his children. Casually delivered school notices, other children's birthday parties, a myriad of other social and community events centered around families. He couldn't protect Ben and Ruby from them all, no matter how much he wanted to. But God, how he wanted to.

He walked slowly to the kitchen and placed the flyer on the counter. He stared at it, trying to work out how to handle the situation. Wait until Ruby brought it up? Mention it himself? Did the fact that Ruby hadn't said anything to his mother tonight and instead chose to cry alone in her room mean he should tackle this more vigorously or give her more space?

He was truly clueless. He rubbed a hand over his face. Then he folded the notice in half and slid it into the junk drawer. He would talk to Ruby in the morning, see if she mentioned the fashion parade. If she didn't... He would cross that bridge when he came to it. If she did, he would offer what comfort he could. Maybe his mother would be an adequate substitute. Or maybe he could offer to do something special with her the night of the parade and turn it into a father-daughter event instead of an occasion of sadness and grief.

Maybe. It was becoming the most overused word in his vocabulary.

THE NEXT DAY, HANNAH exited the workshop and waited for a pause in the traffic before crossing to the small group of shops opposite. She could see there was already a queue forming in the bakery, but she knew Ian would bitch and moan all day if she didn't bring him back the doughnut he'd requested for morning break.

Resigning herself to a long wait, she joined the line and dug her hands into the pockets of her coveralls, jingling her change in the palm of her hand. She was glancing idly out the front window when she saw a dark-haired boy walk past with a couple of taller, older kids. She'd have to be blind not to recognize the younger boy as Joe's son—she'd seen him coming and going from the house often enough.

She checked her watch. It wasn't even close to lunchtime, which meant Joe's kid had no legitimate reason for being on the street during school hours.

Unless he was ditching, of course.

She turned her attention to the menu board behind the bakery counter and concentrated on choosing between a Danish and a vanilla slice for herself. So what if Joe's kid was sneaking off from school with what looked like older, meaner kids? It was none of her business.

It was harder to stick to her decision when she exited the bakery and spotted Joe's son emptying his pockets near the corner while the older kids inspected his haul. It had been a while, but Hannah recognized the classic signs of shoplifting when she saw them. The furtiveness, the repressed excitement and fear. She could imagine how it had worked, too—the older kids distracting the shopkeeper while the younger, more innocent-looking kid played mule and stuffed his pockets.

She hesitated on the curb, watching the smaller boy shake his head in response to something one of the older kids said. Joe Junior or whatever his name was looked a lot like his old man—same dark hair, same blue eyes. No doubt he'd grow up to be as big and strong, too. As though he felt her regard, Joe Junior looked up and for a moment they locked gazes. He looked away first, but not before she saw the sadness in him. Another thing in common with his father.

She crossed the street and reentered the workshop, tossing Ian the bag with his doughnut in it.

"Thanks, boss lady," he said with a grin.

"Just don't blame me when you have diabetes."

She leaned her butt against the rear workbench and bit into her Danish, frowning fiercely as she chewed. For the life of her, she couldn't get the little scene from across the road out of her mind. The way Joe's son had hunched his shoulders when the older kids were talking to him, the patent unhappiness in his eyes—he hadn't looked as though he was having a good time to Hannah. He was new to the area, too. Who knew what kinds of pressure he was experiencing at his new school and what he felt he had to do to fit in with his new peers?

"Shit."

She screwed the remains of her Danish up inside the bakery bag and tossed the lot in the garbage. She couldn't believe she was about to do what she was about to do.

"Ian, I'm heading out for half an hour or so. Cover the phones, okay?"

"Sure. Don't forget Mrs. Lockhead wants her wagon back by three."

"Yeah, I'm on it."

She didn't bother to check her hair or change out of her coverall. This wasn't a social call, after all. She walked around the corner, and down the block to The Watering Hole. It was dim inside after the brightness out of doors so she stopped on the threshold and blinked, waiting for her vision to clear.

It was quiet, since it was only half past ten. Staff were busy cleaning tables and stacking glasses. The smell of beer and fried food hung in the air.

Second thoughts bit hard. She had no business being here. Then Joe exited the office, a stack of papers in hand.

Fine. Get it over with if you're going to be a do-gooder.

She took a deep breath and crossed to the bar. "You got a minute?"

Joe's head came up and his eyebrows lifted. He didn't bother pretending to look pleased to see her. They didn't have that kind of relationship.

"What's up?"

Hannah glanced at the bartender pouring ice into a bucket nearby. "Is there somewhere more private we can talk?"

She figured he wouldn't be thrilled to have his staff learn about his renegade son. Not that he was going to be thrilled at all, of course.

There was a short pause before he gestured with his head for her to follow him. She kept her eyes on the back of his neck as he led her into the manager's office. Boxes of supplies were stacked along one wall and a battered desk filled the corner. He turned to face her, eyes wary.

"If this is about Ruby, if she's been getting in your way when you're trying to work, just say the word and I'll find something else for her to do."

"You have a boy, right? Dark-haired, same eyes as you? I've seen him in the street."

"Yeah, Ben. Why? What's happened?"

"I just saw him at the local shops."

Joe frowned. "He's supposed to be at school."

"I figured." She hesitated a moment, unsure how he was going to take her next bit of news. "I think he was shoplifting."

"What?" He straightened, took a step forward.

She held up a hand, all too familiar with his temper. "Before you start turning green and busting out of your clothes, you might want to hear me out."

She could tell he didn't like the reference but he nodded to signal she should continue.

"He was with a couple of older kids, and it looked like they were using him as their mule, if you know what I mean. That's why I figured you ought to know, since maybe he wasn't doing it because he wanted to do it but because he felt like he had to to make friends."

If she hadn't been looking into his face she would have missed the flash of pain in his eyes. She would have only seen the way his body tensed and heard the anger in his voice.

"How long ago was this? Where were they? Can you show me?" He was already striding for the door.

"They're long gone by now. They were splitting up the booty when I left them ten minutes ago. They've probably gone to the mall to play video games or to some kid's house where there are no parents home." She could see her words sink in. Some of the urgency went out of him. He turned to face her, ran a hand through his hair.

"Bloody hell."

"Yeah, well." She looked away from the confusion and concern on his face. "I thought you'd want to know."

"Thanks." He made an effort to pull himself together. "I appreciate you taking the time. Especially considering I haven't exactly given you a lot of reasons to want to be a good neighbor."

"It's no big deal."

His blue eyes were searching as he looked at her. "It's a big deal to me. My kids are all I have."

She didn't know what to say to that. Apparently she could only handle this man when he was having a go at her. Fill his mouth with civilized conversation and take away his frown and she was reduced to shrugging and discomfort.

She made a show of checking her watch. "I really should get back to the workshop. Good luck with it."

"Let me know next time you're in and I'll shout you a meal."

"Sure." There was no way she'd ever take him up on the offer, but he didn't need to know that.

She got all the way to the door before her conscience bit her. She could only imagine how tough it was bringing up two kids solo, trying to be mother and father to them, trying to anticipate and manage all the little things that could go wrong in life.

Her steps slowed and she closed her eyes and made an impatient noise. Then she swiveled and marched back to his office.

He was leaning against his desk again, head lowered, rubbing the bridge of his nose. For a crazy moment she had to fight the urge to go to him and put her arms around him and draw his head onto her shoulder. As though he wanted her sympathy. He'd probably charge her with assault, given their track record.

She cleared her throat and his head came up. "I have this friend. He's a cop. I'm sure if I asked him, he'd be happy to come around and have a little chat with Ben. If you wanted go down that route, that is."

He stared at her and she suddenly felt incredibly self-conscious. She was about to apologize for interfering when he spoke up.

"I was just sitting here racking my brains for ways to handle this."

"I always remember the police making a pretty strong impression when I was a kid."

His mouth quirked a little and she realized he'd almost smiled. A minor miracle.

"Me, too."

She pulled her cell phone from her pocket. "Give me a second and I'll see what I can line up."

Andrew answered on the second ring and she filled him in briefly before handing the phone over to Joe. She watched as he added a few details then confirmed his address and a time for Andrew to visit that evening.

Joe eyed her curiously when he handed the phone back. "He obviously thinks a lot of you."

"We went to school together. And I helped him rebuild his 1970 Capri a few years back."

"Ah."

Her phone was warm from where he'd held it. She slid it into her pocket then shifted her weight awkwardly. "I'm sure Andrew's visit will nip this in the bud. If Ben's anything like Ruby, he's a good kid."

"Despite having me for a father." He was utterly deadpan, but she was almost certain he was joking.

"Took the words right out of my mouth," she said.

His gaze instantly dropped to her mouth. "Ruby tells me you're restoring an old Triumph."

The comment came from so far out of left field it took her a moment to realize what he was doing: making small talk.

"Um, yeah. It's a Thunderbird, 1955."

"Original electrics?"

She narrowed her eyes. "They were redone in the seventies. You know your bikes."

He shrugged. "I had a few growing up. Always wanted a Thunderbird. Anyway, I'm holding you up." He offered her his hand.

As usual, hers were covered with grease and oil and she showed them to him. "Occupational hazard, sorry."

"I don't mind a bit of dirt."

She smiled, couldn't help herself.

"What's so funny?" he asked.

"Ruby said almost exactly the same thing when I first met her."

He smiled, the corners of his eyes crinkling. "A chip off the old block."

All of a sudden she was struggling to form a reply. He looked utterly different with a smile on his face. Younger, lighter—and so attractive she had trouble breathing properly.

Yeah, right. Like you hadn't noticed before.

But she hadn't. Not consciously, anyway. Men simply hadn't been on her agenda. Certainly Joe hadn't been.

He offered his hand again and this time she had no choice but to take it. His hand was bigger than hers—no small feat, since she wasn't exactly a shrinking violet.

She pulled her hand free as soon as she could and shoved it into her pocket. She jerked her head toward the door. "Gotta go."

He nodded and she hustled out. She didn't slow her pace until she was outside, breathing in the cool spring air. She pressed a hand to her chest, feeling the fast thump-thump of her heart against her breastbone.

Crazy. She had no business getting flushed and flustered over her new neighbor. And over a *handshake*, for Pete's sake. For starters, she didn't even like the guy. And beyond that, she was months, perhaps years off being ready to date again after what Lucas and her sister had done to her.

She let out a bark of laughter as she registered her own thoughts. As if Joe Lawson wanted anything to do with her. As if dating him was even an option.

Absurd. Utterly, completely absurd.

Telling herself she was relieved, Hannah headed back to work, her small moment of madness forgotten. Almost.

CHAPTER FIVE

JOE KEPT AN EYE on the clock that night, watching the minutes tick toward six. Ruby was next door, hanging out with Hannah again. He wasn't sure how he felt about that, and how much of his discomfort came from his inability to deal with his attraction to his new neighbor. A lot, he suspected.

When the doorbell rang a few minutes later, he glanced to where Ben was doing homework at the kitchen table. "Would you mind getting that, mate?"

Ben had been quiet all night. Joe put it down to guilt or maybe fear. But the truth was he had no idea, and he hated that most of all.

Joe waited until Ben had left the room before moving to the kitchen doorway, one ear cocked to hear what was happening at the front of the house. He heard the door open, then the sound of a man's voice. He couldn't quite make out the words, but there was no missing the high note of fear in Ben's voice when he announced that he would go find his dad. Joe crossed to the fridge and collected two beers. Ben appeared in the kitchen, his face ashen.

"The police are here. They want to talk to you," Ben said. His hands were trembling.

Joe laid a hand on his shoulder. "You okay?" he asked.

Ben nodded quickly. "I might go finish my homework in my room."

"Why don't you hang around here for a minute?"

Ben swallowed audibly. Joe steered him toward the front door. Hannah's police buddy stood on the doorstep, resplendent in full uniform. Joe offered his hand.

"Joe Lawson. I appreciate you coming around like this."

"Andrew Bower. And like I said, it's not a problem. I owe Hannah, big-time."

The other man was tall and athletic looking with dark blond hair. Joe guessed he was in his early thirties, maybe a little younger. Ben was looking from the policeman to his father with dawning understanding. Joe met his son's eyes.

"Why don't we all go into the kitchen?"

He led the way and slid a beer in front of Andrew.

"You're off duty, right?"

"On my way home," Andrew confirmed as he twisted off the cap.

Ben stood between them, rigid with fear. Joe put his hand on his son's shoulder again. "I know what happened today at the corner store. You and I are going to talk more about how that all came to pass. But I asked Constable Bowers if he wouldn't mind having a word with you about how the law treats shoplifters."

Ben swallowed again. He hung his head, then sniffed mightily. After a long moment, Ben lifted his head. Joe was proud of the way his boy squared his shoulders.

"Okay," Ben said. He couldn't quite look the policeman in the eye, but he drew up a chair at the kitchen table and sat dutifully.

"So, Ben, I thought it might be good if we talked about Mr. Balas," Andrew said.

Ben's forehead wrinkled. "Who's he?"

"He's the man who owns the corner shop. He and his family moved here from India ten years ago because they wanted better opportunities for their children. The whole family works in the store and lives in the house out the back.

"They work every night and every day. And every time someone steals from them, they have to work a little harder and a little longer."

Ben shifted uncomfortably.

"I'm guessing you probably didn't think about them when you were stealing all that chocolate?" Andrew said.

Ben shook his head.

"That's the thing about stealing. About most crimes, actually. Most of the time, you're hurting someone else. A lot of people don't take the time to think about that."

Joe could see Ben was really listening to what the policeman was saying.

Over the next half hour Hannah's friend shared what happened to shoplifters when they got caught, and the kind of trouble he'd seen other kids get into. After the policeman had gone, Joe talked some more with his son. It became clear that Ben had been having trouble making friends at his new school and he'd fallen in with the older kids because they were the only ones who'd shown any interest in him.

"Now I know why," Ben said darkly as he sat at the kitchen table. He looked up at Joe, trepidation in his gaze. "Are you going to ground me? Take away my Nintendo?"

"No. I think it might be best if we leave it up to Mr. Balas to decide how he wants you to make this up to him."

Ben's face went chalk-white. "No. No way. I'll do anything, anything you want, but not that," Ben said, blinking rapidly.

"Ben…"

"He'll think I'm a no-good thief, Dad," Ben said, the words wrung out of him.

Joe took his son's hand. "I'll go with you, okay? We'll do it together. But you need to face up to what you did."

For a moment Ben struggled with tears. Then he took a deep breath and sniffed. "Okay. Can I go to my room now?"

"Sure, matey."

Joe was sure Ben was going to his room to shed the tears he couldn't let himself cry in front of his father.

For a moment, he was besieged by doubts. Every word, every decision was a minefield. He had no idea if he was helping steer his son in the right direction or scarring him for life.

He missed the support and reassurance of having Beth to talk things over with. The reality was, however, Beth was gone. He'd wasted enough time willing it to be otherwise. He needed to get on with living his life.

He pushed to his feet and crossed to the front door. It was time for Ruby to come in for dinner. He ran a hand through his hair and straightened his shirt before he realized what he was doing—primping for Hannah Napier.

Stupid. And completely pointless, for so many reasons he couldn't even be bothered enumerating them.

He could hear Ruby chattering away as he entered the Napiers' garage. She was telling Hannah about the dog they'd had when she was younger and he could hear Hannah laughing.

"Time to come in for dinner, Rubes," he said.

Ruby's expression instantly became mulish. "But we're not finished yet. We've only pulled apart one wheel."

He saw they'd been working on the Thunderbird, the disassembled pieces laid out on an old sheet.

"I'm sure it can wait. We need to get you fed and washed and into bed."

Ruby opened her mouth to protest but Hannah beat her to it.

"I'm about to call it quits, anyway. We've done more than enough for one night."

She met his eyes and he saw the question in them. He nodded slightly to indicate things had gone well with her friend.

"Why don't you head inside and set the table?" he said to Ruby.

She moaned some more before finally saying good-night to Hannah. Joe waited till she'd gone beyond hearing range before speaking.

"Andrew was great. Thanks for arranging for him to come over. Ben and I had a good talk."

Hannah smiled. "I suppose Ben's grounded for the rest of his natural life?"

"Nope. I'm taking him to apologize to Mr. Balas tomorrow. Mr. Balas can decide how he wants Ben to make it up to him."

She winced. "Ouch. That's gonna sting. But he's never going to forget it, either."

She squatted to place another piece of the bike on the sheet. Her jeans pulled tight across her thighs and he had to work hard not to stare. She had great legs. Firm and strong looking.

He looked away.

"I meant what I said about letting me know the next time you're at the pub. I'll shout you dinner," he said, mostly because he didn't know what else to say. Certainly not any of the entirely inappropriate things that were suddenly floating around his head.

She stood, shrugging dismissively, a gesture he was becoming increasingly familiar with. He remembered the fierce, protective look in her eyes in the family portrait in her mother's foyer. He bet she was the kind of person who struggled to let anyone do anything for her while bending over backward to help other people out.

He pointed a finger at her. "You're going to eat that dinner."

"Yeah? Who's going to make me? You and whose army?"

A smile was tugging at her mouth. He wondered how those plump lips would feel beneath his. They looked so damned soft...

"Don't forget, I have a secret weapon," he said.

She raised an eyebrow in silent question.

"Ruby. I bet you wouldn't say no if she asked." He was aware that he sounded more than a little smug and that he was starting to enjoy himself.

"A child. You'd be willing to stoop that low?"

"Hell, yeah. When there's a point of honor at stake."

They both grinned at his twisted logic. A wariness came into her eyes after a few seconds, however, and she dropped her gaze to the rag in her hand.

"I'd better start cleaning up." She glanced around, almost as though she'd rather look anywhere else than at him.

"I'd better make sure Ruby isn't trying to cook again. Last time it was not pretty."

He raised his hand in farewell and she nodded an acknowledgment before turning away and starting to load tools into a rolling tool chest.

He walked slowly back to the house. If he were a younger man, with less weighing him down... But he wasn't. He definitely wasn't.

AFTER DINNER, BEN WENT to his room to finish his homework and Joe ran Ruby a bath. As usual, he had to go roust her out after half an hour.

She was splashing happily when he entered the bathroom. She'd molded her hair into a bubbly bouffant on top of her head and was singing to herself as she made shapes in the strawberry-scented bath foam.

He smiled. At least he still had a few more years before he had to worry about shoplifting, surliness and silence where she was concerned.

"How you doing in here?"

"Good. You should try some of this strawberry bubble bath, Daddy. It smells good enough to eat."

"Hmm. I'm not sure if strawberry is really me, sweetheart."

Ruby shrugged with one shoulder, the gesture oddly familiar. Then he realized she'd stolen it from Hannah.

As though she could read his mind, Ruby suddenly piped up. "Daddy, do you think Hannah's pretty?" She watched him from beneath her eyelashes, trying to appear disinterested in his answer.

"I don't know, I haven't really thought about it," he lied.

"Do you think she would like to dress up and have fun?"

Joe had a feeling he knew where this was leading. And though he thought it was sweet—if disconcerting—that his daughter was trying her hand at matchmaking, he wasn't about to encourage it. Even if he had just been wondering what it would be like to kiss his prickly next-door neighbor.

"I'm sure Hannah has lots of people she likes to have fun with," he said. "It's time for you to get out now. You want to wash your hair and get into your pj's?"

"It's just that there's this thing happening at school. And I was thinking that maybe Hannah wouldn't mind being my partner in it. But I wasn't sure if she would want to or not," Ruby said in a rush. Her hands were twisted together and she was watching him uncertainly.

He stilled as he understood what she was referring to: the mother and daughter fashion parade. He'd waited for her to bring it up this morning, but she'd been so chirpy and bright over breakfast he'd struggled to find a way to introduce the subject into their conversation. He'd been planning to tackle it tonight before Ben's misadventures had intervened.

He moved into the bathroom and sat on the edge of the tub.

"I saw the flyer for the mother-daughter fashion parade. Is that what you mean?" he asked.

She nodded. "Do you think Hannah would like to be my partner?"

Joe took a moment to choose his words carefully. "I'm not sure. I know she seems to enjoy working on her bikes with you. I was thinking that maybe we could ask Nana Angela to do it with you."

Ruby squashed some bubbles with her hands. "Nana Angela is going to Queensland with her friend next month. Remember?"

Damn. She was right—his mother was attending a rose-lovers convention on the Gold Coast in early October. Which explained why Ruby had cried in her room last night rather than share her misery with her nana. Ruby was smart enough to know that her grandmother would cancel her trip in a blink if she felt either of her grandchildren needed her. His mother was all too aware that Beth had been an only child and that because Beth's parents were deceased, Angela was the extent of their extended family.

For the second time that night he was filled with a fierce pride in his children. They were good kids, despite the shit life had thrown at them. Despite his own shortcomings.

"So do you think I should ask Hannah?" Ruby prompted.

Joe frowned. What were his options here? Say no because he was wary of further entangling his life with that of his compelling neighbor and disappoint his daughter? Or risk a messy situation in order to ensure Ruby didn't miss out on something she wanted very badly?

It was a no-brainer. When push came to shove, his own discomfort or wariness was nothing compared to his daughter's needs.

"I'll have a word with her tomorrow," he said. "Leave it to me."

Ruby slapped both hands down into the water.

"Really? Really, truly?"

"First thing," he promised.

Ruby surged out of the water and flung herself, bubbles and all, against his chest.

"You're the best, Daddy."

He knew he wasn't. Not even close. But he was doing what he could. Even if it meant spending more time with a woman he had no business being attracted to.

HANNAH WAS ABOUT TO HEAD off to work the next day when she had the distinct sensation of being watched. She was astride the bike, the engine running, but she pushed up the visor on her helmet and glanced over her shoulder. Ben stood on the curb in front of his house, his face impassive as he watched her.

They locked gazes for a moment and Hannah felt an absurd stab of guilt when she saw the accusing light in his eyes. She'd only done what was best for him, but she was sure he didn't see it that way. He probably thought she was a squealer of the highest order.

She switched off her bike and tugged her helmet off. Yesterday had been a big day for him and she'd played a part in it. It seemed only right to acknowledge that.

"It's Ben, isn't it? I'm Hannah."

"I know who you are."

"Because of what happened yesterday."

"You ratted me out."

"I did. I was worried about you. You didn't look like you were having a great time with those older kids."

"I can look after myself."

"Sure. The thing is, I don't know you, so I had no idea what you were up for. All I saw was those big kids standing over you, and I figured I'd better talk to your dad about it."

She could see the play of emotions across Ben's face. Surprise, thoughtfulness, wariness. She let the silence stretch for a moment.

"I need to get to work, but I'll see you around, Ben," she said.

He frowned, then he nodded. She slid her helmet on and started the bike. She checked the mirror before riding off and saw him starting up the street, hands deep in his jeans pockets, schoolbag on his back. He looked as though he had the weight of the world on his shoulders.

Not your problem.

She knew it was true, but she couldn't help feeling for Ruby and Ben. Losing their mom so young must have been scary and hard.

She shook the thought off. Her first impulse was right— it wasn't her problem.

They had a busy day scheduled and she threw herself into work the moment she arrived at the garage. She'd just finished flushing the fuel injector on a Honda Civic when something made her look up and she saw Joe walking toward her, his long stride eating up the ground. She quelled the impulse to slip into her office and let Ian deal with his enquiry, whatever it was. She'd never backed down from a challenge, even one as annoying and confusing as Joe.

"Hey," he said as he stopped in front of her. "You got a minute?"

She glanced at the clock. "If you don't mind talking while I work. We're under the hammer today."

"Okay."

She crossed to the Honda. Joe followed but didn't say anything immediately. For some reason she was all fingers and thumbs as she bolted the injector rail back onto the engine. The silence stretched and finally she glanced up at him.

"Is this a quiz? Am I supposed to guess what you want?" she asked lightly.

He met her gaze and she realized he was nervous.

Huh.

"It's about Ruby. Her school is holding a mother-daughter fashion parade."

She winced. "Just what she needs."

"Yeah. I was hoping my mother could do it with her, but she's going to be away."

"Right." She had no idea where he was going with this and she propped an elbow on the rocker cover, waiting for him to get to the point.

His gaze flicked up to hold hers, then quickly flicked away again.

"Ruby and I were talking last night and she suggested that maybe you wouldn't mind doing it," he said, his tone absolutely neutral.

Hannah straightened so quickly she knocked her shoulder on the hood of the car. She rubbed it absently, staring at him.

"You want me to go in a fashion parade?" she asked incredulously.

"Not me. Ruby. And I absolutely understand if you're not up for it. It's a hassle, and you've already been very kind to Ruby—"

"My God, you're really serious, aren't you?" She couldn't quite believe it.

"Well, yeah. Ruby's not something I usually joke about."

She laughed and slid the spanner she was holding into the pocket of her coverall. "Sorry. I'm not laughing at you. It's just the idea of me in a fashion parade… It's pretty funny." She gestured toward her attire. "I couldn't tell you the last time I wore anything except jeans."

"Does that mean you're not interested?"

"It means I'm probably not a great choice. Surely there must be someone else? A family friend?"

His face was utterly impassive as he nodded briefly.

"Sure. I'm sure we'll think of someone." He glanced at his watch. "Thanks for your time, anyway. I appreciate it."

He headed to his car.

She watched him, feeling as though she'd let him down. Worse, she felt as though she'd let Ruby down. But the idea of her in a fashion parade… It was absurd, it really was. Surely Joe could see that? She barely knew how to put on mascara and lipstick, and she'd practiced for weeks before the wedding so she'd be able to walk down the aisle in her stiletto heels. She was so not what Ruby needed.

And yet Ruby had thought of her and sent her father to ask her. And Joe had swallowed his pride and God knows what else to give his daughter what she wanted.

"Damn it."

She took off after Joe, catching him just as he was sliding into the front seat of his SUV.

"Wait a minute."

He looked at her, his hand on the door, waiting.

She shook her head, still unable to quite get her head around it. "It's not that I don't want to do it. It's just… Are you sure? I mean, does Ruby have any idea how much of a handicap I'll be?"

"Ruby thinks you're the bee's knees."

"Which shows how much she knows," Hannah said, but she could feel heat rising into her face.

She was so tragic. It wasn't as if he'd said she was beautiful or anything—he'd compared her to insect appendages, for Pete's sake. What was there to feel self-conscious about in that?

"When is it?" she asked to cover her embarrassment.

"A week from Friday."

She took a deep breath. "Okay. If Ruby wants me, I'm all hers. God help her."

The tight look left his face but his eyes were still wary. "If it's too big a deal, it's fine. Like I said, I'm sure there's someone else."

She gave him a look. "Didn't anyone ever tell you to quit while you're ahead, Lawson? You just got me to agree to wearing high heels and makeup. My advice is to drive away like a bat out of hell before I come to my senses."

She was smiling, suddenly feeling unaccountably goofy. Slowly his mouth curved into a smile. Just like last time, it almost knocked her back on her heels.

"Okay. Thank you. I'll tell Ruby after school. She'll be dancing on the ceiling, no doubt."

"That's because she hasn't seen me in a dress yet," Hannah said darkly.

"I was going to take her shopping on the weekend. I guess maybe we should all go together, make sure your outfits coordinate. That's the way it probably works, right?"

She held up both hands helplessly.

"You're asking a mechanic. But you're probably right. What time do you want me to meet you at the mall?"

"Seems stupid to take two cars. Why don't we plan to leave at around ten or so and meet out the front of your place? Does that suit?"

"Sure. Wait till Mom hears about this. She'll be in heaven."

They finessed the details for their outing then Joe drove away. Hannah remained where she was for a good minute or two.

A cocktail of thoughts and emotions swirled inside her. Warmth that Ruby wanted her to be her partner in fashion crime. Surprise at herself for saying yes to such a ridiculous proposal. And something else. A sort of strange, foreign excitement that she wasn't quite sure she even wanted to name.

Brow furrowed, she strode to the workshop. Hopefully Ruby wouldn't have cause to regret her decision.

CHAPTER SIX

RUBY WAS SO EXCITED about the shopping trip that Joe had to send her back to bed three times on Friday night. She was almost jumping out of her skin Saturday morning as he made pancakes for her and Ben.

"Can I wear a tiara in the parade, like my Barbie doll?" Ruby asked.

"Sure. If that's what you want and we can find one. Remember, though, that you and Hannah need to complement each other in some way."

They'd gone over the guidelines for the parade when they filled out their entrance form the previous night, but Ruby was too caught up in the prospect of shopping to remember the rules.

"There's no way Hannah's going to wear a tiara," Ben said.

Ruby shot him a dirty look. "How would you know? She's my friend, not yours. You hardly know her."

Ben squeezed a small bathtub's worth of maple syrup onto his pancakes. "I don't need to know her. She rides a motorbike. There's no way you're going to get her to wear some stupid tiara."

Even though Joe privately agreed with his son, he had the good sense not to say so out loud.

"I think we should wait until we see what we can find at

the mall before we start worrying about stuff like that," he said diplomatically.

Ben must have caught something in his tone because he looked at Joe suspiciously. Joe couldn't resist winking, and Ben hid a smirk behind his fork as he lowered his head. The small moment of connection almost made Joe grateful for the shoplifting incident. Ever since their trip to Mr. Balas's corner store earlier in the week, Ben had been smiling more and actually volunteering conversation rather than having to have it dragged out of him monosyllable by monosyllable.

Not that the apology had been a walk in the park. Far from it. Ben had been so nervous beforehand he'd been trembling. Joe had kept his hand reassuringly on the back of his boy's neck throughout the whole encounter, squeezing occasionally when he could feel Ben's wiry body tensing with anxiety. Mr. Balas had been stern but fair as Ben explained his part in what had taken place, offering his apology in a shaky but clear voice. Joe had offered to repay Mr. Balas whatever he was owed for the stolen items, in addition to whatever punishment he deemed fit for Ben. The shop owner had surprised them both by refusing the money. Instead, he'd offered Ben the chance to work off his debt by helping out in the store after school.

Ben's relief had been palpable when the ordeal was over. Even though Ben had avoided hugs for the past few years, he didn't resist as Joe pulled him into his arms once they exited the shop.

"You did good," Joe had said. Ben had let his head rest on Joe's shoulder for a few seconds, his arms tightening around him. Joe had had to exercise real self-control to avoid squeezing his son too fiercely.

This morning, Joe slid another stack of pancakes onto a plate and sat next to Ruby.

"What time do you finish at the shop this afternoon?" he asked as Ben helped himself to a second helping.

"One o'clock, I think. Mr. Balas said he only needs me to help sort out the milk delivery and crush the boxes, then I can go."

This would be Ben's third shift. So far, so good.

"We'll be back by then to pick you up. If not, I'll call you."

"Three hours isn't long for shopping, Daddy," Ruby said reprovingly.

"It's going to have to be. We can't chew up all of Hannah's weekend. She might have other things she needs to do."

For all he knew she might have a hot date tonight that she needed to prepare for.

Joe frowned as he sliced into his pancake. What Hannah did in her spare time was nothing to do with him. He didn't even know where the aberrant thought had come from.

"I'm going to go wait out front for Hannah," Ruby said, her chair legs scraping across the floor as she pushed her chair back.

It was still only a quarter to ten, but he figured there was no harm in letting her wait outside. Kicking her heels for a few minutes might even calm her down a little.

He should have known better. He'd just finished rinsing the fry pan when Ruby banged her way back into the house.

"Daddy, we're ready to go now. Hurry up, slowpoke."

He turned to find Ruby had dragged Hannah into the house behind her. His gaze ran over Hannah's damp hair, pulled back into a ponytail.

"Ruby, I hope you didn't hassle Hannah to come early," he said.

Ruby closed her eyes for a long blink before shaking her

head, a sure sign she was prevaricating. "No. Hannah was already up and dressed, weren't you, Hannah?"

Hannah smiled and pinched one of Ruby's earlobes. "Barely, grease monkey. But it's okay, I'm ready to go now."

Her gaze flicked around the kitchen, and he was immediately aware that the room needed to be painted and that he'd been meaning to do something about the pile of mail stacked on the end of the counter.

"I guess we should go, then," he said.

There was a moment of awkwardness as they sorted out the seating arrangements in the car. Ruby automatically moved to one of the rear doors when they exited the house but Hannah quickly intervened.

"No, sweetie, you should sit up front with your dad," she said.

"I don't mind," Ruby said. She slipped into the back of the car and buckled her seat belt.

Joe met Hannah's eyes over the roof of the car for a brief second before she opened the front passenger door. He was acutely aware of her sitting beside him as he started the SUV and backed into the street. He could see her long, jeans-clad legs out of the corner of his eyes, her hands resting on her thighs.

For Pete's sake, you're not fifteen.

He only felt that way. Which boded well for the day.

It wasn't until they had entered the first clothing store that he realized how tense Hannah was. She was frowning, her shoulders very square, her generous mouth pressed into a thin, straight line as Ruby circled the racks, pulling out frilly dress after frilly dress. Hannah's eyebrows rose when she saw how short the skirt was on one of the dresses and she visibly flinched when Ruby selected a shiny Lycra thing in vivid pink.

"What do you think?" Ruby asked.

"Um. Well. I guess. Is this the sort of thing you were thinking of?" Hannah asked.

Ruby nodded. "My Barbie doll has one just like this."

"Your doll?"

"Yep," Ruby said. She started walking toward the change rooms. "We have to hurry because we've only got three hours."

Hannah closed her eyes for a few seconds and he heard her say something under her breath. Then she followed Ruby to the change rooms.

"I'll wait out front," he said.

"No, Daddy, you have to stay with us. We need a boy's opinion," Ruby said bossily.

"I don't know how much help I'll be, Rubes. This isn't really my area of expertise."

Hannah gave him a dark look. "It's not mine, either, but you don't see me trying to wriggle off the hook."

He gave in, partly because Ruby was watching him with big, expectant eyes and he knew that if Beth was here she'd be all over this shopping trip, and partly because he was curious to see what Hannah looked like in a miniskirt.

Spectacular. That was how she looked. Her legs were long with well-defined muscles. Her waist was small. Her breasts… Well, he'd already done his fair share of staring at them. She filled out the minidress like a supermodel, but even Ruby couldn't help but notice how acutely uncomfortable Hannah was in it. She tugged at the neckline, she plucked at the hem, she pulled the fabric away from her middle. She looked about as happy as a cat being forced into a bath.

"You need to stop fiddling with the hem," Ruby said. "It's hard to see how the dress looks when you keep doing that."

"I don't think this one is a goer," Hannah said. "This hot pink color will be really hard to match when we try to find your dress, and I think blue would probably suit you better."

She slipped back into the change room and whisked the curtain closed.

Ruby sighed. "All right then. But remember, we've only got three hours."

Hannah refused to even open the curtain when she'd changed into the next dress. Ruby finally negotiated her way into the change room, and Joe couldn't help overhearing their conversation.

"The top on this dress looked much bigger on the hanger, didn't it?"

"Yes."

"It looks really small now. Really small."

Joe cleared his throat, his imagination going haywire.

"Here." Ruby stuck her head outside the curtain and thrust two dresses into his hands. "None of these are any good."

One of the dresses—the indecent one, he guessed—was still warm from Hannah's body. His fingers slipped through the fabric as he stepped onto the shop floor.

"Here, let me help you with those," a sales assistant said.

Joe returned to the change rooms in time to see the curtain whisking closed on Hannah as she vetoed the third dress. He caught a glimpse of gauzy floral fabric, spaghetti straps and a deeply ruffled hem.

"No good?" he asked.

"No!" Hannah said adamantly from beyond the curtain.

"I thought you looked beautiful," Ruby said wistfully.

"It's too tight. I think we need to find a winter dress. Something with sleeves."

"What do you think, Daddy?"

Ruby pulled the curtain open before Hannah could

object. Hannah lifted her hands as though she wanted to cover herself, then let them drop to her sides helplessly.

"It's terrible, isn't it?" she said.

The dress had a low, rounded neck that sat over her breasts in soft folds. He was sure there was a technical name for it—all he knew was that the draping fabric did a great job outlining the high, round shape of her breasts. The waistline was fitted and the skirt hugged the lines of her thighs until it reached just below her knees, where it merged into a froth of ruffles which ended just above her ankles.

He shoved his hands into his pockets. "I think this should definitely go on your short list."

Hannah's eyes widened. "No way. It's terrible. I look like a kid playing dress-up in her mom's closet."

He frowned, studying her face. She avoided his eyes, her cheeks flushed.

"Daddy likes it, and I get a vote, too, so it's on the short list," Ruby said triumphantly. She herded Hannah back into the changing cubicle. "Now get changed and we'll go to Myer's. They have lots of nice things."

Ruby started gathering dresses at the speed of light once they hit the big department store, once again going for what he could only describe as couture à la princess. Hannah accepted the hangers with a resigned stoicism that would have been funny if it didn't come from genuine discomfort. When Hannah disappeared into the change room with Ruby's selections, he caught his daughter's elbow before she could follow Hannah inside.

"Rubes, wait a minute. I think maybe we need to rethink the fashion direction a little."

Ruby's face wrinkled with confusion. "What?"

"I don't think Hannah's very comfortable in the dresses you're choosing for her."

"But she looks so good in them. She looks like a super-model."

"Yeah, but you've got to remember she's used to wearing jeans and T-shirts most of the time. I think maybe all the pink and frills are a bit too much for her."

Ruby stared at him as though he'd grown another head. "But they're pretty."

"I know. What I was thinking was, maybe we could find an outfit that was somewhere in between what you like and what Hannah likes. That way you'd both be comfortable."

"But Hannah said I could choose whatever I wanted. She said I was in charge of the fashion decisions." Ruby was starting to pout.

He touched her cheek. "You are. But Hannah isn't going to have much fun if you choose something for her that she's not very comfortable in, is she?"

Ruby's forehead puckered into a deep frown as she thought it through. "No more pink?" she asked after a long moment.

"Maybe a little less pink."

"No more frills?"

He held his thumb and forefinger an inch apart. "Just a few, not too many."

Ruby finally nodded. "Okay. If you think it will make Hannah more comfortable."

"I do."

A martial light in her eye, Ruby disappeared into the change rooms. A few seconds later, she reappeared with a pile of dresses in her arms. Hannah trailed after her, looking both confused and relieved.

"You don't want me to try them on anymore?"

"I've decided that maybe you should pick something. So I know what you like," Ruby said.

"Ruby, honestly, whatever you want is fine with me," Hannah said.

Ruby darted Joe a hopeful look, but he shook his head subtly. Ruby sighed. "No, it's better this way. Let's look around together."

Ruby looked to him again and he gave her a thumbs-up. She smiled. Then she slid her hand into Hannah's and led her into the ladies' department.

"Maybe we should look at the trousers," Ruby said.

Joe hung back for a moment, smiling at his daughter's handling of the situation. Just before they disappeared amongst the clothing racks, Hannah glanced over her shoulder. For a second their gazes met and held. Then the moment was gone and he'd lost sight of her behind a display of coats.

Hands shoved into the back pockets of his jeans, he started after them.

"WHAT ABOUT THESE? You'd look great in these," Ruby said.

Hannah surveyed the white jeans the girl was holding up. Sequins and embroidery glittered under the shop lights. They were the kind of jeans Mariah Carey might wear, dripping with bling and sex appeal.

Dear God. Was this morning never going to end? She felt as though she'd been ushered into her own personal version of hell.

"Wow. They're… great," Hannah said.

She'd hesitated just a moment too long. Ruby's bottom lip pouted. "You don't like them." It wasn't a question.

"But you do, sweetie, and I'm happy to wear them if you love them," Hannah said. Especially if it meant she got out of wearing one of the microdresses Ruby had been keen on initially and it meant this shopping expedition was over.

"No, *you* have to be comfortable," Ruby insisted stubbornly. "Daddy said you have to be happy, too."

Hannah frowned. "When did he say that?"

"Before, while you were in the change room. He said you didn't like pink and that you wouldn't have fun if you had to wear something you didn't like."

Hannah was nonplussed. How on earth had Joe picked up on her reluctance? She'd thought she'd been turning in an Academy Award-winning performance yet he'd been perceptive enough to register her discomfort. Further, he'd taken steps to remedy the situation.

"Come on, let's take a look around some more," Ruby said, not giving Hannah a moment to dwell on the realization.

They found the navy linen pants in the corner. Wide-legged, they featured a cute row of buttons across the front, giving them a stylized nautical appeal. Hannah pulled them from the rack and considered them briefly before putting them back. They were way too plain for Ruby's flamboyant taste.

Her pint-size shopping companion stepped forward and took the pants off the rack again.

"Let's try these on," she said.

Even Hannah was surprised by how good she looked and felt in the beautifully tailored pants. They made her butt look high and firm and were so long she'd have to have them taken up a little, a rarity indeed for a five-foot-eleven-inch woman. She stepped out of the changing room feeling good, a sensation that only intensified when she saw the look on Joe's face. His gaze went straight to her legs, lingered around her hips and thighs, then finally made it to her face.

"Okay?" she asked, smoothing a hand down her hip.

"Ah, yeah. You could say that."

He could have just been being polite, but she didn't think so. There was something in his eyes as he looked at her, something dark and intense…

The day was a downhill run once the pants had been given the thumbs-up by all parties. The moment they stepped into the children's department Ruby spotted a cute sailor dress in navy and white, complete with matching hat. Given the nautical feel of Hannah's trousers, it was love at first sight. Another hour was spent looking for a shirt to complete Hannah's outfit, then matching shoes for both her and Ruby. By the time Hannah was ready to pay for her share of the booty, she felt as though she'd run a marathon.

"This shopping business is exhausting," she said in an aside to Joe as they waited to be served.

"Tell me about it. And she's not even a teenager yet."

His tone was wry but the expression on his face was indulgent. Hannah felt an odd squeeze in her chest as she looked at him.

He was a nice man. They'd gotten off to a bad start, but now that she knew him a little better she understood that while he might be taciturn sometimes and stubborn as all hell, Joe Lawson had a big heart and a fierce determination to do right by his kids. Coupled with his undeniable physical attractions, he was a pretty compelling package.

She ducked her head and fished in her wallet for her credit card, thrown by her own thoughts. She wasn't interested in packages, compelling or otherwise. She was heartbroken, angry, bitter.

Right?

She slid her credit card from its slot and held it in readiness as the cashier began to key in her sale.

"Uh-uh. No way. I'm getting this," Joe said.

"What? No, you're not buying me clothes."

"Hannah, come on. You've already given up your Saturday for Ruby, and I saw the look on your face when you tried on those high heels. You're never going to wear them once the fashion parade is over."

"I might. I might go out to dinner one night or something. I'm not a complete scruff, you know."

"Nobody called you a scruff."

"Yeah, but you were thinking it."

He waited a beat before responding. "You have no idea what I'm thinking."

There was a low, slightly rough note to his voice and she jerked her head up and caught the intent look in his eyes again. Her heart did an odd little two-step. She suddenly felt overheated, as though she'd been working over a hot engine for too long.

While she was staring at him like a landed fish he reached out and plucked the credit card from her fingers.

"Hey!"

"You can have it back afterward."

She protested some more, but he was immovable, and afterward he insisted on buying her and Ruby an ice cream each, as well. Only then did he hand her credit card back to her.

"You were born about five centuries too late, you know that?" she grumbled as she put the card back in her wallet. "You need some serfs and peasants and whatnot to boss around."

"Shut up and eat your ice cream," he said mildly.

Ruby sucked in a shocked breath at his deliberate rudeness then pressed her fingers over her mouth to smother a giggle. Hannah couldn't stop the smile curving her mouth, either. She knew it would only encourage him in the mistaken belief that he knew best, but she couldn't seem to help it. He grinned back at her. It was the most relaxed she'd ever seen him, the deep lines by his mouth not so obvious, his big body loose.

"I'll just leave the money in your mailbox," she said.

"Then I'll give it back to you."

"I don't think you have any idea how determined I can be when I put my mind to it."

"I have a fair idea. And I guarantee you I'm more stubborn."

"There's no need to sound so proud of it."

"Oh, I'm not. I know it's a curse. Sometimes it stops me from being gracious when I really should be."

Hannah paused mid-bite, her gaze locking with his. His blue eyes were dancing with mischief and challenge.

"If you think being called ungracious will shame me into giving in, you've got another think coming. I've been ungracious all my life," she said.

"I bet."

She choked out a laugh, couldn't help herself. She pointed her ice cream at him.

"You want to wear this?"

He simply quirked an eyebrow as if to say "I dare you." Hannah stared at him, unable to stop smiling, sorely tempted to follow through with her threat.

"Dad? Don't we have to pick up Ben at one o'clock?"

Hannah blinked, suddenly aware that they were in the middle of the food court, people brushing past them, Ruby watching them quizzically.

"That's right. We do, don't we? Thanks for the reminder, sweetheart."

Joe moved away from Hannah then and the loss of his attention and charm was like the sun disappearing behind a cloud. Hannah blinked, then gave herself a firm shake.

What is wrong with you?

But she had a fair idea, although she didn't want to acknowledge it. Her life was complicated and messy enough without adding any new problems to the mix.

And Joe Lawson was definitely a problem—a big, broad, tall one.

"HANNAH, YOU NEED TO SIT still or I'll never get this done."

Joe hid a smile at the frustrated note in Robyn's voice. She'd volunteered to help both Hannah and Ruby with their hair for the fashion parade, but he figured she'd planned on working on a serene, calm model and not the fidgety, nervous recalcitrant in the chair.

"You've been at it for hours. Surely it's done now? You didn't spend this long on Ruby's hair," Hannah said.

"That's because I didn't move around so much," Ruby said.

Hannah's mom had curled Ruby's hair so that it sat in fat spirals on her shoulders. Once she donned her sailor's hat she was going to look exactly like Shirley Temple, minus the dimples.

Joe watched her, enjoying the light in her eyes and her air of suppressed excitement. By hook or by crook, he'd managed to ensure she took part in the parade. It felt like a minor victory.

In the week since their shopping expedition, Ruby had disappeared before dinner most nights. Each time he'd had to collect her from the Napiers' garage where the Thunderbird was now spread in all its many parts on the sheet. He found it not a little baffling that his daughter could be so interested in fashion and dolls yet revel so much in getting dirty alongside Hannah. Maybe, as his mother said, Ruby was simply exploring different aspects of herself, trying on the mantle of tomboy for a while without completely forgoing her love of sparkles and frills. Lately she'd taken to wearing jeans more, and he'd dodged more than one not-so-subtle suggestion that her wardrobe would never be truly complete without her own leather jacket. Biker style, naturally.

Joe glanced at Hannah's profile as she submitted to a final blast of hair spray. He wondered what she thought of her little shadow, whether she'd noticed Ruby's hero worship or not. His gut told him no. She was completely unaware of the power and appeal of her own personality. No doubt she thought that Ruby was simply a little mechanic in the making.

"All right. That's your hair done," Robyn announced.

"Thank God."

Hannah stood, shaking her head as though she could shake off the last few minutes.

"Don't do that! The pins will come out!"

Hannah's mother sounded so exasperated Joe grinned.

"Sorry. Can we go now?" Hannah asked.

"I guess I could put on the rest of your makeup at the school," her mother said, starting to pack things away into a hefty-looking makeup bag.

"I was kind of thinking I could wear some mascara and lipstick," Hannah said. "Let the clothes do all the talking, you know."

"Well, you were thinking wrong, weren't you?" Robyn said crisply.

Hannah rolled her eyes and Ruby giggled. Joe figured it was time to step in.

"How about we start loading up the car?" he suggested.

An hour later, he stood in the audience beside Robyn, waiting for Ruby to have her moment in the sun. His slim-line digital camera was tucked into his front pocket, and he was under strict instructions from Ruby to take lots of photos. Ben shuffled restlessly at Joe's side as he checked the camera battery one last time.

"How long is this going to take? Do we have to stay for the whole thing?"

Joe took pity on him and gave him some money to buy a drink and something to eat from the refreshments table at the rear of the school gym. When he turned back to the runway, he noticed Robyn was twisting and turning the bracelet on her wrist, her gaze darting back and forth between the clock on the wall and the curtained-off area behind the runway.

"They're running late, aren't they?" Robyn said. She sounded worried.

"I'm no expert, but I'm guessing that with that many women and only a limited number of mirrors there's a pileup."

Robyn didn't so much as crack a smile at his small joke.

"I hope everything goes okay. Hannah needs something to boost her confidence," she said. "She took such a blow when the wedding was called off…."

Joe couldn't hide his surprise. "Hannah was engaged?"

She was so prickly and independent, he couldn't imagine her letting anyone close enough to propose.

Robyn bit her lip, obviously debating whether she should say more or not.

"It's okay. I don't want to pry," he said quickly. Even though he did. Big-time.

"Oh, it's not like it's a state secret or anything. Everyone knows. I guess that's part of the problem. Lucas swept her off her feet, romanced her till she was so dizzy she didn't know which way was up. She was so happy…. And then Kelly came home from her job in the U.K. and everything went bad from there."

Joe wanted to ask who Kelly was, but he was afraid to

interrupt Robyn's train of thought. Hannah's mother shook her head as she remembered something.

"I should have seen it coming. I mean, Lucas and Kelly had so much more in common. They both worked in the IT industry, they shared so many opinions and dreams and ambitions. If only they had handled things better, told Hannah how they felt sooner rather than leaving it so late…."

Robyn was tearing up. He reached into his back pocket for the handkerchief he always carried.

"Here."

"Thanks." Robyn dabbed at her cheeks. "You'd think after six months I'd be a little more resigned to it all, but it's so damned hard watching my two girls torn apart when they used to be such great friends. Kelly didn't mean to hurt Hannah, I know that, but she did. And Hannah feels so hurt and angry and betrayed. Honestly, I don't see how this thing will ever resolve itself."

Joe stilled. Was he getting this straight? Had Hannah's *sister* stolen her fiancé? Could that possibly be right?

It was such a huge betrayal that he couldn't get his head around it. No wonder she preferred working alone in the garage at night to going out and partying or dating. Suddenly every encounter he'd ever had with her was cast in a different light. Her defensiveness, her silent stoicism, her uncertainty.

Before he and Robyn could talk further, music blasted out of the speakers and the lights dimmed. The crowd turned toward the T-shaped runway as one of Ruby's teachers, a tall, slim woman in her fifties, took up her post behind the podium to the far left of the runway.

"Welcome, ladies and gentleman. Elsternwick Primary wants to thank you all for your time and for your generous donations tonight. We've got lots of excited models backstage, so I'm going to dive straight into things. We hope you enjoy our parade as much as we enjoyed putting this night together for you."

She turned toward the stage, then consulted a sheet of paper in her hands.

"Our first models are Melinda and Liana. Let's give them a big welcome."

The crowd dutifully clapped as the first mother and daughter stepped onto the runway. Joe was too busy thinking about what he'd just learned to pay them much attention as they walked to the top of the runway to pose and turn and pose some more while the MC described their outfits.

He could only imagine how humiliated Hannah must have felt to be rejected by her lover in favor of her younger sister. And from what Robyn had intimated, the rejection had come late in the day. He stared blindly at the stage as he wondered how late. Had Hannah bought her dress? Chosen the menu for the reception? Booked the honeymoon?

What kind of an asshole would do that to a woman he'd been prepared to marry? What man could claim to have ever loved her, only to hurt her so badly? As for Hannah's sister...

"Our next models are Hannah and Ruby. Don't they look great?"

Joe lifted the camera, yet he could do nothing but stare. Something warm and primitive expanded in his gut as he stared at the woman holding his little girl's hand. She looked amazing. With her hair piled on top of her head and her eyes done in smoky makeup, Hannah's beauty was undeniable. The navy trousers clung to her long legs as she and Ruby began walking, the fine fabric of her ruffled, sleeveless white blouse betraying the sway of her breasts. But it wasn't simply her many physical attributes that held his gaze, it was the way she lifted her chin as she walked, the look in her eye as she took on the challenge of the fashion parade. She'd rather be anywhere else, he knew, was probably nervous and self-conscious as hell, but she was doing Ruby proud because she'd said she would.

What man could ever walk away from you?

The thought should have been disturbing since it had no place in his world, but it wasn't.

"Hannah wears a pair of Trent Nathan tailored trousers teamed with an Alannah Hill blouse and Marc Jacobs shoes," the MC said. "Ruby wears a sailor dress by Osh Kosh B'Gosh and shoes by Petit Shoes."

Realizing he had yet to take a single shot, Joe lifted the camera and hit the shutter button.

Hannah and Ruby got to the end of the runway and performed the little crossover maneuver he'd seen them practicing the past week. Ruby stuck her left hip out and propped her left hand on it, then Hannah followed suit. Then, unexpectedly, they saluted one another with their right hands, in keeping with their nautical theme. Joe was surprised into laughter, as was the rest of the audience. Hannah's smile was genuine as her gaze swept the audience. For just a fraction of a second their eyes caught and held as he lowered the camera. Then she and Ruby strutted their way back up the runway, Ruby clearly having the time of her life. One last wave, and they disappeared behind the curtains.

Joe could hear Robyn sniffing beside him as he flicked the camera off and tucked it back into its case. She gave him a rueful smile when he glanced across to check if she was okay.

"At least I'm getting good mileage out of your handkerchief," she said.

"I think they both had a good time."

"Oh, I know. That's why I'm crying," Robyn said. She laughed at her own logic.

The next mother and daughter team stepped onto the stage. Joe consulted his program. There were twenty entries in all, and they weren't even a quarter of the way through. He checked his watch, then made a decision. He leaned toward Robyn.

"I'm going to go backstage and check on Ruby. If Ben comes back, would you mind...?"

"Sure. I'll keep an eye on him."

He flashed her a grateful smile and started angling his way through the audience toward the back of the hall. Hannah and Ruby had attended a rehearsal on Wednesday evening and he knew that models who had walked the runway waited in a separate area to those yet to go on. One of the organizers pointed him in the right direction. Ruby leaped out of her seat when she saw him and practically bounced into his arms.

"Did you see, did you see?"

"I did. You were wonderful," he said.

Hannah remained seated, her expression unreadable as she watched them.

"Did you like our salute? That was Hannah's idea and I wasn't sure but everyone seemed to like it." Ruby's cheeks were pink, her sailor's hat tilted on a rakish angle.

"Everyone loved it," he said. "You were both beautiful. The stars of the show."

One of the organizers stepped into the holding area.

"Ruby, we need you to come line up with the other students now," she said.

"Oh, okay." She turned to Joe. "Just us kids are going to do our thing again at the end of the parade so I have to go now."

"Off you go, then," he said with a smile. "I'll keep an eye out for you up front."

"And take lots of pictures."

"Lots of pictures," he promised.

She ran off, curls bouncing. When he turned to talk to Hannah, her chair was empty. He frowned. Then he caught sight of her disappearing through a side door.

He followed her, finding himself in a dimly lit corridor. She had a head start on him, her high heels echoing loudly on the concrete floor as she walked briskly toward the exit sign at the end of the corridor.

"Hey. Wait up," he said, lengthening his stride to catch her.

She stopped, but even in the bad light he could tell she didn't want to.

"Where are you going?" he asked when he reached her side.

She gestured toward the exit sign. "Outside. It's too hot in there."

She fanned her shirt and a waft of something sweet and spicy hit him. With her high heels they were eye to eye and his gaze was drawn to her mouth. She was wearing gloss and her bottom lip looked very full and soft.

"Did you want something?" she asked, and he realized he'd been staring.

"I just wanted to say thanks. You did a great job out there. And Ruby loved every minute of it."

She shrugged. "Honestly, it was no big deal. And it was fun."

He couldn't stop himself from looking at her mouth again. "I also wanted to tell you how great you look."

She made a rude noise. "It's okay, you don't have to suck up to me."

"I wasn't," he said. "You look beautiful."

She frowned and shifted uncomfortably. "Well, don't be fooled. Underneath I'm still the same old grease-stained Hannah Napier."

"Maybe that's what's so good about it."

She stared at him. She looked deeply uncertain. Almost afraid. "I need some fresh air," she said in a subdued voice.

She started to leave. He didn't want her to go. He moved his body to block her path. Didn't think about it, or where it might lead. Just did it.

He felt the warm brush of her body against his side.

"Hannah," he said, but words failed him as he caught another waft of her perfume. "Hell," he said. And then he was leaning toward her.

She gasped with surprise as his mouth found hers. Her lips were incredibly soft against his. His tongue dipped briefly inside her mouth and he tasted her for the first time. Sweet and fresh. He went back for a second taste and after a small hesitation her tongue slid along his, tentative, searching.

Hot desire exploded in his belly and thighs and chest. He crowded her against the wall, his body pressing against hers, hip to hip, chest to chest, as his arms wrapped around her. He angled her head back, deepening the kiss. Her hands grabbed his shoulders as her tongue met his, stroking and challenging and tasting him as avidly as he tasted her. Her hips pressed forward and he could feel her breath coming in fast pants. He slid a hand down her back to her backside, his fingers gliding over the taut, round curve of her ass cheek.

She felt good. So firm and strong. He curled his fingers into her backside and used the grip to pull her more closely against his hips. She made an encouraging sound in the back of her throat. He left the sweet heat of her mouth to taste the skin of her cheekbone and explore the intimate whorls of her ear. She shuddered as his tongue dipped inside her ear, then she grabbed his hand from where it was clamped on her shoulder and dragged it down to her breast. She arched her back, filling his palm, her breast warm and heavy, her nipple already stiff with desire. He ran his thumb over her nipple once, twice, then rolled it between his thumb and forefinger. She shuddered and her hands slid onto his butt, guiding his hips closer as they kissed and caressed and rubbed against each other in the dark.

He was so hard it hurt. He wanted to get her naked and he wanted to be inside her. His frantic, horny mind started making plans. They could go out to the car. Or find a dark, private corner somewhere. Anything, anywhere, as long as he could satisfy the need building in his body.

She seemed to have the same thought. One of her hands slid from his ass to start fumbling with his belt. He found the buttons on her blouse and slid one free, then another, then another. He slid his hand into the gap and found warm, rounded flesh cupped in lace and satin. He pushed her bra aside and groaned as he felt the slide of her silky skin against his hand. She finished with his belt and popped the button on his jeans, reaching for the tab on his zipper. He got harder still as he imagined her hand on him, sliding up and down his—

Music and light blasted into the corridor as the door to the hall opened. Two women approached, talking and laughing. Joe jerked his hand from inside Hannah's shirt. Her hand slid from his waistband. They moved apart and she angled her body toward the wall as she fumbled with her shirt buttons.

Joe pasted on a polite smile and nodded as the women passed, aware he and Hannah probably looked as guilty as hell. God knows what the women were thinking, but he didn't really care. He was too busy trying to understand what had happened.

One minute they'd been talking, the next he'd been ready to throw Hannah over his shoulder and go find a handy cave.

It seemed to take a long time for the two women to reach the exit. He waited until he and Hannah were alone again before speaking.

"I'm sorry. I didn't mean for that to happen."

"It's no big deal."

They were both lying. She couldn't look him in the eye, and he'd wanted to kiss her, touch her from the moment he first saw her, even if it had taken him until this moment to admit it to himself.

He didn't know what to do, what to say. He simply hadn't been looking for anything like this. He'd loved Beth and he'd believed his capacity for this kind of need had died with her. Apparently it hadn't.

"I'm sorry," he said again because he didn't know what else to say.

"You already said that. I get it," Hannah said. "Let's just forget it ever happened."

Before he could respond, she walked away, heading for the exit.

Forget it ever happened.

It was a great idea, in theory. In practice, he knew it was going to be a long time before he was able to forget the feel of Hannah's breast in his hand and the sound of her breath in his ear and the feel of her long, strong body pressed against his.

The door opened and she was silhouetted against the night sky for a handful of seconds. The door swung shut, throwing him back into darkness. After a long moment, he turned and walked the other way.

CHAPTER SEVEN

HANNAH WAS STILL REELING from Joe's kiss when she woke
the next morning. She lay in bed and stared at the patterns
the morning sun made on her ceiling and relived the feel of
his big shoulders beneath her hands and the slide of his
tongue inside her mouth.

God, she'd wanted him. Right there, right then. Even
with Lucas she'd never gotten so hot and heavy so quickly.
With him sex had always been more fun and playful than
hot and fiery. Lucas had never rubbed her the wrong way as
Joe did, either. But maybe that was part of it. Maybe the rub
was part of the tension, part of the heat.

She shook her head, trying to shake the memory loose.
It had been a mistake, a big one. They'd both agreed that
was the case. So there was no point closing her eyes and remembering how hard he'd felt through his clothes, how
much she'd wanted to press her lips to his skin and slide her
hands over his body.

She shifted in the bed, feeling hot and sticky all over
again.

All those years out on the oil rigs had given him a fantastic body. There had been no softness to him, no hint of
weakness in his broad shoulders and muscular arms....

Hannah threw back the covers. Lying in bed fantasizing
about Joe Lawson was the biggest waste of time under the

sun. What had happened had been a freak occurrence, never to be repeated, brought about by too much makeup, a dimly lit hallway and a pair of well-cut trousers. And even if it hadn't been, there was no future in it. He was a widower with two kids, and she was about to set out on a round-Australia trip.

She dressed in her usual jeans and T-shirt after her shower then entered the kitchen. Her mother was making tea and she gave Hannah an assessing look as she poured milk and spooned in sugar.

"You were very quiet last night after the parade. Did you enjoy yourself?" Robyn asked.

"Sure. Ruby had a great time and I didn't take a dive into the audience. What was not to like?"

Hannah collected the cereal box and a bowl, hoping all the activity would hide the slow tide of warmth she could feel creeping up her face. She could only imagine what her mother would say if she knew Joe had kissed her. And that she'd kissed him back and the only reason things hadn't gone any further was because they'd been interrupted.

God, what if we hadn't been? What would have happened if those two women hadn't come along?

"Hannah! You're getting corn flakes all over the floor."

Hannah blinked and realized she was pouring cereal into an already full bowl.

"Sorry. Must have inhaled too much hair spray last night."

Her mother sighed and put down her teacup. "Was it so horrible, getting all gussied up for a change?"

Hannah thought about the way she'd felt when she looked at her made-up face and hair last night—like an impostor, a fake.

"It's not me, all that stuff. You know that," she said. "I know you wish I was more girlie like Kelly, but I'm not, Mom."

Her mother's face clouded. "I don't wish you were like Kelly. I love you the way you are."

"Right."

"I just want you feel good about yourself, Hannah. I don't care how you do it."

Hannah scooped the spilled cereal into the box, using the small task to buy some time. She wanted to tell her mother that she did feel good about herself, that she knew she was a good mechanic and a good person, but she knew that wasn't what her mom meant. The truth was that Lucas's betrayal had knocked her already fragile sexual confidence. She'd never been very good at playing the man-woman game. She didn't know how to flirt. Pretending she was helpless or that she needed a man had never been her style. And she'd never been adept at working out when a man was interested in her or not.

Case in point: Joe Lawson. Until the moment he'd blocked her body with his own and leaned toward her, she'd been almost one hundred percent certain that he considered her a nuisance to be tolerated because his daughter had formed an attachment to her. But then he'd kissed her and she'd realized that the awareness she felt when she was around him wasn't one-sided. Not by a long shot, if his heated response was anything to go by.

"Hannah?"

Hannah glanced up and saw her mother was frowning at her. She'd zoned out again, thinking about Joe. What on earth was wrong with her? It wasn't as though she'd never been kissed before, for Pete's sake.

"Sorry, did you say something?"

"I did." Her mother hesitated a moment, studying Hannah's face. "Lucas called earlier. He'd like to speak to you."

Hannah waited until she'd finished pouring milk on her corn flakes before responding. "What does he want?"

"I'm not sure. To talk to you, I suppose."

Hannah could feel her mother watching her. She crossed to the fridge and put the milk away. What on earth could Lucas have to say? He'd already apologized. She'd refused to take his money more times than she could count. What more was left?

An insidious, dark thought wormed its way into her mind. What if he and Kelly had had a falling-out? What if he'd decided that he'd made a big mistake, choosing her sister over Hannah?

What if he wanted Hannah back?

A few months ago, the thought would have made her heart thump with nervousness and a twisted form of hope. Today, it made her frown.

She didn't want Lucas back.

She froze. When had that happened? When had the wishing for what-once-was faded away to nothing?

She had no idea, but it felt good. As though she'd shed a weight. Without giving herself a chance to think, she walked to the phone and picked it up.

"What's his number?" she asked.

Her mother's eyebrows rose toward her hairline, but she reeled off the number without comment. Lucas picked up on the third ring.

"Lucas speaking."

"It's me. Hannah."

"Hi." There was a short pause. "Thanks for calling." As always, he sounded uncomfortable. Awkward. Regretful. One of the many reasons why she'd gone out of her way to avoid any contact with him or her sister. She didn't want Lucas's pity.

Apparently she didn't want his anything anymore.

She was still getting used to the feeling.

"Mom said you wanted to speak to me."

"I did. I mean, I do. Would it be okay to meet for coffee?"

Her mother was making a big show out of pouring more water into the teapot, but Hannah knew she was listening.

"Can't you just say what you need to say over the phone?"

"I'd rather do it in person. I can meet you at The Watering Hole or wherever you like," Lucas said.

"Not The Watering Hole," she said instantly. The last thing she wanted was to see Joe again so soon. There was no way she'd be able to look him in the eye without blushing from head to toe.

"What about the coffee shop near the workshop? Ten minutes?"

"Twenty. I need to finish my breakfast."

"Okay."

Her mother deliberately talked about every other subject under the sun while Hannah finished her cereal, but she gave Hannah an extra-fierce hug goodbye when Hannah stood to leave.

Lucas was waiting at an outside table when she pulled up, his sunglasses resting on the table before him. He was looking the other way, his foot tapping restlessly, but his gaze swung around when he heard the rumble of her bike.

He stood when she approached the table. He was wearing jeans and a white linen shirt and he needed a shave.

"Hannah."

"Lucas."

They both sat at the same time.

"Thanks for coming at such short notice."

Hannah put her gloves on the table and shrugged out of her leather jacket.

"What's up?" she said, meeting his eyes squarely.

He laughed self-consciously. "You never did beat around the bush, did you?"

"Nope. Life's too short."

"Yep." He rubbed his hands down the front of his jeans and for a moment she worried that she'd guessed right, that he really was trying to find some way to reconnect with her.

"I wanted you to be the first to hear. Your mom doesn't know yet, or my parents. Only me and Kelly. She's pregnant. We're having a baby."

Hannah blinked, waiting for the old pain to reignite in her chest. Kelly was having Lucas's child, something Hannah had once dreamed of doing herself. She'd had it all planned—two children, eighteen months apart. She hadn't cared what sex they were, as long as they were healthy and as long as they had Lucas's deep green eyes.

But the pain didn't come. Slowly her shoulders relaxed. At long last, after six months of dragging her ass around, she'd finally let go of some of her anger and hurt and pain.

"Congratulations," she said after a short, intense silence. "When is she due?"

"The end of March."

Hannah did some mental arithmetic.

"So she's only eight weeks?"

"That's right. We found out yesterday. Like I said, I wanted you to be the first to know."

She looked at him, really looked at him, for the first time in six months. Apart from his obvious nervousness and discomfort at meeting with her, he looked well.

"Are you happy?" she asked suddenly.

"About the baby? Of course. You know I've always wanted kids."

"I meant in general. Are you happy with life, with Kelly, with everything?"

He glanced down at his sunglasses, clearly struggling to find the right thing to say.

"Just tell me the truth, Lucas."

He met her eyes. "Yes. I'm happy. I wish it hadn't been at your expense, but I love Kelly."

His declaration stung a little, but that was more pride than anything else.

"Did you ever love me?" She wasn't going to go home and cry over the answer, but she'd always wanted to know.

"Yes. I still do. But it's different with Kelly. I can't explain it. It's just…right. With you, it was like we were best friends and you happened to be a woman. It was comfortable. I'm never comfortable with Kelly."

She stared at him, trying to understand. "And that's a good thing?"

He smiled and focused on something over her shoulder for a second or two, thinking it over. "Yeah, it is."

She looked away. "Well, I guess we're all better off, then."

Lucas focused on her again. "There's no excuse for what we did to you, Hann. It was the last thing you deserved. If I could change it, I would."

She smiled faintly. "No you wouldn't. Not if it meant giving up Kelly."

He looked as though he was going to argue for a moment, then he shrugged. "More of that Hannah Napier no-bullshit honesty. I miss it."

"Well, you know, I'm happy to be honest with you anytime you like," she said drily. He laughed and she found herself joining in.

Incredible. She was sitting with her ex-fiancé at a coffee shop on a Saturday morning and *laughing*. She wondered if she should pinch herself, to make sure this was real.

Lucas relaxed into his chair, the smile still playing around his mouth. "You going to have a coffee with me?" he asked.

"You paying?"

"Yep."

"Then I'll have a large mochachino. And a piece of orange poppyseed cake."

His smile broadened. She stretched out her legs as he called over a waitress and placed their order. He waited until the girl was gone before leaning forward and putting his elbows on the table.

"There's something else I wanted to talk you about," he said.

"Let me guess—the money." In the past six months she hadn't had a conversation with him or Kelly that didn't include some mention of her debts.

"Yes." He pulled a piece of paper from his back pocket and put it on the table between them. It was a check, and when he folded it open she saw it was made out to her for $20,000.

"Let me cover the loss we took on the apartment," he said.

She opened her mouth to speak but he held up a hand.

"Before you rip my head off and stuff it down my neck, let me say my bit. It's my fault this mess happened. The moment I realized I felt something more for your sister than I should have, I should have put the wedding on hold. But I didn't. I let things play out because I couldn't believe that what I was feeling was real and that Kelly felt the same way. And because I knew I was going to hurt you."

He paused as the server delivered their order. Once they were alone again he leaned forward, elbows on the table, expression intense.

"I'm the one who screwed things up. Why should you suffer? Why should you carry the can for my mistake? Give me one good reason."

Not so long ago, Hannah would have had half a dozen good reasons, all of them angry and bitter. She looked at the check and thought about what a difference it would make to her life. She wouldn't have to delay her road trip any longer. No more scrimping and saving. No more feeling trapped. She could hit the road and follow her dream. North first, to the New South Wales coast. Then on to Canberra to see the nation's capital. Sydney, Byron Bay, Coffs Harbour—there were so many places she'd circled on her map. And that wasn't even including the less-traveled parts of the country. The red heart, the small bush towns, the tropical communities at the northernmost tip of the continent.

"It won't put it right. It won't come close to making it up to you, I know that. But at least it will make life easier for you," Lucas said.

She turned away from him, trying to think and unable to do it properly while he was watching her with those familiar green eyes. Was she letting her sister and her ex off the hook by taking the money? Or was she being smart, looking out for herself?

A dark navy SUV pulled up at the curb. Joe swung out of the driver's seat, Ben exiting the passenger side. Joe slung his arm around his boy's shoulders as they walked toward the Balas's corner store, bending to say something that made Ben laugh and squirm out from under his father's arm.

She told herself to look away, but she couldn't take her eyes off Joe. There was so much arrogant masculinity in the way he walked. As though he owned the world. It made her remember the way he'd pushed her against the wall last night, the utter solidness of his body pressed against hers.

Just before they entered the store, Joe turned his head. He was wearing sunglasses, but she knew he'd caught her watching him. She jerked her gaze away, but not before he'd nodded his head in acknowledgment.

"So, what's it going to be, Hannah?" Lucas asked.

Her hand closed around the check without her even willing it. She folded it in half and slid it into the front pocket of her jeans. Lucas smiled.

"Thank you," he said. "You have no idea what this means to me. And to Kelly."

She looked him dead in the eye. "I'm not doing it for you. I'm doing it for me."

"I'm just glad you're doing it."

She took a mouthful of her coffee. Lucas looked as though he was ready to break into song and skip up the street. He hadn't been lying when he said he was relieved.

She searched her heart and realized she was relieved, too. She'd cut the last tie that bound them all together. What happened next, she had no idea. But she was sick of living in the past.

JOE TRIED TO CONCENTRATE on what Mr. Balas was saying, but his mind was outside, wondering what Hannah was doing with the blond-haired guy in the white shirt. Was he a friend? A customer?

He kept thinking about the way the guy had been watching her, as though right at that moment she was the most important thing in the world to him.

So not a friend, then. Something more.

It took Joe a moment to recognize the emotion burning in his belly as jealousy. It had been a while since he'd had reason to be jealous of anyone.

"So, Dad, I'll see you after two, okay?" Ben said.

"Sure, no problems. Call my cell if you finish early."

He kept his gaze on his car as he exited the store, but he could still see Hannah and her friend out of the corner of his eye. They were talking, leaning toward one another. He told himself what she did and who she did it with was none of his business. It didn't make any difference to the burn in his gut.

Ruby was having a playdate with one of her friends from school so Joe had the house to himself when he got home. He tidied the kitchen, then threw on a load of washing. By the time he'd straightened the living room and cleaned the bathroom, he was all out of busywork. He did a lap of the house, walking from the living room to the kitchen and through the hall to the bedrooms, restless energy and a vague sense of dissatisfaction gnawing at him. Finally he came to a halt in his bedroom doorway.

The bed was a mess, a tangle of sheets and quilt, a couple of pillows thrown on the floor. He'd had a bad night's sleep, tossing and turning, his mind full of images and sense memories: Hannah's breast, full and warm in his hand; the taste of her in his mouth; the feel of her firm, rounded ass. Somehow, somewhere in the dark hours, Hannah and Beth had gotten mixed up in his dreams and he'd found himself looking into Beth's face but pressed against Hannah's body, guilt and desire twisting inside him until he didn't know which was which. He'd woken sweaty and agitated, the sheets wrapped around his legs in a confining snarl.

Now, he sat on the end of the bed, thighs wide, hands on his knees, his unfocused gaze on the carpet.

When Beth had died, the emptiness she'd left in his life had seemed so profound, so all-encompassing that he hadn't been able to see past it. He hadn't been able to imagine ever wanting another woman again, let alone taking the risk of loving someone again.

And then he'd met Hannah.

He'd tried like hell not to notice her, but his body had had other ideas. She fascinated him and aggravated him in equal measures. She made him laugh. And she made him want things he had no business wanting. He wanted to touch her, slide his skin against hers, lose himself inside her. He wanted to make her smile. He wanted to tease her, just to see her rise to the bait. And he wanted to chase away the shadows in her eyes.

He didn't know how to reconcile all that want with his memories of Beth and what they'd once had together. The reality was that he and Hannah hardly knew each other. There was a physical attraction. There was the potential for more, maybe. But he had to take the next step to find out. And he wasn't sure if he was ready to do that.

By the time he'd stripped all the beds and remade them and put on yet another load of laundry, it was time to collect the kids.

"I've decided what I want to get for Hannah," Ruby said the moment she climbed into the car.

They'd discussed buying Hannah a thank-you gift on the way home from the parade last night, in between Ruby scrolling through the photos he'd taken with the digital camera.

"Okay. What did you come up with?"

"Perfume. Carly's mom has this really pretty stuff in a bottle shaped like a lady's body, but with no arm or legs or head."

"Right. Well, perfume it is, then. We can swing by the mall after we pick up Ben."

Once they got to the mall he sent Ben off to prowl the video game shop while he and Ruby hit the department store. Ruby sampled almost every perfume on display until she spotted one with a bottle shaped like a shiny red apple. Joe suspected it could have smelled like insect repellent and she'd still have chosen it.

"Can we take it to her now? Please?" Ruby pleaded in the car on the way home.

"Sure, if she's home."

He wasn't sure if he wanted her to be or not. He still didn't have his head on straight after last night. But he also wanted to see her.

What are you doing, man? What are you thinking? She kissed you, that was all. You have two kids and so much baggage it's ridiculous. You're not exactly a great catch.

But apparently that didn't matter, because when they pulled into the street and he saw Hannah in the garage at her mom's place, his gut tightened and his palms got sweaty.

What are you, a teenage girl?

Ruby was out of the car in a flash, running next door to the Napiers'. Joe followed more slowly, Ben trailing behind him. Hannah was holding the wrapped gift in her hands by the time they reached the garage.

"You didn't have to do this," Hannah said, but the smile on her face said she was pleased.

"I wanted to. I had such a good time last night and we had the best clothes in the whole parade and no one else looked as good as we did," Ruby said.

Ben made a rude noise at his sister's shameless vanity.

"Ah, the modesty of the young," Joe said.

Ruby frowned. "But it's true, Daddy. None of the other women looked even close to as good as Hannah did."

Hannah gave Ruby's shoulder a light nudge. "I think you might be a little biased there, sport."

"No, I'm not. You're beautiful," Ruby said.

Deep color stained Hannah's cheeks. She didn't seem to know what to say and she shot him an anguished, self-conscious look.

"Open your present," he said, a little amused and a lot touched by her reaction.

She seemed grateful for the diversion. She ran her thumb

under the tape and pulled the paper open carefully. Not a ripper, like his kids, Joe noted. But her spotless workshop and attention to detail showed that she was a woman who appreciated order and workmanship.

"Oh, wow, this is lovely, Ruby," she said as she discovered the perfume.

Ruby was bouncing on her toes, thoroughly enjoying her moment of generosity. "I picked it because of the bottle. It's shaped like an apple."

"Cool. I can't wait to try it."

"You should put some on now," Ruby said.

"Okay." Hannah glanced at him quickly from under her lashes before she pried the box open. He wondered what she was thinking, if she was remembering last night.

The smell of sweet toffee apples and something more floral filled the air as Hannah sprayed her wrists.

"Mmm, that's really nice. Thank you so much for such a great present, Ruby," she said. She pulled Ruby close for a hug.

Warmth spread through Joe's chest as he watched the way Ruby hugged her back, her small hands clenching Hannah's T-shirt.

Ben had been lingering on the threshold, but now he stepped inside, drawn to the bike parts laid out on the garage floor. He touched a rusty mudguard with his toe, curious, and the piece of metal teetered for a few seconds before falling over with a loud clang.

"Sorry," Ben said, starting guiltily. "I didn't mean to break it."

Hannah shrugged. "There's nothing you can do to hurt that big old lump of rust. I've got a lot of work to do before it's worth anything," Hannah said. "Go ahead and check it out all you want."

Ruby tugged on the hem of Hannah's tank top to regain

her attention. "We got lots of pictures last night. Do you want to see?"

"Sure," Hannah said.

"Okay." Ruby promptly turned and bolted for home.

"Nothing like an instant response," Joe said drily.

"I'd better make sure she doesn't break the camera," Ben said.

Hannah was smiling as she watched him go, but the moment their eyes met she sobered.

It was the first time they'd been alone since the kiss, and Joe was acutely aware of it. Hannah seemed just as uncomfortable, shuffling her feet and reaching for a rag to clean her already-clean hands. He watched her twist her hands in the soft cloth and wondered if he should apologize for what had happened between them. He'd initiated it, after all. He'd been the one who pushed her against the wall. But she'd hardly been a reluctant participant.

The memory made his blood heat. He shoved his hands into the front pockets of his jeans and did some foot shuffling of his own.

"Listen, about last night," he said.

Hannah's gaze flew to his face. "I know, it was a mistake. It was stupid—"

"It wasn't a mistake," he said before he could edit himself. "That wasn't what I was going to say."

"Oh." She reached for her ponytail, combing her fingers through the ends of her hair for a beat or two. Finally she met his eyes again. "What were you going to say?"

"Come out with me?"

She looked as surprised as he felt. Hadn't he decided this morning that whatever he was feeling for Hannah was too hard, too confusing, too much for a man in his position?

"You mean on a date?" She said it as though he'd suggested they attempt nuclear fission rather than share a meal.

"Yeah. You, me, no kids. The usual kind of thing."

"Why?"

She was asking him that after last night? But he could see she was serious and he reminded himself what her mother had told him last night. Hannah's confidence had taken a huge knock recently.

"Because I like you."

"Oh." Her gaze dropped to her feet, but he could see the corners of her mouth curling into a smile.

"What's so funny?"

"Um, I think I like you, too," she said.

"You *think* you like me?" he asked lightly, something inside him relaxing at her words. She was going to say yes. He could feel it.

"Yeah. But we don't really know that much about each other, do we, to know if we really like each other?"

He knew enough. He knew that she was sexy and strong and too damned appealing for his peace of mind, which was why he was standing in her garage despite his many misgivings.

"That's what dinner would be about. Getting to know each other a little better, no distractions."

"But—" She didn't finish whatever it was she'd been about to say, instead lapsing into a frowning silence.

He took a step closer. "But what?"

She lifted her head and looked straight into his eyes. In an instant all the heat from last night was there between them. He could feel himself growing hard, just from a look.

"Okay. Yes." She sounded a little breathless. She licked her lips. "I'll go out with you."

She looked as dazed as he felt. But she'd said yes. He smiled, and she smiled back at him.

She'd said yes. Now he only had to worry about what the hell that meant, and what happened next.

CHAPTER EIGHT

HANNAH COULDN'T BELIEVE she'd said yes. What had she been thinking? Even if she hadn't still been grappling with the aftermath of her failed wedding, there was the small matter of her imminent trip around Australia and the fact that Joe had two children to consider. Not exactly your ideal dating scenario.

And yet she'd said yes.

You like him. At least be honest with yourself. You like him, and you think he's sexy.

Which was why she shaved her legs for the first time in months on Sunday night, and why she chose her best underwear and sprayed on a generous amount of her new perfume. She balked at spending too much time on makeup, however. The Hannah he'd kissed at the fashion parade was not the real her. If he wanted that woman—and she was almost convinced that must be what was going on, since he'd never grabbed her and pressed her against a wall when she was in her work coverall—then he was in for a rude awakening. She chose jeans and a shirt for the same reason, refusing to pretend to be anything other than who she was. She'd played that game with Lucas—grown out her hair, worn more makeup, bought more dresses. Then her sister had come home and cast Hannah well and truly into the shade.

She hadn't told her mother about the date. She didn't

want Robyn jumping to conclusions or assuming anything. Probably it would be a one-off. No point getting her excited over nothing.

Good advice, Napier. How about taking it yourself?

Because there was no denying the anticipation tap-dancing in her belly. She was half scared, half excited about the prospect of spending a whole evening with Joe. Sitting across the table from him. Talking to him. Thinking about that kiss.

Even if it was probably only going to be a one-off.

She gave herself a quick head to toe. Fitted black shirt with tiny black flowers embroidered on it. Her good dark denim jeans. Her favorite black boots with the Western heel. Her hair was long and loose and she was wearing a touch of mascara and lipstick. She looked about as good as she was ever going to.

She shrugged into her leather jacket and grabbed her wallet. Her mother was chopping vegetables at the kitchen counter and she looked surprised when Hannah appeared in the kitchen doorway.

"You're going out?"

"Yeah. Sorry. I meant to tell you, but it kind of slipped my mind," Hannah fibbed.

Her mother took in her loose hair and good shirt in a single glance. The corners of her mouth twitched for a second before she returned her attention to the chopping board. "Not a problem. Have a nice time."

Hannah suspected her mother knew exactly who she was going out with. She hovered for a moment longer, trying to decide if she should address the issue or not. But her mother didn't look up again, so Hannah simply shrugged and headed for the door. Joe was waiting by his car already, his hair damp from the shower. He looked good in a dark brown shirt and black jeans. Maybe a little too good—one look at him and her palms got clammy.

"Hi," he said.

"Hi."

"You look great," he said, his gaze running appreciatively over her body.

She shrugged, unsure what to say. She'd never known how to handle compliments. Probably through lack of practice. Guys tended not to tell you how nice you looked while you were helping them strip a carbie or beating them at touch football.

"Shall we get going? I booked us a table at an Italian place," he said.

"Okay."

She rolled her eyes as she walked to the passenger door. Could she be any less sophisticated? So far she'd managed two words and a shrug. Next she'd be grunting in response to his questions.

She stopped in surprise when she realized Joe had rounded the car to open her door for her.

She muttered a disconcerted thanks as she slid into the car. She wasn't used to having men wait on her.

She concentrated on securing her seat belt, but she was very aware of his aftershave as he got in beside her and started the engine. Something spicy and mellow that made her think of wood and leather.

She smoothed her hands down her thighs. "So where is this place you're taking me, anyway?"

"It's called Il Solito Posto. It's in a laneway off Collins Street. One of the guys at work recommended it."

"Cool."

"If it sucks, you can help me come up with a suitable punishment for him."

She laughed. "That'll teach him to recommend anything."

"Exactly."

The restaurant turned out to be partly underground, with windows high in the wall that offered glimpses of the legs of passersby in the bluestone alleyway outside. They were seated in a corner, the fat candle on the small wooden table casting a warm light over them.

"You want something to drink to start with?" Joe asked as they scanned their menus.

Hell, yeah.

Maybe some alcohol would make her feel less stiff and on edge. "That sounds good."

He ordered a bottle of red for them to share and a plate of antipasto. She chose gnocchi for her main. He chose osso bucco. With the ordering out of the way and wineglasses in front of them, they stared across the table at each other.

"This is nice," she said lamely.

Good one. Hit him with more of that sparkling banter, Napier.

"Yeah. Place seems good." He took a hefty slug from his wine then shifted in his chair.

He was regretting his decision. She could see it in every line of his body. He'd asked her out on impulse, maybe because he had been misled by all that hair and makeup the other night, maybe because he'd felt grateful on Ruby's behalf. And now he was willing the minutes to pass.

"Listen," they both said simultaneously, leaning forward. Hannah laughed awkwardly. "You go first," she said.

Joe cleared his throat. "I was just going to say sorry if I'm a bit rusty. Haven't done this sort of thing for a while."

Dull color traced his cheekbones.

Huh. So she wasn't the only one flailing around here. The

knowledge helped loosen the band of tension around her chest. "Well, in case you hadn't noticed, I'm not exactly a social butterfly myself," she said drily. "I've kind of been keeping a low profile lately."

She took a deep breath, then let it out again. She hated telling anyone about the wedding, but he was bound to hear it from someone eventually. The whole neighborhood knew about it, and if he heard it somewhere else first then he'd think she'd kept it secret on purpose, which would give the wedding far more importance than it deserved.

"I was engaged last year, but the wedding was called off at the last minute," she said before she could change her mind.

There was a short pause before he answered. "That must have been tough."

She checked to make sure he wasn't giving her the pity look. She'd seen it often enough over the past six months to be able to spot it at ten paces. But he simply looked straight at her, his deep blue eyes giving nothing away.

She tightened her grip on her wineglass. Might as well reveal the full horror. "It was called off because my fiancé fell in love with my sister."

His expression didn't change; he simply ducked his head in acknowledgment. She narrowed her eyes.

"You already knew, didn't you? Who told you?"

"Your mom."

She sat back in her chair, expelling her breath on an exasperated sigh. "Bloody hell. Is nothing sacred?"

"Not where moms are concerned. Talk to mine long enough and she'll tell you I took twice as long to toilet train as other kids and that when I was fifteen she caught me with my hand up Sally Perkin's blouse."

She smiled, even though she made a mental note to have

a word with her mother on the subject of discretion. "I guess there's not much left for me to confess, then."

"Was that who you were talking to yesterday at the coffee shop? Your ex?"

"You don't miss much."

"Used to work on an oil rig. Keeping an eye on what's going on around me is pretty much a survival skill."

"Hmm. You know, in a woman that would simply be called plain old nosiness," she said.

He smiled. "Lucky I'm not a woman, then."

Her gaze ran over his shoulders and broad chest. He was *definitely* not a woman. "Lucas wanted to tell me my sister is pregnant."

Joe went very still, then swore under his breath. "I hope you told him where to get off."

She liked that he was angry on her behalf. "Not exactly. I congratulated him. I'm not going to waste the rest of my life being angry with them."

"You a Buddhist or something?"

"Nope. Just sick of feeling like I want to punch something."

He smiled and she found herself smiling in return. They both sat back as the waiter put a large white platter on the table between them. Hannah surveyed the tempting array of antipasto. Her mouth watered.

"Yum," she said.

Joe laughed. Then he lifted his glass and tilted it toward her in a toast.

"You're a gutsy woman, Hannah Napier. But I guess I already knew that about you."

Because she didn't know what to do with the warmth in his eyes and tone, she reached for the serving tongs and started filling his plate.

"Thanks," he said when she'd finished.

She shrugged and slid some stuffed mushrooms onto her own plate.

"So, Ruby tells me you've got a big trip planned. Any idea when you're going to hit the road?" Joe said as he picked up his knife and fork.

"Soon." Hannah thought about the check she'd deposit first thing Monday morning. "Sooner than I thought, actually. I really only need to wait for the owner of the garage to find someone to take over from me, buy some gear then I'm off."

There was a small silence. When she glanced up he looked…disappointed. That was the only way she could describe the mix of frustration and regret she saw in his eyes. Then he blinked and it was gone.

"Ruby's going to miss you," he said, spearing a chunk of fried polenta with his fork.

What about you? Will you miss me?

She shook the thought off. They hardly knew each other. How could he miss someone he barely knew?

"I'll miss her, too. She's been a fantastic help with the Thunderbird."

"You won't get to finish restoring it."

"No. I guess I won't."

Their gazes met across the table.

"So, where are you heading for first?" he said, breaking the small silence.

Hannah spent the next twenty minutes doing her bit to clear the platter of delicious Italian morsels while detailing her planned route to him.

"So you're going to camp most of the time?" he asked.

"If I can. The weather is good and I think it's the best way to see the country."

"Not going to miss hot and cold running water and all the mod cons?"

She cocked her head and raised an eyebrow. "Not a fan of the great outdoors, Joe?"

"Me? I love it. Always have. Beth couldn't stand it. Had to have a roof over her head, air-conditioning, running water, you name it."

The name came out of his mouth so casually, so naturally, but they both stilled. It was the first time he'd ever mentioned his wife to her. He fiddled with the stem of his wineglass for a few seconds. "Beth was my wife," he said.

She nodded. She could see this was hard for him, and she guessed that it wasn't something he talked about very often.

"How did she die?" she asked, trying to make it easier for him since he seemed determined to address the issue.

He frowned slightly. "How did you...?"

"Ruby."

"Ah."

"Seems the family telegraph has been working for both of us," she joked. Anything to ease the desolate look that had come into his eyes.

"It was a car accident. I was up north on the rig and she was driving to collect Ben from karate practice. A driver ran a red light, smashed into her car."

His knuckles were white, and she was afraid he was going to snap the stem in half. She reached across the table and laid her hand over his.

"It's okay. We don't have to talk about it."

He stared at her, his expression bleak. Then something in him seemed to relax. "It's more that I'm out of practice. It's been two years. And people don't exactly line up to talk about it."

"I can imagine," she said drily.

"The worst of it was that she didn't die straightaway. She had massive head and internal injuries. They operated while I flew down to Sydney from the rig. She died before the plane landed."

She tried to imagine the torture of sitting on a plane, hoping against hope that her loved one would survive, willing the plane to fly faster, get there sooner, only to arrive to the worst possible news.

"I'm so sorry. That must have been a terrible thing to come home to."

"Yeah. Worst flight of my life. I was almost too scared to turn my cell phone on when we landed. Then my mom called."

He blinked a few times and her chest ached for him. She had no words of comfort to offer. What was there to say, after all? If she knew him better, she would have simply stood and rounded the table to put her arms around him. But she didn't, so she sat quietly while he took a swallow of wine.

"Sorry. Like I said, out of practice," he said.

"Tough memories."

He nodded.

The waiter cleared the platter and their side plates. Hannah took advantage of the moment to pull herself together. Watching the grief on Joe's face, it had suddenly hit her that he was still hung up on his dead wife. And that meant that anything that happened between them was, by definition, doomed to failure.

Hello? You're about to hit the road. What does it matter if he's over his dead wife or not? It means nothing to you. He means nothing to you. One kiss does not give you the right to feel disappointed.

But the fact was that she couldn't help looking at Joe and

seeing a world of what-ifs. What if they'd met at another time, when she'd been less angry and he'd been less hurt? What if either of them had been prepared to take the risk of loving someone again? Because she had the feeling that Joe Lawson was a man it would be very easy to love.

The buzz of a cell phone interrupted her thoughts. Joe pulled a face and reached for his back pocket.

"Sorry. I told the sitter to call if there were any problems."

"Of course."

She hadn't dated a man with children before, had never really thought about all the extra complications and problems a woman would have to be prepared to take on. It would be daunting, becoming part of an instant family. A real baptism of fire.

She fiddled with her cutlery, not wanting Joe to think she was eavesdropping, but it was hard to avoid overhearing his conversation even though he was talking quietly. It quickly became obvious from his tone and what he was saying that he was talking to Ruby.

"The spider's not going to hurt you, honey," he said. "It's probably more afraid of you than you are of it."

Joe flicked her an apologetic glance, but she shook her head to indicate she wasn't fussed. His kids needed him. She had no issue with that.

"Well, if it ran under the bed, it's probably not going to come back out again." Joe smiled as he listened to his daughter. "Okay, how about this? You bunk down on the couch and I'll check your room out when I'm back from my meeting? How does that sound?"

Meeting?

Joe said good-night to Ruby and ended the call. "Sorry. Ruby had a spider in her room. It only sounds like a huntsman, but she's terrified of the things."

Hannah nodded. She told herself to ignore what she'd heard, but she couldn't help herself. "You didn't tell her about our date?"

He looked uncomfortable for a moment, then he shrugged. "I haven't dated anyone before and I wasn't sure how she'd react. I know she loves you, but I didn't want her getting the wrong idea."

Hannah stared at him, wondering what he thought the *wrong idea* was. Then she thought about the sad, awkward little confessions they'd just made—her failed wedding, his dead wife—and her planned trip and his fierce protectiveness and sense of duty toward his kids.

She shook her head slightly. "Who are we kidding?"

He raised his eyebrows. "Sorry?"

She gestured toward the table, the candle, the wine. "All this, what happened the other night… I'm about to head off for months. You've got your kids. We're both walking wounded. This was never going to happen."

He looked arrested for a moment, then his shoulders visibly relaxed. "You're probably right. I'm not exactly the best catch at the moment."

"Second only to me, owner of a never-worn wedding dress." She raised her wineglass. "To a bold attempt."

His eyes were warm with appreciation and humor as he lifted his own glass. "To bad timing."

She laughed and Joe joined in.

The rest of the evening flew by. With the possibility of anything romantic developing between them well and truly put to bed, the tension dissolved and conversation flowed freely, ranging from childhood anecdotes to favorite movies to most coveted vintage car. Joe had a dry, quick sense of humor and he loved to tease her, his blue eyes dancing as he threw a contentious comment onto the table and waited for her to take the bait. He had a great laugh and she found herself doing everything she could to amuse him. She told him stories from her apprenticeship, shamelessly embroidering them so she could see the corners of his eyes crinkle and his mouth curve into a grin. He countered with his adventures as a young roustabout on the rigs, and they wound up comparing scars on their hands and forearms.

"This one was completely my fault," Joe said, tracing the wicked-looking curling scar she'd noticed when she first met him.

"Let me guess—you were juggling knives?"

"Close. A couple of guys and I were fishing off the platform one afternoon—"

"You can fish off an oil rig?"

"Hell yeah. Fish love it around a rig. They're like shipwrecks, covered in barnacles below the water. Once you've got barnacles, you've got fish."

"Huh. Sorry, I interrupted. You were explaining how your tomfoolery scarred you for life."

He let her gibe pass. "We'd been out there for a few hours when I got a big tug on the line. A beauty, a giant trevally, looked about a hundred and eighty pounds."

"*Looked about?* Uh-oh, I sense a bad ending to this fishy tale."

"Yeah, well. He was a big boy, and it took me ages to bring him in. The other guys were hooting and hollering. When I finally landed him he was all snarled up in the line. Mick told me to let him be a while before cutting him free, but I was too impatient. So I grabbed my fishing knife and knelt down to cut the line, and the fish bucked like a bronco. I nearly took off my hand as well as cutting through the line. Meanwhile, the trevally slid off the platform and back into the ocean without so much as a goodbye and good luck."

"Selfish bastard. How many stitches did you need?"

He shrugged. "Enough to learn my lesson."

"Which was what? Never take a knife to a fish fight?" she asked, deadpan.

"Anyone ever told you you've got a mouth on you, Ms. Napier?"

"Frequently and at great length."

"I bet."

They shared a dessert and lingered over coffee. By the time they were walking back to Joe's car, Hannah was feeling warm with goodwill and the mouthful of hazelnut-flavored liqueur she'd had with her coffee.

"Definitely you shouldn't sack him," she said as they walked along the Paris end of Collins Street—so-called because of the ornate European-influenced buildings lining either side of the road.

"The guy who recommended the restaurant?" he asked.

She smiled. She liked that he'd been able to follow her chain of thought without her explaining. "Yep. He did good."

"I know. I'm thinking of giving him a raise."

She spluttered out a laugh. "It wasn't that good."

"Speak for yourself."

She nudged him with her elbow. "You're easily pleased."

"You have no idea."

She laughed again, aware that he was flirting with her but knowing it was meaningless. They'd both agreed that there was no future in the attraction between them. What was a little harmless flirtation between friends, after all? It had been a while since she'd felt this light and frivolous and had so much fun.

They bantered some more in the car on the way home, the radio playing softly in the background. She was surprised when the car pulled into their street.

"We're here already," she said stupidly when he pulled into the driveway of his house.

"Seems like it."

"Huh." She reached for her seat belt and slid it free. She started to frame a thank-you in her mind, but she didn't want the evening to end yet. If she wasn't living at her mother's place, she'd invite him in for coffee. But she was. And he had kids and a sitter at his place....

"Well, I had a great night. Thanks," she said.

"We'll have to do it again sometime."

"Yeah. Although I'll probably be pretty busy getting stuff ready for my trip."

"Right. I'd forgotten about that for a moment."

His face was in shadows and she couldn't read his expression, but there was a note of regret in his voice. Or maybe she was imagining it, because suddenly she was wishing all over again that things could be different between them.

She shook her head minutely. Stupid to wish for things that were never going to happen.

"Anyway, thanks," she said again.

"It was my pleasure."

She didn't consciously think about her next move, she simply leaned across to press a quick kiss to his cheek. Except he turned his head, and instead she found herself kissing the warmth of his mouth. She pulled back a fraction and for a moment the car was very still, then Joe made an unintelligible sound—or maybe it was her—and they came together again, hands reaching for shoulders, heads angling, mouths pressing together and opening.

He tasted of coffee and hazelnuts and the touch of his tongue against hers sent a thrill all the way through her body. In no seconds flat her heart was galloping and her body was on fire.

His fingers slid into her hair, the pads of his fingers pressing into her skull as he urged her closer. She was only too happy to oblige. She wanted to taste him until the craving inside her was gone. She wanted to slide her hands over his body to discover if he really was as hot and hard as he looked. She wanted him to touch her, and she wanted to answer the question that had been echoing deep inside her ever since she'd first met him: what would it be like to be skin to skin with this man? To have him inside her?

She made an encouraging noise as his hand slid down her shoulder to her breast. Her nipple was already hard and he rolled it between his thumb and forefinger. Desire pierced her, so sweet it made her shudder. She felt a tug as he opened her shirt and then his hand was sliding inside her bra to cup her bare flesh.

"Yes," she whispered against his mouth.

He pulled her closer and the hand brake pressed into her belly. She broke their kiss long enough to throw a leg over the center console and scramble over it. Then there was nothing between them as she straddled Joe's lap.

His stubble rasped against her as he trailed kisses up her neck. She gasped as he tongued her ear. She could feel how aroused he was, his erection a thick, hot presence pressed against her wide-open thighs. She rotated her hips and it was his turn to groan. Hungry for more, she slid a hand beneath his shirt and pressed her palm against the firm muscles of his belly. He felt incredibly hot, and she slid her hand up to cover one of his firm, rounded pecs, her thumb finding his nipple.

He tugged on her shirt some more until he was pushing it open, his gaze taking in her breasts with a single-minded intensity that made her feel like the most desirable woman on the planet. He lowered his head and ran his tongue along the lacy edge of her bra, then he used his teeth to pull her bra cup free even as his hands were busy behind her, undoing the clasp. His mouth closed over her nipple, hot and wet and she lost all power of thought. She wanted. That was all. The rest of the world ceased to exist.

She slid her hand between their bodies to grasp the thick, long ridge of his erection through his jeans. His body tensed and his hips pressed upward encouragingly. She began to stroke him while he suckled and teased first one breast then the other.

She was panting, mindless. His body was bowed toward her, tense with desire and need.

"Hannah," he said, his voice low and deep.

"Yes. Please," she said. "Hurry."

He reached for the stud on her jeans and she leaned backward to help him out. The sound of the car horn cut through the night like a siren. They both started and Hannah jerked away from the steering wheel.

"Shit," she whispered.

A porch light came on. She had a sudden vision of a sleepy-eyed Ruby or Ben coming out to see what was keeping their father from coming inside.

Joe must have shared her vision because they both scrambled for her shirt buttons at the same time.

She threw a leg over the console and slithered awkwardly into the passenger seat, twisting around so she was facing the right way even as her fingers worked furiously at her buttons. By the time the front door was opening she was decent, even if her bra was hanging loose around her rib cage.

"The babysitter," Joe said as a young girl stepped onto the porch and looked curiously toward the car.

"Grace Melville," Hannah said, recognizing the teenager from across the street.

"Yeah."

Joe gave Grace a reassuring wave and the girl ducked back into the house. He ran a hand over his face and exhaled loudly.

"Probably just as well," he said after a moment.

She nodded.

"It's not like it was ever going to go anywhere," he added.

"No."

"And we're both too old for car sex. So, really, being interrupted was a good thing."

"I wouldn't go that far," she said drily.

He looked at her, startled. She didn't bother trying to hide how frustrated she was, how much she still wanted him. His mouth crooked into a faint smile. "Yeah, well, there is that."

They stared at each other for a long moment. She held out her hand.

"I had a nice time. Thanks."

"Nice?" He raised his eyebrows, clearly unimpressed with the lukewarm adjective.

"Parts of it were exceptional, but I'm marking you down for failure to complete."

"You're the one who sat on the horn."

"Don't I know it."

He laughed at her double entendre. At last he took her hand. His fingers closed around hers, warm and firm. "There we go with the bad timing again."

"And then some."

She slid her hand free. "Good night, Joe."

"Good night."

She exited the car, closing the door quietly. She let herself into the house and walked on her toes across the tiled floor, in case her mother was still awake. She didn't want to talk right now. She was still buzzing with arousal, disappointment and frustration. She reached her bedroom and eased the door closed. For a moment she simply stood there, her back pressed against the door.

She felt as though she'd just had a glimpse of something wonderful and impossible. Something good and real.

Her gaze fell on the road atlas she'd been using to plan her route and she straightened.

They'd already agreed at dinner: it wasn't going to happen between them. Too many problems, too many obstacles, too much baggage. A handful of great kisses and some heavy-duty lust didn't change any of that, no matter how much her frustrated body wanted it to.

Heavy with regret, she got ready for bed.

CHAPTER NINE

JOE FELT LIKE A KID. A horny, dumb, inarticulate kid. It didn't matter how many times he told himself that Hannah Napier was a dead end, he couldn't stop himself from wanting her. He slept badly after their interrupted tryst in the car and the next day he kept one eye on the door of The Watering Hole for most of the afternoon until he realized he was waiting for her to enter. As soon as he acknowledged his own subconscious desire he also acknowledged that she wouldn't be coming into the pub that day, not after what had almost happened between them. She wasn't the kind of woman who played games. She was going away, he was staying. There was no point pretending otherwise, even if the physical chemistry between them was hot enough to launch a rocket. He appreciated the clear-cut honesty of it, of her. But he still wanted her.

That night when Ruby asked if she could go next door to help Hannah with her bike, he found himself making the short walk next door alongside his daughter. Hannah was hunkered down cleaning the rusty front forks of the Thunderbird with some steel wool and she glanced up with a smile when Ruby said hello.

"I was wondering if I was going to see you tonight," she said. Her gaze flicked to him and away again, but the extra color in her cheeks told him she was every bit as aware of him as he was of her and that last night was still on her mind.

"I was thinking you might need an extra pair of hands," he said.

Her eyebrows rose. "You want to help me strip rust off old bike parts?"

"Sure. Why not? Ben's doing his homework, I'm finished at the pub for the night. And like I told you, I always wanted one of these things."

And he wanted to be around her, even if it meant nothing and went nowhere.

He had the good sense not to say the last part out loud.

"Okay, sure. Grab some steel wool." She darted a sideway glance his way as he helped Ruby tear off a chunk of fine-grade steel wool, but she didn't say anything more.

"Maybe we could do this bit together, Daddy," Ruby suggested, pointing to the rear wheel rim.

"That sounds like a plan."

Ruby sat cross-legged on the concrete and began to attack one end of the once-shiny rim. He squatted and began working on the other side.

"Guess what we did at school today, Hannah," Ruby said.

"Um, reading? 'Rithmatic? 'Roo wrestling?" Hannah guessed.

Ruby laughed. "None of those things. We had to make a car of the future in art class."

"Wow. I bet you a million dollars egg cartons and pipe cleaners were involved." Hannah was smiling, her attention on her work.

"How did you know?" Ruby asked, eyes wide.

He laughed and Hannah glanced up and met his eyes. For a moment something warm and bittersweet unfolded inside him.

I could get to really like you, Hannah Napier. I could get

*to really admire your salty wit and your take-no-prisoners
attitude and that sexy, curvy body of yours.*

Too bad she was going away.

HE HELPED RUBY AND HANNAH out again on Wednesday
after dinner but when he was about to slip next door on
Thursday night Ben looked up from his Nintendo game with
a frown.

"What's so good about next door, anyway?"

"Why don't you come with us and see? I'm sure Hannah
would welcome the extra pair of hands."

"That would be so cool. If we all work together we can
finish the bike really quickly," Ruby said enthusiastically.

Ben scowled at the TV screen, his thumbs twiddling aim-
lessly with the game controls.

Joe stepped into his son's line of vision. "Come on, it'll
be fun."

Rolling his eyes, Ben tossed the game controller onto the
couch. "This had better be good," he said as he slouched
toward the front door.

Joe suppressed a smile and followed his kids out into the
street. Hannah looked surprised to see her new recruit, but
she quickly recovered. "Excellent. More slaves to do my
bidding. Hope you like grease, Ben."

Ben shrugged, eyes downcast. Hannah didn't let his
manner put her off. Over the next hour, she checked in with
him regularly as they all worked at cleaning bike parts. Joe
watched surreptitiously as Ben slowly thawed and relaxed.
By bedtime Ben was laughing at Hannah's jokes and trying
out a few of his own.

Joe lingered for a moment after he'd packed the kids off
to clean up and brush their teeth. "You handled him just
right."

"I treated him like any other apprentice."

"Ah. Is that how you see us? As your apprentices?"

She shot him a look from beneath her eyelashes. "Not all of you. Some of you have more than your fair share of experience."

He grinned. "I'm going to take that as a compliment."

She frowned. "There's no need to look so pleased about it."

"I can't help it. I've been staring at the ceiling all week thinking about Sunday night. It's good to know I'm not the only one it left an impression on."

She smiled ruefully. "Yeah, well, next time we decide to quit while we're ahead, let's quit while we're ahead."

She stooped to collect some discarded steel wool, and Joe stepped in front of her when she straightened.

She looked at him steadily. There was wariness in her eyes as well as frustrated desire. He couldn't help himself—he ran his thumb along the slope of her cheekbone. Her breath caught, and her eyelids swept down over her eyes, hiding her reaction from him. But he knew. If he kissed her right now, it wouldn't take much to get either of them back to the same hot, heavy place they'd been in his car the other night.

If only she wasn't going away…

It was on the tip of his tongue to ask if she really had to go, if maybe she couldn't delay her departure, hang around and explore this feeling between them.

But she'd been planning this trip for a long time. She'd told him over dinner how she'd already put it off once for her ex-fiancé. He couldn't ask her to put it off again for him. What did he have to offer, after all? Neither of them had any idea what the future held. He couldn't ask her to delay her dream on the chance that things might work out between them. And what were the odds of that? Her broken heart, his blighted one. His kids. Plus all the usual misapprehensions and problems most couples dealt with. It would be a miracle if they lasted a week.

She took a step backward.

"It's not that I don't want to kiss you again, but I'm really not into self-flagellation. I'm trying to be smart here," she said.

"Yeah, I know." He turned and started down the driveway. "Good night."

"Thanks for the help with the bike," she called after him.

He simply raised a hand in acknowledgment and kept walking. It wasn't like he had much of a choice.

WHEN BEN AND RUBY WENT next door the following evening, Joe stayed behind, pleading bookwork for the pub as an excuse. It was too hard being near Hannah and not being able to touch her or look at her the way he wanted to.

He was hunched over the calculator, trying to reconcile the hard spirits inventory when he heard the front door open. He finished adding a column of figures, then glanced up to see Ruby standing in the doorway to the living room, her face twisted with emotion.

"She's going," she said. "She's leaving next week!" She hurled herself across the room and into his arms, pressing her face into his neck.

He closed his arms around her and cupped the back of her head with his hand.

"It's okay, Rubes."

"I don't want her to go."

"I know. But we always knew Hannah was heading off on her big trip, didn't we?"

"But I didn't think it would be for ages and ages. I don't want her to go."

He didn't know what to say. He couldn't make promises on Hannah's behalf. He had no idea when she planned to come back, or if she planned to come back at all. He suspected Hannah didn't know herself. That was part of the appeal of the open road.

He heard the sound of the front door opening again and a couple of seconds later Ben entered the living room, Hannah hard on his heels. She looked stricken when she saw Ruby in his arms.

"Oh, man," Ben said, his voice filled with brotherly disdain for his sister's tears.

"She'll be all right," Joe said to Hannah. "I think you just took her by surprise."

"I didn't mean to upset you, Rubester," Hannah said. "I thought you knew I was going soon."

Ruby spoke into his shirtfront. "I did. But I don't want you to go."

Hannah met his eyes over Ruby's head.

"I wish I could stay, sweetheart. But this is something I've dreamed of doing ever since I was your age. I've been collecting maps and tourist guides for years and years."

"I know. You showed them to me, remember?" Ruby said.

"That's right. I forgot. Look, it's not like I'll be gone forever. I'll come back. My mom lives right next door—I have to come back or she'll kill me."

He glanced down and saw that Ruby was smiling a little now.

"Will you send me postcards?"

"Every week," Hannah said. "I promise."

Finally Ruby pushed away from his chest. He loosened his arms and she turned to face Hannah.

"What's going to happen to the Thunderbird while you're gone?"

"I'm going to pack the parts away so that I can take them to be rechromed when I come home. You can help me put it together when it's all done, if you like. That's if you're not too busy doing your nails and going shopping by the time I return."

"I can do both," Ruby said.

"Good. Because I'd miss having my ace right-hand woman working beside me." Hannah paused to eye Ruby carefully. "So are we okay?"

Ruby shrugged her shoulder in perfect imitation of Hannah. "Yeah." She walked across the room and wrapped her arms around Hannah's waist, laying her head against Hannah's hip. "It's going to be weird without you."

Hannah blinked rapidly. "Yeah."

Joe became aware of Ben standing to one side, the expression on his face an odd mixture of scorn and envy as he watched Hannah embrace his sister. Joe had a sudden memory of Beth sitting on the couch, Ben snuggled in her arms as she read him a book. She'd been a very demonstrative woman, warm and affectionate. Kisses and cuddles before bedtime, the casual brush of a hand over one of her children's heads when they passed in the hallway, tickle wrestling on the living room rug.

Ben missed being held by his mother, just as Ruby clearly craved a woman's touch. For a moment Joe felt heavy with regret. There were so many losses he could never hope to replace, too many gaps in their lives for him to even come close to filling them all.

"I was thinking that maybe before you go I could go for a ride around the block on your bike," Ruby said. She kept her voice carefully innocent, but she knew what she was asking.

For a second he locked eyes with Hannah. Her lips twitched into a smile, and he couldn't help but respond.

"Nice try, sweetheart," Hannah said.

"I couldn't have put it better myself," he said.

"You are such a doofus, Ruby. No way is Dad going to let you go on a motorbike," Ben chipped in, but even he was smiling at Ruby's opportunistic audacity.

"It was worth a try." Ruby's grin was cheeky.

"Yes, it was," Joe agreed. "Now, who wants a hot chocolate before bed?"

"Me. But I want double marshmallows," Ruby said, twisting away from Hannah and racing for the kitchen.

Ben wasn't far behind her. "I'm measuring out the cocoa. You mucked it up last time."

Joe looked to Hannah. "Can we tempt you?"

She was silent for a shade too long. "Thanks, but I'd better go. Maybe another time."

"Sure."

He pushed his disappointment aside. Hadn't he decided to minimize his contact with her before she left for the sake of his own sanity? And yet here he was, leaping on the first opportunity to prolong her visit. He was as bad as Ruby, a desperate opportunist.

He followed Hannah to the door. "I take it you're leaving next weekend?" he asked.

She nodded. "Saturday."

"Right."

Another long silence.

"I'd better go," she said.

"Okay."

When she turned away, her movements were jerky, almost as though it had taken an effort to drag herself away.

He closed the door after her, staring at the wooden surface blindly.

One more week, then she'd be gone.

Damn.

THE FOLLOWING FRIDAY NIGHT, Hannah checked her camping gear one last time before strapping it to the accessory rack she'd bought for the back of her bike. Her mother stood to one side of the garage, arms crossed tightly over her body.

"I can't believe you're really going. You've talked about this for so many years, and now this is finally it," her mom said.

"Yep."

"What time are you leaving tomorrow?"

"Ten. Traffic should be fairly light heading north."

Her mother pressed her lips together, but Hannah could see she was close to tears.

"Mom, I'll call every week, I promise."

"I know. It's just been lovely having you back home again."

Hannah hid her smile. She'd hardly been the most gracious houseguest, but her mother was feeling sentimental and there was no point letting the facts get in the way of a good farewell.

"It's been great being here. You've been a lifesaver, Mom."

Her mother waved a hand dismissively, but Hannah could see she was pleased.

"I must admit, I was holding out hope that something might happen to give you an incentive to stay."

Her mother's gaze was assessing. Hannah busied herself checking the oil level on the bike.

"Fine," her mother said. "Make me come right out and ask, then. Is anything happening with Joe or not?"

"He's got two kids to consider and I'm hitting the road. What do you think?"

"I think you should hang around and see what happens."

Hannah screwed the cap back on the oil tank. "I can't."

"Australia will still be out there in six months' time."

Hannah turned on her mother. "And what if it doesn't

work out again? What if I'm not the woman Joe thinks I am or something else goes wrong? Am I supposed to pick myself up and dust myself off all over again?"

"You're scared." Her mother said the words as if they were a huge revelation.

"Of course I'm scared. I'd be stupid if I wasn't. We're supposed to learn from past mistakes, aren't we?"

Hannah's mother smiled sadly. "Loving someone is always a risk, sweetheart. That's why it's so exciting and terrifying all at the same time."

"Right now I'm willing to pass on the excitement if it means I don't have to put up with the terrifying."

"If you could see the way Joe looks at you when you're not watching…"

Hannah's chest tightened. She took a deep breath. "Mom, I don't want to talk about it. I've made my decision, I've said my goodbyes. I'm leaving tomorrow."

Her mother flinched and Hannah knew she'd hurt her feelings.

"Okay. Well, I'll leave you to it and I'll see you in the morning."

"Mom…"

"It's okay, Hannah, I understand."

Hannah kissed her good-night and gave a sigh of relief when her mother had disappeared into the house and she was once again alone. She couldn't wait to be on the road, all of this far, far behind her.

Maybe that made her a coward, but so be it. She wasn't ready to risk her heart again. Especially with a man who almost definitely hadn't come to terms with his grief for his dead wife.

She checked a few more last-minute things then went in to the house. She'd written out a detailed outline of her proposed route and a bunch of contact numbers for her mother, and she stuck the page to the fridge with a magnet. Then she went to her bedroom and sorted her rucksack. She was traveling light by necessity: a few pairs of jeans, underwear, a swimsuit, T-shirts, a couple of warm sweaters. If she needed anything else, she'd simply buy it on the road.

Satisfied she had everything in order, she shed her clothes, brushed her teeth and crawled into bed. She wasn't even close to being able to sleep, however. Her thoughts kept circling around tomorrow, her last goodbyes, the first hours on the road. She planned to camp at Albury her first night before making her way to Eden on the New South Wales coast. She'd check out the scene there, spend a few days fishing and swimming, then head north again.

It would be good. Free, easy. At last she'd get a chance to see the country the way she'd always wanted to.

She rolled onto her side and stared into the darkness.

I wish he'd never kissed me. I wish he was just a man with two kids and a dead wife who happened to live next door.

But Joe had kissed her, and he'd become more than her neighbor. A lot more.

"So stupid," she muttered.

She'd known she was going on this trip, so why on earth would she start feeling something for a man she was always going to leave behind? It was dumb, plain old dumb.

Eventually she fell asleep but she woke feeling gritty-eyed and grumpy. Her stomach was tense with nerves and she had to force herself to eat a decent breakfast. As ten o'clock drew closer she grew more and more nervous, her gaze darting to her watch every few minutes.

Ruby had made a point of saying she'd be over at ten to

see her off. Hannah was dreading saying goodbye to her little buddy. She was also terrified Ruby would be accompanied by her father. She didn't trust herself not to say or do something embarrassing and revealing. Like throw herself at him and ask him to tell her to stay.

She was in the garage tugging on her leather jacket when Ruby appeared. Joe was with her, and Ben. A lump formed in the back of Hannah's throat.

"Hey," she said. Somehow her voice sounded normal, even though her throat felt constricted.

"We bought you a going-away present," Ruby said.

"You didn't have to do that." She looked to Joe, frowning. "You guys have given me enough already—the perfume, all the help with the bike."

Joe lifted a shoulder. "Don't look at me. It was Ruby and Ben's idea."

"Here," Ruby said, holding out a neatly wrapped parcel.

Hannah accepted the parcel. "You guys," she said, shaking her head in admonishment.

Ruby moved closer and Hannah could feel the little girl watching and waiting for her reaction. Hannah eased the tape free of the paper and didn't have to feign appreciation when she saw what they'd bought her: a pair of beautiful leather motorcycle gloves, complete with high-end carbon knuckle guards.

"Thank you. These are wonderful."

Ruby looked at her brother. "You were right," she said, resigned. She turned back to Hannah to explain. "I wanted to get you more perfume but Ben thought you'd prefer these."

"Perfume would have been lovely but these are perfect, Ben. Thank you."

Ben's cheeks were a fiery red as he shuffled his feet, the picture of teen discomfort. "It was just an idea, that's all."

"A great idea. I love them. They're miles better than my old gloves."

She ceremoniously picked up her old ones and flung them onto the workbench at the back of the garage. Ruby and Ben both looked thrilled by the gesture. Joe simply watched, his face utterly impassive. She flicked him a quick glance, then looked away again.

"I have something for you guys, too. Nothing fancy, but I thought it might be fun for you to keep track of where I'm going on a map."

Hannah collected the small bag of supplies she'd put together and offered it to Ruby.

"There are some pushpins in there and a big map of Australia. I figured each time one of my postcards arrive you and Ben could stick a pin in the map and keep track of my progress."

Ruby clutched the bag to her chest. "Thank you."

Hannah sank to one knee and opened her arms and Ruby stepped into them for one last hug.

"You've been great. The best apprentice ever," Hannah said.

Ruby sniffed and nodded her head. With a shuddery sigh she stepped back, using her forearm to wipe her eyes.

Hannah glanced at Ben but his body language told her he wouldn't welcome a hug the way his sister had. She held out her clenched hand instead and they bumped fists.

She flicked another look at Joe. He was staring at the ground, his mouth a firm, straight line. There was no way she was hugging or kissing him in front of his kids. There was nothing platonic or friendly about their relationship.

Because she didn't know how to say goodbye to him, she zipped her jacket and reached for her new gloves.

"I guess I'd better get this show on the road."

Her mother came out of the house, a wad of tissues clutched in one hand.

"Don't start, or you'll set me off," Hannah said. "I'll call you from Albury, okay?"

"Don't forget. And I want weekly updates."

"I promise."

Hannah flexed her hands in her new gloves, smiling to show Ben and Ruby how much she appreciated them. She slid her helmet on, pushing the visor up. "Okay. I'm as ready as I'll ever be."

Ruby moved closer to her father, reaching for his hand. Hannah turned the key to start the bike. The engine fired and she rocked the bike off its stand.

She was acutely aware that she and Joe had barely exchanged a word. She had no idea what he was thinking or feeling, if the uncertainty and regret she felt were one-sided or shared. For a moment she hesitated, gripped by the urge to say something, anything to connect with him.

But he wasn't rushing forward to talk to her. Hadn't even offered her his hand or his best wishes.

She twisted the throttle, and the bike rolled out of the garage and into the street. Joe and his kids and her mother walked after her. She paused for a moment, one foot on the ground, and glanced over her shoulder. She lifted her hand in a last farewell. Her mother mopped at her tears with the tissues. Ben stood off to one side, a frown on his face. Ruby had turned her face into her father's belly, her arms wrapped around his waist. Joe's attention was on his daughter. He didn't so much as glance up.

Well, I guess that answers that question. No goodbyes, no regrets. Time to haul ass, Napier.

She turned away and eased the throttle open. The bike

took off down the street. She told herself not to look back again, but she couldn't resist a glance in the rearview mirror.

Her mother was turning toward her house, but Joe and Ruby and Ben still stood watching her. For the first time she saw emotion on Joe's face—disappointment, frustration, regret. Then the road demanded her attention and she turned the corner and they were gone.

For a moment her grip eased on the throttle and the bike slowed.

He feels it, too. The pull of what might have been.

But she'd made her decision. As she'd told her mother last night, she wasn't prepared to gamble with her heart again, and she was at the beginning of a lifelong dream. There was nothing to do but look forward.

JOE WENT OVER AND OVER those last few minutes with Hannah during the following weeks. He should have said something. Given her his best wishes. Made a joke, at the very least. Instead, he'd stood there and let her ride away.

He told himself it was for the best. Safer. Easier. But when he came home at night and saw the garage door at the Napier house firmly down, he remembered what it had been like to make Hannah laugh, and how soft her skin was and how kind she'd been to his children. It was the same at work—every time a slim, brown-haired woman walked into The Watering Hole his gut got tight, then he'd blink and realize it wasn't Hannah and that she wasn't coming back anytime soon.

For the first time in two years Beth was absent from his dreams. There was only Hannah, her body firm and warm under his hands, her taste in his mouth. Teasing him, then walking away. Or staring at him expectantly, waiting for him to say or do the one thing that would make her stay.

The first postcard arrived on the Wednesday after she left. It was from Eden and showed a fishing fleet sailing out into the ocean, an arc of golden sand marking the shore. Hannah wrote that the weather was fine and that she'd stopped on the way north to help a couple with a broken-down car on the freeway. She missed Ruby and her new gloves were the best she'd ever owned. Lastly, she asked Ruby to say hello to everyone for her.

Ruby read it out loud three times before solemnly pressing the first pin into the map. She'd mounted it on the cork bulletin board on her bedroom wall and every time he tucked her into bed he saw that lone pushpin and thought of Hannah.

"Do you think she's thinking of us the way we're thinking of her, Daddy?" Ruby asked exactly one week after Hannah had departed.

"She sent you a postcard. That means she must be thinking of you," he said.

Ruby stared hard at the map. "Do you think she'll be back by Christmas? I really want her to be home for my birthday."

"I don't know, sweetheart. It's three months away, but Australia is a big country, there's a lot for her to see. You probably shouldn't bank on it."

He felt like a complete fraud since he'd been doing the exact same calculations in his head. How long till she reached Queensland? How long till she'd traversed the Northern Territory? How much time to explore Central Australia? When would she head west? And, finally, when would she make her way home again?

Might as well ask how long a piece of string was. Part of the appeal of this trip for Hannah was the freedom of the road, the ability to move at her own pace and explore at her leisure. She'd explained it all to him over their one-and-only dinner, her eyes alight with excitement and anticipation. If she found somewhere she loved, she planned to stay awhile, get some casual work, get to know the locals. If she heard about an amazing place that wasn't on her route, she'd divert and go find it. This was her dream. He was just the idiot she'd left behind.

The second postcard arrived like clockwork a week after the first. Sydney this time, a classic shot incorporating the Harbour Bridge and the Opera House. Ruby pressed another pin into the map. He told himself that soon he would stop thinking about Hannah. They'd had one date and shared a handful of kisses. It was stupid to be so hung up on someone and something that had never really happened.

But it seemed he was destined to be stupid. He wanted her, and her being gone didn't seem to make a damn bit of difference to that fact.

THREE WEEKS AFTER her departure from Melbourne, Hannah stood on the beach in Townsville in Northern Queensland. A strong offshore breeze blew the hair off her face and pressed her clothes against her body. She squinted her eyes against the brightness of the rising sun and told herself how lucky she was to be here, seeing this, experiencing this moment.

After a few minutes, she started back to the campground where she'd pitched her tent last night. It was going to be another stinker of a day, with the mercury predicted to hit forty degrees. The beach would soon be filled with tourists and locals keen to claim their patch of sand. If she wanted to, she could put on her swimsuit and take a towel and a book down to the water to join them. There was no work to get to, no one else's needs or desires to consider. She could laze the day away and work on her already impressive tan.

The problem was, she didn't want to. She'd woken this

morning with Joe's face in her mind and her hands clench-ing the fabric of her sleeping bag. This was supposed to be her dream, but every day she'd had to remind herself how lucky she was, how beautiful the landscape was and how much she'd looked forward to finally seeing all the places she'd circled on the map over the years.

Her heart wasn't in it. That was the truth of the matter. Her dream had changed.

The realization had sat like a lead weight in the pit of her belly for the past few days. Her heart—her stupid, incon-venient, badly house-trained heart—was back in Melbourne, fixated on a tall, dark-haired man with sad eyes and the most incredible smile in the world.

Every postcard she'd sent to Ruby had taken her hours to compose. She'd told Ruby about her adventures and the people she'd met. She'd made jokes at her own expense and included tidbits of history and local lore. And all the while, the only thing she wanted to write was: *Does he miss me? Does he think about me? Does he feel the same way I do?*

She had no idea when she'd become so involved, so enmeshed with Joe Lawson. Somewhere between him chewing her out for working on her noisy bike at night and the moment she'd turned the corner and left him standing in the street with his children on either side of him. It was crazy. They'd had one date, shared one meal. She didn't know half the things she used to think were important to know about someone. His birthday, whether his childhood had been happy, what political party he voted for. And yet she knew how to make him laugh. She knew he felt deeply and loved with everything he had to give. She knew he was a great dad, even though he suffered doubts over some of his decisions. She knew he was honest, even if the truth was sometimes hard to hear. She knew that he was as scared to love again and trust another person as she was, even if he was motivated by very different reasons. And she knew that when she'd ridden away from him and Ruby and Ben she'd made what was possibly the biggest mistake of her life.

She stared at her meager campsite—the tent, her bedroll, her rucksack of clothing. She turned and squinted toward the rising sun. She thought about the years she'd planned this adventure. Then she knelt and began to pull the tent pegs from the ground. Within twenty minutes she had the tent packed away. Half an hour later her worldly goods were once again strapped to the back of her motorcycle. She didn't look back as she rode out of Townsville.

CHAPTER TEN

JOE WOKE EARLY. HE rubbed his tired eyes and stared at the ceiling. So much for the blissful escape of sleep. Hannah came to him every night, and every night he wrestled with his subconscious for control of his dreams. If he could make his dream go the way he wanted it to, if he could just hold her and say the things he wanted to say... But he never seemed to find the words to stop Hannah from walking away.

He had half a dozen sleeping tablets left from the time after Beth died. If he'd wanted to, he could have taken one and slept the night through, deep and dreamless. That was the worst part of the whole mess, because, as tired and irritated and frustrated as he felt dreaming of chasing Hannah and never catching her every night, he'd choose the dreams over nothing any day. He knew it made him a tragic, laughable figure of the highest order, but there it was. If he couldn't have the real Hannah, he'd settle for a dream of her, even if it was driving him slowly crazy.

You pathetic bastard.

He glanced at the alarm clock. Just after 6:00 a.m. Great. The kids had stayed at his mother's last night since it was a Friday and he'd had to work late due to staffing problems at the pub. He'd arranged to pick them up at midday, which left him with a whole six hours to fill.

There was laundry to do—there was always laundry—and a host of other domestic chores. Maybe if he really threw himself into the housework he'd stop his mind from running in a continuous loop, thinking about Hannah then reminding himself how pointless it was.

He rolled out of bed and reached for his jeans. He smoothed a hand over his hair as he walked up the hallway to the kitchen. Pizza boxes were stacked beside the counter, even though he'd asked Ben to put them out at least twice during the week. He flicked the kettle on and picked the boxes up, making a mental note to have a word with Ben about doing his chores.

Barefoot and bare chested, he made his way to the carport where the recycle bin lived, then walked to collect the newspaper from the mailbox. He was scanning the front page when he heard the low rumble of a motorbike engine in the distance. His head came up and his muscles tensed.

Which was stupid, because there was no way it was Hannah.

The engine noise grew louder as he started toward the house. He glanced over his shoulder, his pace slowing. Sure enough, a motorbike turned into the street.

His hand tightened around the newspaper. He stopped in his tracks and turned and stared as the bike slowed and then stopped in front of his house.

It was her. It had to be.

He barely stopped himself from breaking into a run as he made his way down the driveway, dropping the newspaper on the concrete behind him. Hannah slid off her helmet, shaking out her hair. He stopped in front of the bike.

"You're back," he said, then gave himself a mental kick. Talk about stating the obvious.

"Yeah."

She dismounted and placed her helmet on the seat. He couldn't take his eyes from the long line of her jeans-clad legs. She was so bloody sexy. How had he ever kept his hands off her?

Belatedly it occurred to him that something pretty serious must have happened to bring her home so early.

"Is everything all right?" he asked. "Is Robyn okay?"

"She's fine. I came back because I forgot something."

There was a look in her eyes....

"What did you forget?"

She held his gaze and stepped closer, so close the front of her leather jacket brushed his bare chest.

"This," she said. "I forgot to do this."

She reached up and curled a hand around the back of his neck and pressed a kiss to his lips. Her body leaned into his, the leather of her jacket supple and warm against his skin. For a moment he was passive, blown away by her return, by the fact that she was kissing him, that this was real. Three weeks of dreams. Three weeks of calling himself an idiot for letting her go without even trying to get her to stay...

Hunger and lust and relief rose inside him in equal measure. He wrapped his arms around her, sliding his palms across her back, hauling her close. Her mouth opened under his.

She tasted of sunlight and ocean breezes. She tasted like salvation, a new beginning. Hope.

He slid his hands into her hair, grabbing handfuls of it as he angled her head to deepen their kiss. She spread her palms flat against his back and pressed her length against him. She felt so good. So warm and alive.

After long, breathless moments they broke apart to stare at each other.

"Come inside?" he asked.

She flicked a glance toward his house. He knew what she was thinking, what she was worried about.

"The kids are with Mom."

She huffed out a sigh of relief. "Thank God, because I don't think I can wait a minute longer."

He laughed, loving the boldness of her. When had Hannah ever given him less than the truth? "Come on." He slid his hand down her arm to weave his fingers with hers.

He started toward the house, towing her after him. His mind sprinted ahead to the bedroom, imagining peeling her out of her clothes, seeing her for the first time, exploring her soft curves. His body swelled, growing even harder. He quickened his pace, almost dragging her over the threshold.

"Where's the fire?" She laughed.

"I'll show you in about ten seconds."

Then they were in his bedroom and she was standing in front of him, a smile on her face.

"If you had any idea how many times I've imagined being here like this with you…" she said

He reached for the tab on her jacket zipper.

"In *my* fantasies, you're always wearing a lot less," he said.

Her smile turned into an outright grin as he tugged her zipper down and pushed her jacket open and down her arms. Underneath she was wearing a tight-fitting black tank top. He stared at her breasts for a moment, simply appreciating the sweet perfection of her.

"You're good for my ego," she said.

"Baby, I haven't even started."

She laughed and reached for the hem of her top, pulling it over her head in one smooth move. Her eyes locked with his, she reached behind her back for her bra clasp.

"Next time, we'll go slow. But I've been thinking about you, about this, for too long to wait," she said.

He didn't respond because he couldn't. Her breasts were bare and all rational thought fled his mind. He ached to taste her, to shape her with his hands. Instead, he reached for the stud on his jeans. The soft denim gave easily and within seconds he was pushing his jeans down his legs, his erection springing free.

"Oh, man," she said, her gaze on his groin. Her movements became frenzied as she tugged at her belt and shoved her own jeans down her legs. She kicked her shoes off and at last they came together, skin to skin, mouth to mouth.

"So good," she murmured against his lips.

"Tell me about it."

He slid his hands onto her backside and snugged her hips against his, his erection pressed against her belly. She made an approving noise and circled her hips. He ducked his head and kissed the smooth valley between her breasts, scattering kisses across the curves until he found a nipple and pulled it into his mouth. She shivered, then her hand slid between their bodies and down his belly until she was curling her hand around him.

He lost track of time for a while. The world became only her and him and soon they were on the bed, touching one another, exploring, encouraging, discovering.

"Joe," she whispered after a while, her body trembling in his arms. "Please."

He was only too happy to oblige. He took a moment to protect them both, then he slid inside her. She made a small, satisfied noise in the back of her throat. He clenched his hands into the sheets on either side of her body. For seconds neither of them moved, both of them marking the moment. Then he shifted his hips and she moved with him and soon they found their rhythm.

Her hair was spread across the pillow, her eyes dreamy

and unfocused. He kissed her, riding high inside her, feeling how much pleasure she took from his body. She started to pant, her hands clutching at his back and his butt, one leg wrapping around his waist as she urged him on.

Pleasure rushed through him and he tried to hold off, but it had been so long and he'd been dreaming of this for weeks. He pulled back, wanting to ensure her pleasure, determined to make it last. She shook her head against the pillow, her hands on his hips urging him to move harder, faster, deeper. He felt her quiver around him. Her head dropped back, then her body arched as she found her release. His breath rushed out as he pressed his face into the soft skin of her neck. He shuddered as his own climax hit him, one hand gripping her hip, the other lifting her so he could bury himself deep inside her.

He dropped his head onto the pillow beside her for a few beats afterward, his breath coming fast, a bead of sweat trickling down his spine. Hannah smoothed a hand around his shoulder to the nape of his neck, her fingers kneading the muscles there. He felt her belly muscles tense as she lifted her head to press a kiss to his shoulder. He closed his eyes, swamped by a swell of emotion. It had been a long time since he'd held anyone or been held.

"I missed you," he said.

"I could tell."

He lifted his head so he could see her face. She was smiling, but her eyes were serious. He curved a hand around her cheek and caressed the soft skin of her temple with his thumb.

Thank God she came back.

She lifted a hand and traced his lips with a finger.

"You have the best smile. When I first saw it my knees literally went weak."

"When I first saw you, I thought you were a man," he said.

She gasped and punched him on the shoulder. He laughed and caught her hand.

"Let me finish. I thought you were a man for about half a second. Then you stood and turned around and I realized I'd made a huge mistake and I couldn't get out of there fast enough, because I was afraid you'd bust me staring at your breasts like a randy schoolboy."

"No one would ever mistake you for a schoolboy. Believe me."

He kissed her, and things soon became heated all over again. Afterward, she fell asleep in his arms, her head a welcome weight on his shoulder. He must have drifted off as well because he woke to a gentle nudge in the ribs, finally opening his eyes when Hannah bit his shoulder gently.

"Wake up, sleepyhead," she said. "What time did you say you had to pick Ben and Ruby up?"

He rolled on top of her so quickly that she could only laugh and weakly try to fend him off.

"Midday. And I was only sleeping so I could recover from being woman-handled twice in a row," he said.

"Well, it's eleven. And if you're complaining about the woman-handling, there's a really quick and easy cure."

"I'm not complaining. Not by a long shot. Handle away," he said.

"You have no idea how tempted I am. But there is no way I'm making you late for picking up your kids. Not exactly the best way to start out," she said.

She rolled toward the edge of the bed. He watched as she stood, the long muscles of her legs rippling. If he was about ten years younger, he'd drag her back onto the mattress and make it three for three. But he wasn't, and she was right about his kids. For the first time he allowed himself to think beyond the here and now and the demands of his body.

"Ruby will jump out of her skin when she hears you're back," he said.

"Yeah? I wondered if she might have gotten over being a grease monkey while I was away."

"Nope. She's been bugging me to show her how to change the oil in the Mazda."

"Really?" She looked delighted.

He watched as she pulled on her underwear.

"How do you think she'll feel about this?" she asked, her gesture taking in the rumpled bed and him lying in it.

He frowned, thinking about how his kids might react to the news he was dating Hannah. Ruby adored her, but that didn't mean she'd warm to the idea that Hannah was dating her daddy. He'd learned enough about the possessiveness of women over the years to know that. As for Ben… Joe had no idea how his son might react. Things had been better between them since the shoplifting incident, but Ben was still not the open, happy boy he'd once been. Maybe some of that could be laid at the door of hormones and puberty, but Joe figured a lot of it was about Beth dying. Was Ben ready to accept that his father might want and need another woman in his life?

"I don't know. This isn't something we've been through before."

"I kind of guessed," Hannah said.

"That obvious, huh?"

"No. But I knew there hadn't been anyone since Beth."

His wife's name seemed to hang in the room for a long beat. He shifted on the bed. "Probably the best thing for us to do is take things slowly," he said.

She nodded. "Sure."

"Maybe you should come out for dinner with us tonight. Let the kids get used to you being around again."

She smiled.

"That sounds good."

She zipped her jeans and tugged her tank top on. He stared at her, barely able to believe that the past few hours had really happened, that she was here. That she'd come back for him. For a moment, all his doubts and uncertainties fell away.

Hannah was home. The rest they could make up as they went along.

HANNAH WAS NERVOUS as she got ready that night. Sweaty palms, queasy stomach, shaking hands—the works, basically. All for a casual dinner at The Watering Hole.

The thing was, she'd thought about Joe and his kids the whole of her journey south. She'd thought about the way Ruby looked at her with so much trust, and she'd remembered the wary curiosity and interest in Ben's face when he'd worked with her on the Thunderbird. They were both good kids. She enjoyed their company, and she hoped they enjoyed hers. But the fact remained that her parenting experience was zero and they'd lost their mother in shocking and sudden circumstances just over two years ago. If things worked out between her and Joe, she would be stepping into some pretty big shoes, and it would be foolish to assume that everything would go smoothly.

She pressed a hand to her nervous stomach. She couldn't believe she was standing in her mother's house thinking about becoming a stepmom. It seemed so presumptuous.

Then she thought about the way Joe had looked standing in the street this morning wearing nothing but his low-slung jeans. The look on his face, the hope in his eyes... This was about more than sex. This was real. And more than anything she wanted it to work.

Her toes curled in her boots as she thought about the way he'd made love to her. He'd been insatiable, attentive, passionate, demanding—everything she'd ever fantasized about and more. He'd made her feel beautiful and sexy and precious.

Which was why she'd come home, after all. And why she was standing in her bedroom freaking out over having dinner with his children.

A knock sounded on the door and her mother popped her head in.

"I thought you might need a little jacket or something in case it got cold," her mother said. She offered a black woolen shrug to Hannah. "This would look so nice with your jeans."

Her mother knew Hannah had about a million jackets she could wear to ward off the coolness of an October night. The truth was, her mother was excited and she wanted in on the action. She'd burst into tears when she'd seen Hannah on the doorstep, her hands pressed to her chest.

"I knew you'd come back! I knew you were too smart to throw away something so good," Robyn had said, throwing her arms around Hannah.

Now, she helped Hannah into the shrug and turned her to face the mirror. "There. Doesn't that look nice? Not too overwhelming, but it will keep your arms warm."

Hannah met her mom's eyes in the mirror. "Thanks for being so patient with me, Mom."

"I had a feeling about Joe the moment I met him," Robyn said. "He's a good man. I think you can make each other happy."

"I hope so."

"And those children need you so much, Hannah."

"They have to get used to their dad dating me first."

"I'm sure they'll be fine with it. It's not like you're some stranger he's bringing into the home."

"Maybe. Anyway, we're going to take it easy to start with."

Her mother frowned. "What does that mean?"

"We're not going to ram it down their throats. Like tonight—I'm meeting them for dinner as a friend, that's all."

Her mother's frown deepened.

"You mean you're going to lie to them?"

"No. We're going to give them a chance to get used to the idea of me being around, then we're going to tell them."

"But they're already used to you being around. You live next door. I don't see why he needs to lie to them about you."

"He's looking out for his kids, Mom. What if things don't work out between us? He doesn't want his kids investing in something that might not go the distance."

Her mother made a rude noise. "You gave up your dream for him, Hannah. You traveled halfway across the country for him. What more does the man want?"

Her mother looked so fierce, as though she was ready to wade into battle on Hannah's behalf.

"It's okay. Really. I understand his kids have to come first."

Her mother eyed her for a long moment, then she shrugged. "All right. I just hope for your sake that this isn't a sign of something else."

"Like what?"

"There's a reason the man hasn't dated anyone else in two years, Hannah. He obviously loved his wife very much."

"Yes, he did. But she's dead, Mom. And Joe deserves some happiness in his life."

"I didn't say he didn't, darling."

Hannah growled in the back of her throat. "Unbelievable. Five minutes ago you were ready to marry the guy yourself," she said.

"Forget I said anything. I'm sure you and Joe will sort

things out. You've managed to muddle your way through up until now without me sticking my oar in."

Hannah grabbed her purse.

"Fine. I'm going now," she said, her tone a little on the sharp side.

Her mother stepped forward to brush some lint off her shoulder. "I want you to have everything you deserve, sweetheart. That's all."

Hannah softened as she saw the concern in her mother's eyes. "Don't wait up for me, okay?"

"I won't."

Joe and his children were waiting for her at a corner table when she arrived. Ruby was sitting on the edge of her chair and she shot to her feet like a jack-in-the-box the moment she saw Hannah. Her small body rocketed into Hannah's with force, her arms wrapping around Hannah's waist.

"Hey," Hannah said, bending to return Ruby's embrace.

"You're back," Ruby said.

"That's right."

"And you're not going away again?"

"Not that I know of."

Ruby's arms tightened even further and Hannah had to blink back tears. It wasn't until that moment that she'd realized exactly how much she'd missed her little helper.

"I missed you, too, sweetheart," she said.

Ben had remained with his father, but he offered her a shy smile when she and Ruby finally made their way to the table. Ruby practically sat in her lap as Hannah explained that she'd come home because she'd been homesick. Every time she met Joe's eyes she flashed to the hours they'd spent in his bed that morning and had to look away again, sure that what was going on between them must be obvious even to the uninformed eyes of two prepubescents.

By contrast, Joe was the most relaxed she'd ever seen him, his blue eyes warm with good humor, his mouth curved at the corners as though he was constantly on the verge of smiling. She very badly wanted to lean across the table and kiss him or simply slide her hand into his. For the first time she had an inkling of how hard it was going to be to play his public friend while being his private lover.

"I thought you'd planned your trip for years," Ben said, his forehead wrinkled with a frown. "I thought it was your big dream."

Hannah met Joe's eyes for a moment before looking away. "It was. But it turned out that I'd outgrown that old dream. I realized I wanted to be here more than I wanted to be there."

Ben bounced a glance between her and Joe, a wary look on his face. "Seems like a waste of a good trip."

Hannah stirred in her seat, sure that any second now Ben was going to ask a more pointed question.

"Can I have French fries *and* a pizza?" Ruby asked.

The conversation shifted to food and Hannah let out a silent sigh of relief. Under the table, she felt a nudge as Joe's leg slid between hers. It wasn't sexual, more reassuring. She pressed her leg closer, letting him know she appreciated the contact.

Despite the awkwardness of having to keep a close guard on herself in regard to her behavior toward Joe, she enjoyed the meal. Ruby and Ben were bright, articulate kids, and they enjoyed teasing and being teased by their father. She found herself laughing a lot and copping her fair share of mock abuse and razzing.

She'd thought the evening was going really well until Joe and Ruby left to check out the cake display and Ben turned and nailed her with a disconcertingly direct stare.

"Are you and my dad going out with each other?"

Hannah blinked, her mind a complete blank for a long, long moment. She'd always been a crappy liar, one of the many reasons why she preferred sticking to the truth. She felt particularly bad lying to Joe's child. No matter what she'd said to her mother about Joe protecting them from the potential failure of their relationship, it felt wrong.

"Wow. Where did that come from?" she finally said.

"I know you like him," Ben said. "You look at him all the time."

Hannah could feel warmth climbing into her cheeks. Good grief, was she that obvious?

"I think your dad's a really good guy. But we're just friends at the moment," she lied.

It was what Joe had asked her to do, after all.

Ben stared at her for a moment longer before shrugging. "Okay. Whatever."

The wrinkle between his eyebrows relaxed, however. He believed her. And he was relieved.

Useless to pretend that it didn't sting a little to know he was glad she wasn't seeing his father. She and Ben hadn't gotten off to the best of starts, but she'd thought they'd developed a friendship during their sessions with the Thunderbird.

His mother died, Hannah. Of course he doesn't want to replace her. Get a grip.

She shook the moment off. This was why she and Joe had agreed to keep things low-key initially, after all—to give the kids time to adjust.

When they walked out to the street after their meal, Joe let the kids go ahead and caught her hand in his in the darkness.

"How're you doing?" he asked quietly.

"Good. How about you?"

"All good."

She took a deep breath. "You should probably know—

Ben asked if we were dating when you and Ruby went to check out the cakes."

There was a short silence.

"What did you say?"

"That we were just friends."

"Thanks for that."

She shrugged. "It's what we agreed to."

They were nearing the car and he released her hand. She was surprised by the sense of loss she felt.

"Well, I'll see you guys later," she said.

"Can I come over tomorrow to work on the bike?" Ruby asked.

"Sure, sweetheart."

Ruby kissed her goodbye. Ben gave her a wary nod. Joe raised a hand in farewell.

She walked to her bike and took her helmet from the storage box beneath the seat. Joe's Mazda pulled away from the curb and drove off. She stared after his fading taillights.

So. Their first family dinner, if it could be called that. She wasn't sure if she should label it a success or not. She'd known she'd be taking on a lot, dating a man with children, but she hadn't expected to feel so…left out.

It's day one, Hannah. Give it a chance. This is new for everybody.

She knew it was true, but it didn't change the way she felt. When she got home, Joe had slipped a note beneath the garage door.

Meet me out front at 10:30?

She had no way of replying, but it wasn't as though she was going to say no. She'd driven thousands of miles to be with him. She'd take whatever she could get.

She'd been waiting for five minutes when she heard Joe's front door close later that night. She straightened from her position leaning against the tailgate of his car. He smiled when he saw her.

"You came."

"Yep."

He stepped closer and slid his arms around her. They kissed long and slow, taking their time, but soon hands were gliding over backs and breasts and hips and bellies.

"You taste good," Joe whispered near her ear.

"So do you."

They fooled around a little more until they were both hot and bothered. Finally Joe broke their kiss and let his forehead rest against hers.

"The kids go to school at eight-thirty on Monday," he said. She could hear the frustration in his voice.

She smiled. Any doubts she had faded away in the face of his very evident desire for her. This was right. Not perfect, but definitely good. They would make it work.

"You wouldn't happen to be setting up a booty call, would you, Mr. Lawson?"

"I'm interested in a lot more than your booty."

She kissed the line of his jaw. "Monday seems like a long way away."

"Tell me about it."

He tucked her hair behind her ear, his fingers caressing her neck.

"Thank you for tonight. For your patience. I know it's not easy—"

She pressed her fingers against his lips. "Don't. You don't have to apologize or explain. This is going to be tough for Ben and Ruby. I get that."

"Yeah. But maybe we need to rethink holding off on

telling them. Ben's obviously picked up on something." He was frowning, clearly troubled.

"Whatever you think is best," she said.

He focused on something over her shoulder, his gaze distant. "It's so hard to get a read on him lately. I have no idea what's going on in his head half the time."

She could feel the uncertainty in his body. He was such a good man. So determined to look out for his kids, even if it meant sacrificing his own happiness and comfort.

She pressed her palm flat against his chest. "We'll work it out."

His gaze returned to her, warm with appreciation. "Have I mentioned yet how happy I am that you came home?"

There was a serious note to his voice. Suddenly she felt very exposed, very vulnerable. As unspoken declarations went, returning early from a lifelong dream trip so you could get busy with a man was right up there. Not much Joe Lawson didn't know about how she felt about him now.

"It's good to be back," she said, mostly to fill the silence.

"Hannah." Joe lifted her hand to his mouth and kissed her knuckles.

Her chest seemed to swell with emotion as she looked into his eyes. She waited for him to say something more, but he didn't. Instead, he lowered his head and kissed her again.

"You drive me crazy, you know that?" he said.

For the second time that night she felt a stab of disappointment. She wasn't sure what she'd expected or wanted Joe to say. That he loved her? It was too early for that. For both of them. Right?

She pushed her stupid thoughts aside. All that mattered right now was that she was in Joe's arms, and he was kissing her as though his life depended on it.

CHAPTER ELEVEN

JOE TRIED TO GAUGE his son's mood as they ate breakfast the next morning. Ben was quiet, chewing away at his cereal mechanically, his gaze fixed on the tabletop. Joe cleared his throat, determined to get this right with his children.

"So how are things at school these days? Everything good?"

Ben shrugged a shoulder. "It's okay."

"Any new friends?"

"A couple."

"Hey, that's great." Joe winced. He sounded like a freaking game show host, stiff and artificial.

This is bullshit. Just tell him the truth and deal with whatever happens.

His gut said it was the right decision. He pushed his cereal bowl away and focused on his son. "There's something I wanted to talk to you about."

Ben fiddled with his spoon. "What did I do wrong now?"

"You didn't do anything wrong." Man, he hated that his son's default position was to assume he was in trouble. Had he really been riding him that hard? "This is about me and Hannah."

Ben's gaze flew to his face. "What about her?"

"Well, she and I have gotten to know each other. And it turns out we both like each other. So, we've decided to start dating." He sounded like a game show host again, but he had no idea how he was supposed to sound when discussing his sex life with his thirteen-year-old son.

Ben's eyes burned with intensity as he stared across the table. "What about Mom? Don't you love her anymore?"

"Of course I still love her. But it's been two years, mate, and sometimes it's nice to have someone to go to the movies with and dinner and stuff."

Ben's lip curled. "You're not going to the movies with Hannah. I'm not stupid. You're *doing it* with her."

"We're dating," Joe said firmly. "I wanted to give you guys a chance to get used to Hannah being back before I told you about us, but she told me you asked her about it last night."

"Yeah, and she said you were just friends."

"Because I asked her to. Like I said, I wanted you kids to have a chance to get used to her being around first."

Ben stood. "Is that all?"

"Do you have any questions? Anything you want to talk about?" Joe asked.

Ben simply stared at him for a long moment. "No."

There was no mistaking the anger and hurt in his face.

"Ben…"

"I've got homework to do."

Ben strode for the hall. Just before he exited the kitchen he ducked his head and dashed his forearm across his eyes. Then he was gone.

Shit. Joe sat back in his chair for a second. That had gone well. Not.

He sighed, wondering if he should go after Ben or give him time to cool down and vent and cry a little.

The doorbell rang, the sound echoing through the house, and he pushed himself to his feet.

"I'll get it," Ruby called. He heard the thump of her feet on the floor as she ran to the door.

He was halfway up the hallway when he heard Hannah's voice.

"Hey there, grease monkey. I came over to see if you wanted to get started early."

A smile curved Hannah's mouth when he entered the entrance hall and she saw him.

"Hi."

Before he could respond, Ben strode between them and pointed a shaking finger at her.

"You're a liar. A bloody liar," he said.

"Ben!" Joe said, startled by the belligerence in his boy's voice.

Ben shouldered his way rudely past Hannah and out the front door. Joe made eye contact with Hannah.

"Sorry." Then he went after his son.

"What's going on?" he heard Ruby say as he took the porch steps two at a time.

Ben hadn't gone far. He stood beside the mailbox, his head bowed, his shoulders hunched. Braced, Joe guessed, for his father's disapproval.

Joe stopped in front of him. "I asked Hannah to keep what was happening between us private. That's why she told you we were just friends last night."

"Then you're a liar, too."

"Yes, I guess I am, in this one case. But do you understand why I made that choice?"

Ben hunched a shoulder.

"Mate. Look at me."

Ben slowly lifted his head. His face was filled with so much misery Joe's chest ached.

"This doesn't change anything between you and me and

Ruby. It doesn't mean I love your mom or any of you any less. It only means that Hannah and I are going to spend some time together."

Ben broke eye contact and returned his gaze to the ground.

"Now, I want you to come apologize to Hannah."

Ben stiffened. "No way. I didn't do anything wrong. She's the one who lied to me."

"Because I asked her to. I thought you liked Hannah."

"That was before she was screwing you."

Joe flinched at the ugliness in Ben's tone. Ben shot him a half afraid, half defiant look, clearly expecting his father to come down on him like a ton of bricks.

Joe leveled a finger at him. "I don't want to hear that kind of language from you. Especially not toward women, and especially not toward Hannah. She's been a good friend to our family."

"She's not my friend. You can't make me like her."

"No, but I can make you apologize. Right now."

"Joe."

He turned to find Hannah standing behind him, a concerned frown on her face.

"It's okay," she said.

"Ben needs to apologize to you."

"He's allowed to have his feelings," she said. "I understand."

Joe wavered, uncertain if he was setting a bad precedent by letting Ben get away with such disrespect. Hannah had a point, however. He'd brought much of this on himself by trying to protect his kids. And Ben did have a right to his feelings.

"I want you to go to your room," he said to Ben.

"Fine."

Ben speared Hannah with a burning look as he strode past her.

"I'm sorry. That was my fault," Joe said.

"It's all right. I'd be angry if I was in his shoes, too."

Ruby appeared on the doorstep, a frown on her face.

"I need to talk to Ruby," he said.

"I think she's heard enough to have a fair idea of what's going on."

He shook his head. "What a screwup."

"Yeah, well, it could have been worse."

"How so?"

"They could have walked in when we were going at it like monkeys yesterday morning."

He couldn't help but laugh. "There is that."

"Let me know if there's anything I can do, okay?" she said.

"Will do."

She gave him a small smile before turning to wave to Ruby and walking away. He watched her for a moment, admiring the swing of her hips.

Then he took a deep breath and went to talk to his daughter.

LATER THAT NIGHT he fielded a call from his mother.

"I thought you should know that Ben phoned and asked if he could come live with me," she announced.

Joe swore.

"That's not going to solve anything," his mother said.

"Thank you, I know that." He took a deep breath and let it out again. His mother hadn't done anything to earn his anger. "Sorry."

"What's going on? Did you two have a fight or some-thing?"

"I've started dating someone. Ben doesn't approve." He filled his mother in briefly.

"Oh, Joe. You've made a real mess of things, haven't you?"

He bit his tongue. She was only speaking the truth, after all.

"I'm open to suggestions," he said.

"Who is this woman, anyway? How come I haven't heard about her before?"

"She lives next door."

"The girl Ruby has taken such a shine to?"

"She's hardly a girl."

"She sounds very young to me from what Ruby has told me."

"She's in her late twenties." He was thirty-six. He figured it was a respectable age difference, nothing to get outraged over. Certainly he'd never given it a moment's thought.

"But she rides a motorcycle, is that right? And didn't she take off on some big road trip recently?"

"She came back. And she's hardly a biker moll. She's a mechanic and she's into restoring old bikes."

"I see."

"I thought you'd be happy I was seeing someone."

"I am. But it's not like you only have yourself to think about. It's not enough that you're attracted to this woman. You have children to consider."

No shit. He rubbed the bridge of his nose.

"I know all this, Mom. The kids already have a relationship with her. And I wouldn't have gotten them involved if this was just some fling."

"Well, that's good to hear. I only hope she feels the same way."

"What's that supposed to mean?"

His mother's sigh filtered down the line. "You're asking her to take on an awful lot, stepping into a ready-made family."

"Hannah knows who we are."

"And is she ready to become an instant mother to someone else's children?"

He tipped his head back and reached for patience.

It had all seemed so simple when Hannah had ridden back into his life yesterday. He'd been thinking about her so much, had been kicking himself for letting her go without saying anything, and it had felt right and good to take her to bed. But it hadn't taken long for reality to intrude.

As his mother said, he wasn't a man alone. He had two children who depended on him utterly for everything. And they had to come first, no matter what.

"Look, it's early days. All I know is that she's great with Ruby and she's been incredibly patient with Ben."

"And what happens when the novelty wears off and the going gets tough? Is she going to stick around?"

"She's not like that, Mom."

"I'm not saying she's a bad person, Joe. I'm just saying that you're asking her to take on a lot. And it's going to take a special kind of woman, a very generous woman, to do that."

He stared at the wall. It wasn't as though he'd never considered the issues his mother was bringing up. But he'd let desire and need override his common sense and caution.

Had that been a mistake?

He flashed to the hot and sweaty hours he'd spent in bed with Hannah the previous morning and the contentment and peace he'd found lying with her in his arms afterward. There hadn't been a doubt in his mind then. He had to hang on to that feeling, to that belief.

"Hannah *is* special," he said.

"I hope you're right. What do you want to do about Ben? And how is Ruby taking the news?"

"She couldn't be happier. She told me she'd been wishing for Hannah to be my girlfriend because she thought we were both lonely."

Despite everything, the memory brought a smile to his mouth. At least one of his kids was happy.

"Hmm. Out of the mouths of babes."

He decided to ignore the skepticism in his mother's tone.

"I'll talk to Ben," he said.

"Maybe he should come stay with me for a couple of days, let him cool down."

"No. We're a family. He can't opt out when it suits him. We have to work this through."

"Good to hear."

"Glad you approve of something," he said drily.

"Joe…"

"I know. And thanks for the call. I appreciate the heads-up. And the lecture."

"Anytime," his mother said, and he knew she was smiling.

They talked a little more before he ended the call. He sat for a moment, going over the conversation again in his mind. Then he pushed himself to his feet and made his way to Ben's room.

His son was lying on his bed, his iPod plugged into his ears. His eyes flicked toward Joe then away again.

"Could we talk for a minute?" Joe asked.

Ben ignored him. Joe walked to the bed and tugged the earphones from Ben's ears. "I asked you a question."

"I didn't hear you."

Joe decided to let the lie slide. "I just got off the phone

with your grandmother. She told me you wanted to come stay with her."

"That's right."

Joe cocked his head and studied him for a moment.

"Is that really what you want? You don't want to be here with me and Ruby anymore?"

Ben shrugged, avoiding eye contact. "At least Nan doesn't lie to me."

"I've explained to you why I felt it was best to hold off on telling you and Ruby what was happening between me and Hannah. You're old enough to understand that there are different kinds of lies. If you tell a lie to hurt someone, or to cover up something bad, that's wrong. But what I did was to protect you and your sister."

Ben simply stared at him, unresponsive. Joe sighed. Clearly there would be no getting through to him tonight.

"Look, all I can say is that I love you kids and you're my first priority, always. I'm sorry if what I did hurt your feelings. But that doesn't mean you can milk this forever. You're not going to your grandmother's, okay?"

Ben looked as though he was going to say something for a moment, then he shrugged and reached for his earphones again. "You're the boss."

He stuck his earphones back in his ears and made a point of focusing on the football poster at the end of his bed.

Not the most satisfactory conversation Joe had ever had, but it would have to do. He couldn't force his son to feel one way or another. He would simply have to wait him out. Ben had liked Hannah before Joe had started dating her, and Joe was confident his son would come around eventually. It would take time, and patience. He crossed his fingers that Hannah was prepared to ride out the storm with him.

If she runs screaming for the hills, then you'll have your answer, won't you?

He told himself it was his mother's voice he was hearing in his head, advising caution, casting doubts. But the fact remained that most of what his mother had said was true: he was asking Hannah to take on a lot.

TWO WEEKS LATER, HANNAH waited on the front porch of Joe's house for him to return from dropping the kids at school. He was running a little late and she checked her watch. If she got the job she was interviewing for this afternoon, it would mean the end of their early-morning meetings.

She stared glumly out at the empty street. Well. They would have to find another way to spend time together without further upsetting the delicate balance in his household. So far, Ben had showed no sign of thawing toward her. She'd come over for dinner on the weekend and he'd steadfastly ignored her through the whole meal. On Tuesday night they were all supposed to go to the movies together, but Ben had claimed he had study group at a friend's place. And last night he'd answered the phone when she'd called and said not a word once he recognized her voice, simply passing the phone to Joe.

She was officially persona non grata where he was concerned, and as much as she told herself he was young and full of grief and entitled to his feelings, she wasn't immune to his tactics. It was hard to take pleasure in the time she spent with Joe and Ruby when she understood that at the same time she made Ben unhappy. She kept telling herself that it wasn't personal, that he'd feel this way about any woman Joe was dating, but that argument was wearing thinner and thinner.

She'd been hoping for some sign of a thaw by now.

Anything—some eye contact, a mumbled word of greeting. Hell, she'd even take a belch if it sounded friendly enough. But Ben was sticking staunchly to his guns, with no sign of a cease-fire in sight.

The sound of a car engine brought her head up and she smiled as Joe pulled into the driveway.

"Sorry, I got held up with one of Ruby's teachers," he said as he exited the car.

He kissed her deeply, his palm curled around the back of her neck. She leaned against his broad chest, savoring the contact. This was the one thing in her world that was absolutely right: being with Joe, holding him, touching him, being touched by him. She'd never had a more considerate or passionate lover.

"You okay?" he asked when he broke the kiss.

"Yeah, of course."

The concern and warmth in his eyes made her chest hurt. Every time she saw him, he asked her the same question, his first thought for her and how she might be feeling. He already had the world on his shoulders, and yet he was prepared to take on her problems and doubts and fears, as well. He had a generous heart.

"As long as we haven't scared you off yet." He said it lightly, but she couldn't help wondering if he wasn't also fishing for reassurance. Did he think her feelings were so small and malleable that Ben's resistance would tip the balance out of his favor?

"I'm hard to scare. I thought you knew that by now."

And I love you. I'm not going anywhere.

The words formed in her mind and were almost out of her mouth before she caught them.

Well. She hadn't wasted any time, had she?

She ducked her head, buying a few seconds to pull herself

together and deal with her realization. Apparently she hadn't ridden halfway across the continent only to see what Joe was like in bed. Apparently she'd fallen in love with him, somehow, somewhere. Go figure.

He tilted her chin up and kissed her again, one hand sliding onto her backside. Familiar heat raced through her body. She flashed to the last time they'd made love, the way he'd kissed her all over and made her crazy using only his hands and his mouth. Thinking about it made her feel liquid with longing again.

He made a frustrated noise as he broke their kiss.

"I've got an appointment at ten o'clock with my lawyer," he said.

She checked her watch. It was nine-thirty.

"How long do you need?" she asked, looking up at him from beneath her eyelashes.

She loved how quickly he hustled her inside. She loved how avidly he gazed at her breasts and belly and thighs as he stripped her. She loved the way he savored her, his eyes closed as he teased her breasts with his mouth then kissed his way down her stomach. She loved everything about him, and as he slid inside her she had to bite her lip to stop herself from saying the words out loud.

She had no idea if her feelings were reciprocated, and he had enough on his plate without having to deal with a badly timed declaration from her. She knew he fancied her like crazy, that he loved sex with her. She knew he laughed at her jokes and appreciated it when she challenged him. But he'd been married for fifteen years to a woman he'd loved passionately, and there was every chance he would be slower and more careful before giving his heart away than Hannah was. She figured she'd already shown her hand enough by returning to be with him—there would be other times to let him know how much he meant to her.

"We're on the clock, pay attention," he said as he moved inside her.

She pushed her thoughts away and followed instructions. Within a handful of minutes she was clutching at his back, his shoulders as he drove into her. Rippling pleasure washed through her and her body clenched his as she climaxed.

"Hannah," he whispered, then he came, too, his cheek pressed against hers as his body tensed and shuddered.

He pressed a kiss to her jaw afterward, one hand curled possessively over her breast.

She traced the arch of his right eyebrow with her fingertip then repeated the gesture with the left.

"I love your eyes," she said, mostly to stop herself from saying something else.

He smiled. Then he tensed as he caught sight of the clock on the DVD player.

"Shit. I'm going to be late," he said. He rolled off the couch and onto the floor.

Hannah laughed as she helped him round up his underwear and shoes, buckling his belt for him as he pulled on his shirt. He left her to lock up the house, kissing her one last time before bolting for his car. She finished dressing and was about to head out the door when she paused.

It was the first time she'd been alone in Joe's house. Feeling somewhat guilty, she crossed to the family portrait propped on a shelf near the TV.

She'd never had a really good look at Beth before. She'd passed the portrait a dozen times but never lingered, for obvious reasons. Now she picked up the frame and studied the photograph. It was an informal shot. The family was gathered on a picnic blanket, the kids sprawled like puppies at their parents' feet, Beth leaning back against a smiling Joe. Joe's wife was small and blonde, with wide blue eyes. She wore a white dress with little yellow flowers on it, and a pair of high-heeled yellow espadrilles had been kicked off to one side. She was beautiful in a fragile, feminine way.

Utterly different from Hannah. She stared at the photograph, trying to understand if what she was feeling was envy or jealousy or something else altogether.

It must be every woman's nightmare not to live to see her children into adulthood. The thought of not being there to guide them through crises, to kiss things better or deliver a serve of tough love…

Looking into the other woman's smiling face, Hannah decided that she felt sad for Beth Lawson, nothing else. She'd had a life, a family, a good marriage. She'd loved and been loved. And it had all been taken away in a split second.

If it was me, I'd want Joe to be happy. I'd want him to find someone else to love, for someone else to love my children.

Hannah placed the frame back on the shelf.

Making peace with Beth had given Hannah new clarity. She loved Joe, and she fell more and more in love with his children every day. Ben could ignore her all he liked, but he couldn't stop her seeing his little-boy's heart or understanding he was hurting. She could wait him out. He needed her. They all did, just as she needed them. At the end of the day, that was what family was about, right?

I want this. I want them.

It was that simple. Now all she had to do was win Joe's son's trust and hope that Joe could find the courage to love another woman the way he'd loved his wife.

Small potatoes, right?

OVER THE NEXT WEEK, Joe swung between two states—stupid, bemused happiness and deeply frustrated sadness.

It seemed crazy to him that both states could coexist, but it was the reality of his life. When he and Hannah were alone, he felt invincible. She was sexy, strong, gutsy, smart—she made him feel seventeen again, the way he couldn't stop thinking about her. If he wasn't careful, one day soon he'd come out of a daze and find he'd etched her name in his desk at the pub. He was that obsessed, that involved.

Then there was Ben. Angry, silent, rude. And that was on a good day. It had been three weeks since Hannah had returned and he'd told the kids they were dating. Ruby was as happy as a clam. Each night she trekked next door to help Hannah with the Thunderbird. Sometimes he joined them, sometimes he didn't. Ben never did. He'd taken to spending time in his room, except when Joe forced him to join them at the dinner table. He'd also had to intervene in more than one row between Ben and his sister, Ben's anger spilling over into other aspects of his life. Joe was waiting for the inevitable phone call from school to tell him Ben had been in a fight—it seemed a logical extension of his son's behavior.

The worst thing was that Joe felt so powerless. He'd tried patience. He'd tried communication. He'd tried bribery, to his shame. Nothing got through to his sullen son. Ben had effectively withdrawn from the family.

Every time Ben turned his back on Hannah or glared at her or avoided spending time with them as a group, Joe remembered his mother's words. *You're asking her to take on an awful lot, stepping into a ready-made family.* Even though his gut told him Hannah would stay, that she would never have entered their lives if she hadn't intended to go the distance, a part of him was afraid that he would lose her just as he was beginning to understand how bloody lucky he was.

The tension within him came to a head when Hannah was over for dinner Tuesday night. Ben opened the door to her knock and walked away without acknowledging her at all.

"Ben!" Joe said sharply, but his son just kept walking up the hallway.

Joe took one look at Hannah's dismayed face and his temper flared.

"That's it. I've had enough." He moved toward the hall-way, but Hannah caught his arm.

"Wait five minutes before you go after him and say some-thing you might regret."

"Something has to give," he said. She might not want to acknowledge it, but Ben's attitude was getting worse, not better. He was becoming openly, aggressively rude, some-thing Joe would not tolerate. Ben didn't have to like what was happening between Joe and Hannah, but he had to respect his father's decision, and he needed to respect Hannah.

"I know. But two angry Lawson men aren't going to get us anywhere."

She was right. He knew she was right. "Okay. I'm count-ing to a hundred."

"Make it two hundred," she said.

Which made him laugh. She always knew how to get to him.

Before he could stop himself, he reached out and tugged her close, kissing her briefly on the lips. She kissed him back and he had to remind himself his children were in the house. Sure enough, when they pulled back he became aware of Ruby standing in the kitchen doorway, a drink in her hand. They'd been very circumspect with physical stuff to date, hand-holding being the limit of their displays of affection in front of the children. Ruby's eyes were wide, as though she'd just spotted a real-life fairy, or some other mystical creature at the bottom of the garden.

Hannah cleared her throat, her cheeks a little pink. "Um, hi, Ruby."

"When are you going to stay the night?" Ruby asked, her small face avid.

Hannah made a choking noise.

"Ruby," Joe said, amused despite himself. She was incorrigible—and he much preferred her this way to the nervous, anxious little girl she'd been when they first moved from Sydney.

"I'm only asking what everyone else is thinking," Ruby said matter-of-factly.

"Everyone? Who's everyone?" Joe asked. Too late he realized he'd been foolish to buy into the discussion.

"Grandma, and Aunty Robyn next door."

"Not quite everyone," he said.

"Close enough," Hannah murmured.

"Staying the night isn't something people should rush into," Joe said.

"Why not? I thought you liked each other. It would be cool to have Hannah here for breakfast," Ruby said.

There was a sound from the hallway and Joe swung around to see his son standing in the living room doorway, his angry gaze fixed on Ruby.

"What is wrong with you?" Ben snarled. "Why are you trying so hard to replace Mom?"

Hannah visibly flinched and Ruby went pale as she stared at her brother.

"I'm not. I'm not trying to replace Mommy," she said. She looked to Joe, stricken.

"Yes, you are. Wanting Hannah to be in that mother-daughter thing with you, always sucking up to her and trying to get Dad to like her more. What do you think Mom would say if she could see you?"

Ben was white with anger, his hands curled into fists by his sides.

"Mate," Joe said, stepping forward.

Ben swung toward him. "You're just as bad. Don't you care that she's not here? Don't you even think about her anymore?"

"Of course I do, we all do—"

"No, you don't. You just want to do it with Hannah all the time and forget about everything else. You don't even care that she's dead."

"You know better than to talk like that," Joe said.

"Don't think I don't know what you do when Ruby and I go to school." Ben's face was red and he was shaking, but he didn't take his fierce gaze from Joe's.

Hannah stepped forward. "Ben, the last thing I want to do is try to take your mom's place. My dad left when I was about Ruby's age, and I know it's not the same as dying, but I missed him like crazy."

Ben refused to even look at her, keeping his gaze fixed on his father.

"I don't want to try and take away your memories of your mom or replace her or anything like that, I promise," Hannah said. "I just like spending time with you and your dad and Ruby."

Joe watched carefully, trying to read his son's response, not sure if he should intervene or not.

"You want more than that," Ben said. "I'm not stupid."

Hannah held up her fingers in a classic Scout's pledge. "I swear, I just want to hang with you guys. No agenda. I like you. Where else am I going to get such cheap labor for the Thunderbird?"

Ben shot her a confused look. Hannah took another step forward and reached out to place a reassuring hand on his shoulder. "Couldn't we at least try to be friends?" she asked.

Ben looked at her, and for a moment Joe caught a glimpse of something desperate and needy in his son's face. Then Ben scowled and shrugged his shoulder, roughly brushing Hannah's hand away. "I told you, you're never going to be my mom."

Ruby was across the room in a flash, throwing herself between Ben and Hannah, reaching out to push her brother away.

"Stop it! You're going to ruin everything! You're going to make Hannah hate us and then she'll go away and we'll never see her again."

"You're a traitor," Ben yelled. "A stinking traitor." He shoved Ruby with all his might. She staggered backward, wildly off balance, then fell awkwardly onto her outstretched left arm.

Her wail of pain made the hairs on the back of Joe's neck stand on end. He was at her side in seconds, cradling her as she hugged her arm to her chest.

"It hurts. It hurts so much," she sobbed.

Grim, he gently tested her wrist joint. Ruby yelped with pain.

"I think it's broken," he said.

Ben stood frozen, so pale Joe thought he was going to pass out. "I didn't mean it. I didn't mean it." Ben bolted for the door.

"Ben!" Joe bellowed. It was dark outside and the last thing he needed was to have to chase Ben down when they had to get Ruby to the hospital.

But Ben was gone, the door banging loudly behind him.

"I'll go after him," Hannah said. "You need to get Ruby to a doctor."

He nodded briefly, giving Ruby a reassuring squeeze. Hannah headed for the door, her stride long, and he gave his daughter all his attention.

"Daddy's just going to go grab a bag of peas from the freezer for you, sweetheart. It'll make the pain a bit better. You keep your arm still and don't move."

By the time he had Ruby in the car and ready to go, Hannah had returned.

"No sign of him. I'm sorry, I have no idea how he disappeared so quickly," she said helplessly.

He stared out into the night. He hated the thought of Ben roaming the streets, upset and alone, but there wasn't much he could do about it right now. He couldn't be in two places at once.

"I need to go," he said.

"I'll find him," Hannah promised.

He looked at her, remembering his mother's warning that once the novelty had worn off and the going had gotten tough, Hannah might want to opt out. He figured tonight definitely qualified under the tough category, but she showed no signs of flinching.

"Thank you," he said.

She simply shook her head. "You don't have to thank me."

He could see what she wasn't saying in her eyes and even though he had a million worries pressing down on him, he couldn't stop the words from rising up inside him.

"Love you," he said, stepping close to press a quick kiss to her lips before turning to slide into the driver's seat.

She looked flustered for a moment, then her mouth lifted at the corner. "Nice timing."

"Figured I'd better get in while the getting was good."

She looked as though she wanted to say more, but she pushed his car door closed. "Call me from the hospital, let me know how Ruby is."

"I will."

She stepped back from the car as he reversed into the street. The last thing he saw was her standing in his driveway, arms crossed over her chest, her stance strong and sure.

LOVE YOU.

Joe's words echoed in Hannah's head as she walked the streets of Elsternwick, eyes peeled for a slim thirteen-year-old boy in baggy jeans and a white T-shirt.

How typical of Joe to blurt it out like that. She'd been biting her tongue for days, waiting for the right moment to declare herself, and he'd just thrown his own declaration at her as casually as goodbye or hello or have a nice day.

Okay, it hadn't been *that* casual. But he'd definitely caught her by surprise. And she'd been very aware of Ruby in the backseat, her face creased with pain. Hardly the moment to tell him the feeling was mutual and that she adored him, body and soul.

She checked her watch. She'd been searching for nearly forty minutes now. She'd checked the school, The Watering Hole and the local shops. She'd run out of obvious options, so it was time to start thinking not so obviously. There always seemed to be a bunch of kids hanging out at the twenty-four-hour convenience store near the highway. Maybe Ben had taken refuge with them. And it might be worth checking in with the Balases. Ben had formed an attachment with the Indian shop owner over the past few months.

Her phone buzzed in her pocket. Joe's name was illuminated on her screen.

"How is she?" she asked as she took the call.

"Broken scaphoid bone in her wrist. When she fell on her arm like that I was pretty sure that'd be the case. Seen it a few times out on the rigs."

"But she's okay?"

"She's fine. Getting a cast put on as we speak, lapping up the attention and the lollipops."

"I was about to check out that twenty-four-hour place over near the highway," she reported. "He's not at the school or the shops or the pub."

"All right. I'll come join you once I've got Ruby home."

"Mom's there to look after her."

"Good, that'll save me calling my mom."

Might as well say what they were both thinking.

"If we don't find him soon, we should probably think about calling the police," she said.

"Yeah, I know." His voice was heavy with worry.

They agreed to touch base again once he was close to home, then Hannah ended the call. She got her bearings and struck out in the direction of the highway. She was passing the local playground, the equipment reduced to vague shapes in the darkness, when she caught a flash of something out of the corner of her eye. She stopped in her tracks. Ben had been wearing a white T-shirt. Was that what she'd seen in her peripheral vision?

She peered into the park. Slowly the vague shapes took form: a swing set, a slide, monkey bars, a flying fox.

"Ben? Are you there?" she called.

She held her breath, waiting. Nothing but silence greeted her. She walked farther into the park and saw there was a log bridge situated beyond the swing, the kind made from two mounds of earth placed on either side of a large section of concrete pipe with a bridge built over the top.

Her heart gave a huge, painful thump of relief when she saw a pale shape huddled in the darkness inside the big pipe.

Ben. It had to be.

She ran the few steps to the bridge and dropped to her knees.

"Ben. Thank God. Are you okay?"

As she'd half expected, he flinched away from her. "Go away."

"I can't do that, I'm sorry. Your dad's worried sick about you."

Silence from the pipe. She could barely see the pale oval of Ben's face.

"Ben, why don't you come out and we can go home and talk? No one's angry with you, if that's what you're worried about."

Ben hiccuped softly, and Hannah realized he was crying. Had been crying for a while, judging from the hiccups.

"Ben, it's okay," she said.

She crawled a few feet inside the pipe so that she was sitting next to him. She wanted to put her arm around him very badly but doubted he'd tolerate it.

"Are you worried about Ruby? Is that it? Because I just spoke to your dad and he said she was going to be fine."

Ben's sobbing increased.

"Come on, let's go home," she said again. "Don't you want to go home?"

He was crying so hard she almost didn't hear what he said. "Can't."

"Why can't you come home, Ben?" She felt woefully out of her depth, but Ben was so miserable she had to try.

His voice was broken and small and Hannah had to strain to hear his reply. "Because it's my fault. They'll all hate me once they know."

She frowned. She might be inexperienced with kids, but her gut was telling her that there was a whole lot more going on here than reaction to the incident at the house.

"I haven't known your dad and Ruby as long as you have, but I know that there is no way they could ever hate you, Ben. They love you. Absolutely they love you."

Ben pressed his hands to his face. "That's only because they don't know."

"I'm sure that whatever it is, it's not as bad as you think."

"It is. It's the worst."

A shiver raced up her spine. Had something happened to Ben? Had someone taken advantage of him? "Would it help if you told me? Maybe you'd feel better if you got it off your chest."

He shook his head.

"What if I promised not to tell anyone else unless you gave me permission? Would that make a difference?" She held her breath, banking on the fact that Ben was clearly aching to tell someone what was on his mind.

Ben sniffed a few times, thinking her offer over. "You can't tell anyone."

"I swear it will be our secret."

There was a long silence. When Ben spoke, his voice was barely above a whisper. "The day Mom died, I was supposed to get a lift home from karate with George Simpkin's mom, but George and I had a fight during class and I called Mom and asked her to come get me."

Hannah closed her eyes, guessing what was coming next.

"If I hadn't asked her to pick me up, she wouldn't have been in the accident. It's my fault she died," Ben said brokenly.

Bloody hell.

For a moment Hannah was swamped with a huge, vast sadness. Joe's son had been carrying this misplaced guilt around with him for two long years. No wonder he'd been so angry and sad and withdrawn.

"See. You hate me now. And Dad and Ruby will hate me if they find out."

Tears pricked the back of her eyes at the depth of his fear and hurt. For a moment she felt overwhelmed. Then she shuffled around so she was facing him. "Ben, I want you to look at me."

His head came up. His face was streaked with tears and his bottom lip trembled with emotion. She held his eye.

"What happened was not your fault. It was an accident. No one could have known that it would happen."

"But she wouldn't have even been there if it hadn't been for me."

Hannah wondered how many times he'd lacerated himself with the exact same thought. "Someone ran a red light. That's why your mom died. You didn't do a thing wrong."

She could see how much Ben wanted to believe what she was telling him. It was bad enough that he had to live with the grief of losing his mother, but to believe he was to blame... It was the sort of misconception that could ruin a life.

"Accidents happen all the time, for no reason," she said. "I know that's kind of scary to think about, but it's true. You can't take responsibility for an accident."

Ben frowned into the darkness. She wished she knew the handful of magic words that would convince him, but she suspected there were none. He'd been living with his mistaken belief for two years, and it was going to take time to convince him he was blameless.

He shifted and sniffed mightily, wiping his nose on the sleeve of his T-shirt.

"Has anyone ever told you how gross that is?" she said lightly.

As she'd hoped, it shocked a laugh out of him. "Yeah. Grandma. All the time."

"You do that in front of your grandma? You're a brave man."

Ben sniffed again, but the look he flashed her was marginally less miserable.

She pulled out her phone. "I'm going to call your dad, let him know I've found you so he can stop worrying. Okay?"

She kept the call short, letting Joe know they were on their way home. When she ended the call, she simply sat in silence for a few seconds.

"You ready to go?"

"I guess."

They crawled out of the pipe. Ben looked so small and young, Hannah had to clench her hands into fists to stop herself from hugging him.

They were both silent as they walked through the park to the street. Ben didn't speak up again until they were about to turn into their street.

"Are you going to tell him?"

"Your dad? No. I promised you I wouldn't, and I won't. But I think you should."

Ben stared at her mistrustfully. She stopped walking to give him her full attention. "What have you got to lose?"

"Only everything."

"And that would make you really miserable and you wouldn't want to hang out with anyone or make new friends and you'd probably spend most of your time in your room on your own listening to your iPod. When you weren't yelling at your sister or ignoring your dad, that is. Does that sound about right?"

Ben blinked. "You're saying I'm already unhappy."

"You tell me."

They both started walking again, Ben's face screwed up in concentration as he thought over what she'd said.

"I guarantee he won't hate you, Ben," she said as they turned onto their street and saw Joe's house, light spilling out of every window, the Mazda parked in the driveway. "I know it's hard, but I think you need to start telling people how you're feeling instead of keeping everything locked up inside all the time."

Ben glanced at her out of the corner of his eye.

"If you want me to, I could tell him with you. Would that make it any easier?" she said.

Ben didn't respond. She bit her lip. She was about out of strategies. They walked toward the house. She could feel the heat coming off the SUV as she passed the hood. Joe must have just gotten home.

"Okay," Ben said, so quietly she almost didn't catch it.

She glanced at him as Joe walked out onto the front porch. Ben stopped in his tracks and the two Lawson men stared at each other across the space of a few feet. A knot lodged in her throat as she saw the fear and longing on Ben's face.

"You okay?" Joe asked, his voice rough with emotion.

Ben nodded. Joe started down the porch steps and Ben made a choking sound before flinging himself into his father's arms.

Hannah sniffed noisily as she watched Joe comfort his son. Lucky she wasn't the kind of woman who wore a lot of makeup or tonight would have left her looking like a panda.

"I'm sorry. I didn't mean to hurt Ruby," Ben said, his voice muffled by Joe's shirt.

"Your sister is fine, although she's probably going to drive you crazy asking you to sign her cast."

Ben made a sound that might have been a laugh. Then he pushed away from his father's embrace. He shot Hannah a quick, nervous glance, then focused on his father and took a deep breath.

"There's something I need to tell you. It's about Mom," Ben said.

Joe's face remained carefully neutral. "Okay. Why don't we go inside?"

He started to herd Ben toward the door, but Ben hung back and glanced over his shoulder.

"Hannah, too," he said.

It was the smallest of shifts, but it pierced her heart.

"It's okay, I'm coming. Try keeping me away," she said with a watery smile.

Then she followed Joe and Ben into the house.

CHAPTER TWELVE

JOE PAUSED IN THE HALLWAY as he shut the door to his son's room. It was late, past one in the morning, and for a moment he felt immeasurably heavy, weighed down by the sadness his son had been carrying for so long.

He closed his eyes and rubbed the bridge of his nose. He should have pushed harder earlier, asked the right questions. He should have somehow seen that Ben's misery went deeper than simple grief.

He walked slowly to the living room. Hannah was on the couch and she looked up when he entered.

"How's he doing?"

"He's asleep."

"No wonder. It's been a big night."

"Yeah."

"Come here." She patted the floor. "Sit between my legs."

He sat on the floor and allowed her to draw him back against the couch, her legs on either side of his shoulders. She began to massage him, her thumbs working at the tense muscles in his back and neck.

"Don't give yourself a hard time," she said quietly.

He shrugged. She found a knot in his neck and worked at it diligently for a few seconds.

"You're a great dad, Joe. One of the best. But you're not a mind reader."

"You didn't know him before the accident. I should have seen it was something more than Beth dying."

"Tell me, how is a grieving kid supposed to act? Moody, angry, incommunicative? Until Ben was ready to tell someone what was going on in his head, you didn't stand a chance of working it out on your own. And blaming yourself isn't going to get anyone anywhere or do Ben any favors, by the way."

Typical Hannah, calling it as she saw it, like always. Despite his weariness and sadness he smiled. "You're a real ball breaker, you know that?"

"You wish."

"You saying I want my balls broken?" He twisted his neck to look at her, one eyebrow raised.

"I'm saying you'll take any attention down there that you can get."

"Really?"

"Really." She raised a challenging eyebrow back at him.

He moved quickly, twisting and hooking an arm behind her neck and hauling her onto the floor. He didn't stop until she was beneath him, her arms pinned to the carpet.

"Thank you for making my point," she said.

He kissed the smile off her lips. "You can break my balls anytime."

"Aren't you supposed to whisper sweet nothings like that in my ear?" she said.

She was such a smart-ass.

He pulled her earlobe into his mouth and bit it gently.

"How about this? I love you, Hannah Napier," he whispered against the soft skin of her neck.

She went very still, and he released one of her hands so he could lever himself up on an elbow and look into her face.

"Something wrong?" he asked, trying to keep his tone

light despite the flutter of nervousness in his belly. He thought he understood her, knew what was in her heart. But he could be wrong. He could be way off base.

"No. You just keep taking me by surprise, that's all."

"You mean it's a surprise to you that I'm crazy about you?"

And here he thought it had been as obvious as hell, that he might as well plaster it on a billboard and shout it to the world.

"Yes. No. You know what I mean. I've been biding my time, trying to find the right opportunity, the right moment, and you just threw it out there...."

It took him a moment to understand what she was saying. He smiled, warmth unfolding in his chest. "Let me get this straight. I'm in trouble because I beat you to the punch?"

"Not in trouble. Just stuck with me for the foreseeable future."

She still couldn't say it. He had her ex-fiancé to thank for that, he suspected. He cupped a hand to his ear, pretending to be hard of hearing.

"Sorry, was that a declaration I just heard, Ms. Napier?"

She stared at him for a moment. Then she took a deep breath, her eyes very serious as she looked into his. "I love you, Joe Lawson. Happy now?"

"Yes."

He wrapped his arms around her and pulled her close, his cheek resting against hers, her scent in his lungs, her heart beating next to his. He thought about the past few weeks, the trials she'd endured, and he squeezed her closer.

"I love you," he said again, just to hear the words out loud.

"I love you, too. So much."

"Let's go to bed."

She hadn't stayed the night before, but he needed her

tonight. Needed her body against his, the simple comfort of having her near.

"Not really the best timing for such a big move," she said regretfully.

He knew she was right, but it was hard not to feel frustrated. And it wasn't about sex. It was about intimacy. Belonging. Comfort. Security.

She traced a finger along his jawline. "What if I just lie down with you for a while? Then I'll go home."

It was something, better than nothing.

He led her to his bedroom and she took off her shoes and jeans and climbed into bed beside him wearing her T-shirt and underwear. He pulled her into his arms and she rested her head on his shoulder, their legs tangling. She felt good, smelled even better. He closed his eyes and pressed a kiss to the top of her head.

Almost immediately his brain circled to the problems of the evening, to his troubled son and his daughter with her arm in a cast. He smoothed a hand down Hannah's arm over and over, wondering what more he could have said to put Ben's mind at ease, if there was something else he should be doing.

"He's going to be all right, Joe. He's a smart kid. He'll work it out."

Somehow, she knew he was fretting again.

"I hope so."

She turned her head to look at him. "I was thinking it might help to find someone for him to talk to. Someone who specializes in kids. What do you think?" She said it hesitantly, as though she was unsure of his reaction. Trust Hannah to have a game plan when he was still floundering and trying to find his feet.

"Good idea. I'll talk to our doctor tomorrow, see if he can

recommend someone." He'd make the call first thing and do whatever it took to get Ben to open up.

"He'll be okay," Hannah said again.

"Yes."

She smiled at the conviction in his voice and lay her head back on his chest. "I'm just going to close my eyes for a few minutes. *Do not* let me fall asleep."

"I won't."

"Because I can't stay the night yet."

"I know."

"Not until Ben is absolutely okay with all of this."

"Yes."

It was one of the many things he loved about her, the fact that she put his kids' welfare first and foremost, always.

"Just a few minutes," she reminded him drowsily.

He smiled to himself. In all likelihood she would fall asleep, and he would let her. Then he would wake her in an hour or two, and if he was very lucky, they might make love before she went home.

And maybe, one day soon, she wouldn't have to go home, and he'd have the pleasure of waking to find her next to him, her brown eyes hazy with sleep, her beautiful mouth curving into the first smile of the day.

Getting a little ahead of yourself, buddy.

But for the first time in a long time it felt okay to dream a little, to believe that maybe they'd turned the corner and that things were going to improve.

And right now he had Hannah in his arms, even if for a few hours. It was enough to be going on with.

"HANNAH, OVER HERE. Come and look at this one."

Hannah looked up from the doll-themed pajamas she was inspecting and saw her mother was knee-deep in the women's lingerie department, a flashy red bra and pantie set dangling from one hand.

"Mom, we're not shopping for me. Or you, for that matter," she said.

It had been nearly six weeks since Ben's big blowup, or what she and Joe now referred to as The Turnaround. Christmas was just around the corner and she was still trying to find a few must-haves for Ben and Ruby. The Nintendo game he'd requested was proving impossible to find, and even though Ruby claimed that with her eleventh birthday looming in late December she was "over dolls," Hannah knew better. Ben had taken it upon himself to do an inventory of his sister's accessories so Hannah would know what not to buy, and Hannah was determined to take home a haul of pink, spangly stuff if it killed her.

She smiled as she remembered Ben's earnestness as he handed over his list to her. He'd been seeing a counselor for about a month and the change in him was nothing short of miraculous. It was as though a huge burden had been lifted from his shoulders—which, of course, it had. Every time he laughed or teased his sister or looked to his father for approval, Hannah's chest ached to see him so changed. Best of all was when he looked at her, or laughed at her jokes, or came over to help her put the finishing touches on the newly chromed Thunderbird. Joe didn't know it yet, but she was giving it to him for Christmas, and both his children had been excellent coconspirators in helping her trick the bike out to suit his tastes. She and Ben had finished buffing the mudguards just last night, in fact.

"It's so beautiful, Hannah," her mother called again. "At least come and look at it. If I had your figure I'd buy it in a snap."

Everybody in a five-mile radius could hear what her mother

was saying and see the red bra and panties. Hannah rolled her eyes, knowing there was only one way to shut her up.

"It's one of those sexy balconette things," her mother said, thrusting the bra into Hannah's hands the moment Hannah joined her. "And feel how soft the silk is."

Hannah dutifully rubbed the silky fabric between thumb and forefinger. As her mother had said, it was very soft. And even though she wasn't particularly into girlie underwear, the red silk and black lace was actually pretty saucy up close.

"Joe loves red," she said absently. He'd commented on her one, rather pedestrian red bra a number of times.

She checked the price tag and almost choked when she saw how much the pair would set her back.

"Get out of town," she said, putting the underwear back on the rack. "No way am I paying so much for so little."

"I'll buy it for you. My Christmas present to both of you." Her mother gave Hannah a cheeky wink.

Somehow, despite her objections, Hannah found herself being herded into the change room.

"We need to go to the men's department next," Hannah said as she started undressing. "I want to get Joe that cashmere sweater we saw last week. I should have bought it at the time."

"I thought you were giving him the bike?" Her mother's disembodied voice floated over the curtain.

"I am. But I want to get him a few other things, as well. He'll be suspicious if there are no parcels for him under the tree."

She was a little embarrassed about how much she was looking forward to Christmas Day. They were going to have a big sit-down dinner with her mother, Joe, the kids and his mother. Between them, she and her mom and Joe's mom were going to cook the meal. It was going to be a real family day, her first Christmas with Joe.

She fumbled the clasp on the new bra and fiddled with the straps until they were comfortable. She laughed a little when she saw how outrageously sexy the bra looked when it was on.

"How does it look?" her mother asked, sticking her head inside the curtain. "Oh, Hannah. Isn't it wonderful!"

"That's one word for it. I don't know if this is really me."

She had a veritable shelf of breast in front of her, packaged in silk and lace.

"Joe will love it. Not another word, I'm buying it," her mother insisted.

Hannah shrugged. She knew her mother well enough not to bother arguing. She reached behind her to undo the clasp and felt a stab of pain near her left armpit.

"Ow!" She tugged the bra away from herself and saw the culprit: the tiny safety pin holding the swing-tag to the bra had popped loose.

"Stupid thing."

She pulled the bra off and soothed the scratch with her hand.

"Give it to me and I'll take it to the register," her mother said.

Hannah frowned as she felt something small and firm beneath her fingers.

"What's wrong?" her mother asked.

Hannah met her mother's eyes in the mirror. "There's a lump."

The smile faded from her mother's eyes. "Are you sure?"

"Yes. It's probably nothing. Hormones or something."

"Let me feel."

"Mom." Hannah wasn't about to let her mother feel her up in a public change room.

"Let me. I have more experience with this than you. My breasts are twenty-five years older than yours."

Hannah sighed and turned so her mother could poke the side of her breast where it tapered into her armpit. "Can you feel it?"

"Yes."

Her mother was frowning now. "When did you check your breasts last?"

"I don't know. Five months ago? Six?"

"Hannah," her mother said reprovingly.

Hannah started pulling on her own bra. "I'm twenty-eight. Hardly in a high-risk group," she said when she caught sight of her mother's worried expression.

She wished she'd never said anything, or that she'd been alone when she tried on the bra. Her mother would be all over her now to get it checked out, and it was probably nothing. Breast cancer was an older woman's disease.

As if she could read Hannah's mind, her mother started counting names off on her fingers. "Kylie Minogue. Christina Applegate. Anastacia. Belinda Emmett. Don't think young women don't need to be careful. I want you to get this checked out, Hannah."

Hannah sighed and tugged on her T-shirt. Clearly, she was never going to hear the end of this until she'd made an appointment with her doctor.

"Fine. I'll go see Dr. Nelson."

Her mother pulled out her cell phone. "I'll see if she can fit you in tomorrow."

"Mom. Will you stop being such a panic merchant? Unbelievable."

"Consider it your early Christmas present to me—peace of mind."

Hannah listened resignedly as her mother spoke to the

receptionist at the medical center, making an appointment for during her lunch break tomorrow. She'd found a new position as senior mechanic with a big, progressive workshop three weeks ago and was glad her mother at least understood that she couldn't afford to take time off so early into the job.

"Happy now?" she asked when her mother ended the call.

"Not yet. But I will be."

THE NEXT DAY, HANNAH greeted her doctor with a self-deprecating smile.

"I feel stupid even mentioning this," she said when she'd explained about finding the lump. "I mean, I'm twenty-eight. Like it's going to be anything to worry about, right?"

"It probably isn't, but you were right to come in. Any changes are worth investigating. The sooner we catch anything, the better," Dr. Nelson said. "Why don't you step behind the screen and take your bra and top off and we'll take a look."

Hannah did as instructed then eyed the examination couch.

"How do you want me?"

"On your back, with your arm behind your head, elbow out."

Hannah lay down and Dr. Nelson pushed the screen back and stepped toward the examination table.

"Sorry if my hands are cold," she said before laying her hands on Hannah's breast.

"I've had worse."

Dr. Nelson smiled. She became more serious as she concentrated on palpating Hannah's breast. Hannah tensed as her doctor located the lump and felt around it.

"Okay, it's definitely a discrete lump. Is there any tenderness when I press it?"

"No, not at all. That's good, right?"

Dr. Nelson's small smile was sympathetic and slightly worried. "Accepted theory is that breast cancer lumps are not generally painful. But there are always exceptions to the rule, especially in younger women."

Hannah frowned. "So is it good or bad that I have no pain?"

The doctor's eyes were unfocused as she concentrated on palpating the rest of Hannah's right breast. "I suspect it's neither here nor there. I'm just going to check your lymph nodes."

Hannah lay still as Dr. Nelson checked her armpit and neck, then examined her left breast.

"Well, Hannah, I'm going to send you for an ultrasound. There's no doubt in my mind that this lump is new and therefore worthy of investigation."

Hannah's stomach was suddenly hollow. "Okay. Um. When should I book the test?"

"I'll ask my receptionist to arrange one for you with a radiologist we have a relationship with. They usually keep a few appointments free for cases like this."

Cases like this. What did that mean?

Dr. Nelson obviously read the uncertainty in her face because she put her hand on Hannah's shoulder. "We're being safe, that's all. Don't hit the panic button just yet. And remember, if we find something, there's an enormous amount we can do."

"Sure."

Hannah dressed in a daze, her cold hands fumbling with the catch on her bra. She'd expected to be reassured and sent home, not sent off for tests.

It's nothing. Dr. Nelson said it herself—she's just being safe.

But the words didn't make the panicky, fluttering feeling leave her stomach. Hannah waited tensely in the reception area for the receptionist to get off the phone with the radiologist.

"They can fit you in first thing tomorrow. How is that?" the receptionist asked.

"I'll have to be late for work, but that should be fine," Hannah said. So much for not looking bad in her new job. She would have to make up the time at the other end of the day.

The receptionist wrote down the address for the radiology clinic and Hannah tucked the card into her pocket. Her first impulse when she stepped outside the clinic was to phone Joe. She hadn't told him about finding the lump or her appointment, hadn't thought it worth mentioning, but now she needed to hear his voice, deep and reassuring. She pulled her cell from her pocket, then remembered that he had a huge function booked for The Watering Hole tonight. An office Christmas party, with over two hundred guests. She didn't want to dump bad news on him when he had to work all night. He'd simply fret and worry, and for what? Tomorrow she'd have her test and get the all clear.

She was about to get on her bike when her cell vibrated in her pocket. It was her mom, surprise, surprise.

"How did you go?"

Hannah hesitated a moment. "Good. Dr. Nelson said not to worry," she lied.

"Oh, that's good. Thank God. You must be relieved."

Hannah closed her eyes. "Yeah, I am."

"And I suppose you're cursing me for making you get it checked out."

"Something like that."

"Well, I'm not sorry. I'd never have stopped worrying otherwise."

Hannah made an excuse to end the call. She had no idea why she'd just lied to her mother. She simply hadn't wanted to say the words out loud. *The doctor's sending me for tests.* It sounded so ominous. Scary.

She went back to work and spent the evening watching DVDs with Ruby and Ben. It was good to force her worries from her mind and give herself over to the here and now of being with Joe's kids. Ruby insisted Hannah sit on the floor so Ruby could sit behind her on the couch and braid her hair. By the time Brendan Fraser had finished journeying to the center of the earth, Hannah had a head full of slightly wonky plaits.

"If you leave them in overnight you'll wake up and your hair will be all kinky," Ruby said.

"And this is a good thing?" Hannah asked.

"Oh, yes. People pay a fortune to have kinky hair," Ruby said knowledgeably.

She hustled the kids to bed at eight-thirty, aware they had school the next day. Ben wanted to read for a little while and she left him to it, figuring he'd probably pass out with his book in his hand and she could swing by in twenty minutes and turn the light out. Ruby wanted to talk, and Hannah sat on the side of her bed and listened to her plan her birthday party.

"Some people think it sucks having your birthday so soon after Christmas, but it's good," Ruby confided. "People always worry that you feel hard done by and you get extra stuff."

"I've never thought of that."

"The only thing is, you have to wait a long time with no other presents to break up the year. Ben's birthday is in

June, so he gets presents every six months. But I only get them once a year."

"That is definitely a bummer. Maybe we should move your birthday, what do you think?"

Ruby laughed. "You can't move a birthday, silly."

"So what else are you going to have at this party of yours? Lions and tigers, dancing horses?"

Ruby rolled her eyes at Hannah's silliness but she was smiling. "No. We're going to have pass the parcel and musical chairs. And blindman's buff. And little sandwiches cut into triangles."

"Mmm. And ice-cream cake. We always had ice-cream cake for our birthday parties."

Ruby's face clouded. "My mom used to make our cakes. She had this cookbook with lots of different cakes in it and each year me and Ben were allowed to pick the cake we wanted her to make. I've had a castle, a turtle, a pony and a puppy. The puppy was the best." Ruby's hands plucked at the edge of the sheet as she remembered.

"I bet they were great cakes."

"They were. They were the best."

Ruby's voice had dropped to a whisper and she blinked rapidly. Hannah patted her knee. "Why don't you squish over and I'll lie down with you?"

Ruby shuffled over without a protest and Hannah kicked her shoes off and lay down beside her, sliding an arm around the little girl's middle so she was snuggling her from behind.

"You give good cuddles," Ruby said.

"So do you."

They were both quiet for a few minutes.

"Hannah?"

"Yes?"

"I'm glad we moved in next to you."

"Me, too, sweetheart."

Slowly Hannah felt the tension leave Ruby's body as she drifted toward sleep.

Hannah started to ease away from her, but Ruby shifted restlessly.

"Don't go. I don't want you to go."

Hannah subsided and waited until Ruby was breathing steadily before sliding out of the bed.

Joe came home late, tired and smelling of beer and cigarette smoke. She swallowed the urge to spill all her doubts into his lap as she listened to him detail the small dramas of the evening. He was tired, and she knew he would be worried if she told him what was happening. It seemed pointless and selfish to do that to him when she would probably get the all clear tomorrow.

Because that was what was going to happen, definitely.

So instead of telling him, she went home to stare at the ceiling and count the hours till morning.

THE RADIOLOGIST WAS a friendly older woman who patiently explained the ultrasound procedure to Hannah before asking her to undress and lie on a table with her arm behind her head. Cool gel was smoothed over Hannah's skin and the ultrasound wand pressed against her breast. Hannah watched the screen intently, trying to understand what she was seeing.

"So is this what you guys do now instead of mammograms?" she asked.

"Oh, no, mammograms are still very much in use. But when we're looking at younger breasts, ultrasound is often more helpful. Younger breast tissue is much more dense and not so easy to look at with X-ray."

"Oh, right."

The radiologist paused as she ran the wand over the area near the lump. Hannah watched the screen, her heart in her mouth. "Is there something there?"

"There's an unusual mass, yes," the radiologist said slowly.

Hannah had to swallow before she could speak again. "Is it cancer?"

"I'm afraid I can't tell you that just by looking. We need to take a biopsy. But we can do that now."

Hannah nodded dumbly. She'd stand on her head if only this woman would give her the all clear.

The radiologist started to assemble a tray with needles and swabs and other medical paraphernalia. After a local anesthetic, she used the ultrasound to target the lump in Hannah's breast and then drew some cells out of it using a fine needle.

Hannah watched as the woman smeared the cells onto a glass plate.

"These go off to the lab now. You should have the results within forty-eight hours."

More waiting. Hannah tried to smile and failed. She dressed slowly and rode to the garage. For the rest of the day she threw herself into her work, trying to drive fear and uncertainty away through sheer willpower.

She was supposed to have fish and chips on the beach with Joe and the kids for dinner but she called and told him she thought she was coming down with a cold. She couldn't look into his eyes and not tell him what was going on. And she wanted to, so much. Wanted his support. His concern. But she'd already decided to spare him the worry she was going through. Joe had been through enough.

She was inspecting the shock absorbers on a Range Rover when her phone vibrated in her pocket the following day. She closed her eyes when she heard her doctor's voice. Dread thumped in her belly. There was no reason for her doctor to call her before her scheduled appointment tomorrow afternoon unless there was bad news.

"Hannah, I'd like you to come in today if possible," Dr. Nelson said. Her voice was calm but serious.

"Oh, God."

"Can you make it this afternoon? Let me know and I'll shuffle appointments around."

A great rush of fear surged up inside Hannah and she pressed her forehead against the cool metal of the car.

"Hannah?"

"I'm still here." Just. Barely.

"Can you come in?"

"Yes. I think so. I need to talk to my boss."

"Look, why don't you just come when you can. We'll work around you."

Hannah nodded, then realized Dr. Nelson couldn't see her. "Sure."

"Hang in there, okay?"

Hannah ended the call. She felt dizzy. Her stomach was tight; it was hard to breathe.

She had cancer. That was the only reason Dr. Nelson could possibly want her to come in so urgently.

She couldn't think. Her brain was resounding with the shock of it. Adrenaline was surging through her body, but there was nothing for her to fight or flee from. Whatever was attacking her was inside her body, inescapable, unavoidable.

After a few minutes she took a deep breath and forced herself to push away from the car. She concentrated on the short-term goal of getting to the doctor's. That was the most important thing right now.

Her boss took one look at her bloodless face and gave her

the afternoon off, no questions asked. She rode to the clinic and the receptionist notified Dr. Nelson the moment Hannah announced herself. Within five minutes she was sitting opposite her G.P.

"As you've probably guessed, your tests have come back positive. Hannah, you have what's classified as invasive ductal carcinoma. It's the most common form of breast cancer. Basically, it means the cancer started in one of your milk ducts and has spread into the surrounding breast tissue."

Hannah's hands were clamped to her knees, her knuckles white. "Am I going to die?"

"You're young, the lump is small, there are some excellent treatments for breast cancer. You have every chance of surviving," Dr. Nelson said.

Hannah stared at her. She'd been looking for a one-word response: no. She hadn't gotten it.

"I'm referring you to an excellent surgeon. He works at the Peter Mac Hospital in the city. He's very highly regarded."

Hannah tried to marshal her thoughts. There were things she ought to ask, but for the life of her she couldn't think of what they were.

"Hannah, is there someone I can call for you? Maybe someone who can come and give you a lift home?"

Joe's face filled her mind and her eyes flooded with tears. She blinked a few times, then straightened her shoulders. "I'll be fine. I just need to get my head together."

"Are you sure?"

"Yes."

By the time she left the doctor's office she had an appointment to see a surgeon on Monday of the following week. Dr. Nelson explained that they would want to operate quickly as breast cancer in younger women could sometimes be more aggressive than in older women.

"And we'll want to test you for the breast cancer gene. That might make a difference to your treatment. But Dr. Minton will go over all of that with you."

Hannah rode home, but instead of parking her bike and going inside to tell Joe and her mother and the rest of her world that she might be dying, she rode straight past.

She wasn't ready to go home yet.

She rode hard and fast down the highway until she hit the beach. Then she parked her bike and strode the length of the St. Kilda Pier. She stared out at the ocean and took in big gulps of fresh air, her hair tangling around her face in the breeze.

After a while she sat and leaned her back against one of the weathered wooden pylons. Tears leaked from the corners of her eyes as she watched the ever-moving blue of the ocean. A ship crawled slowly across the horizon. Seagulls flew overhead.

It's not fair. I'm too young. I just found Joe.

The three thoughts looped through her mind as she cycled from anger to despair to fear and back.

Her life had just started coming together. She had a future planned out, with Joe and Ben and Ruby at her side. This wasn't supposed to happen.

Finally her thoughts settled. She hugged her knees to her chest, willing herself to calm. She didn't have the luxury of wallowing in self-pity. She needed to get her shit together. She was about to take on the battle of her life.

And she was going to have to do it alone.

She choked on a sob as she consciously acknowledged her decision for the first time. She wasn't sure when she'd made it. When she decided not to tell Joe about the lump on that first day? When she lay in bed next to Ruby the other night? It didn't really matter. The fact remained that there was no way she could put Joe and his kids through the trauma of surgery and chemo and God knows what else. No. Way.

Joe had barely recovered from the loss of his wife. Ben was seeing a counselor to help him come to terms with his grief and guilt. And Ruby needed someone to make her feel safe, not a woman who may or may not be around to see her next birthday.

She couldn't do it to them. That was how much she loved Joe Lawson and his children.

She huffed out a humorless laugh. She was so freakin' noble it made her sick.

No matter how much she needed Joe or wanted Joe, no matter how much she wanted to be a part of his children's lives, she had to face the fact that she had now become a liability. Joe could not afford to have someone like her in his life. Certainly his kids couldn't. It simply wouldn't be fair to expect them to take this journey with her.

She pressed her knuckles into her eyes, willing the tears to stop. She had to stop crying. No matter how scared and sad and angry she was, throwing a pity party was not going to get her through this. She was going to have to be tough. She was going to have to stand her ground and then some.

She waited until the tears dried on her cheeks, going over and over what had to happen next in her mind. Finally she scrubbed her face with her hands and stood.

It was time to go do what had to be done.

CHAPTER THIRTEEN

JOE STEPPED FROM HIS CAR, the heat of a Melbourne summer's day hitting him like a wall after the air-conditioning in the SUV. He frowned when he saw the kids hadn't drawn the curtains to keep the afternoon sun out as he'd asked. Great. Now the living room would be like a sauna all night.

"Hey, Daddy," Ruby said when he entered the living room.

The kids were sprawled on the floor with Hannah playing cards, all of them stripped down to shorts and tank tops. He tried not to stare at Hannah's long, tanned legs. Maybe there were advantages to having a hot living room, after all.

"Hannah and Ben and I have been playing poker and Hannah says that cheating is wrong but I can't win otherwise," Ruby explained.

"She's right. Cheating is wrong," he said.

Ruby pouted.

"Told you," Ben said triumphantly. "You want to win, you got to play smarter, that's all."

Joe sensed an argument brewing and decided to head it off at the pass. He reached for the envelope in his back pocket.

"I have something I wanted to discuss with you guys," he said, his gaze taking in all of them.

Ben and Ruby stared up at him, their faces expectant. Hannah's face was lowered as she fiddled with her cards.

"Is this about Christmas?" Ruby asked.

"No, this is about Easter. How do you guys feel about a trip to Movie World and Sea World on the Gold Coast?" he asked.

He knew they'd been disappointed they weren't going away for Christmas, but the pub was too busy to leave at this time of year. The Easter trip was his way of making it up to them.

Judging by the shocked delight on their faces, he'd done all right.

"For real?" Ben asked, his face splitting into a big smile.

"Yeah, for real. Got the plane tickets right here. Four of them." He glanced at Hannah to check her reaction. There was a look on her face he couldn't quite define.

Ruby and Ben whooped with delight. He cocked his head in enquiry as he caught Hannah's eye. What was going on?

"Surprise," he said wryly, waiting for her to smile.

She didn't. Instead, she frowned, then lowered her head and fiddled with her cards some more.

Ben and Ruby were too busy enthusing over the holiday to notice. As they enumerated to each other the rides they'd go on and the sights they'd see, Joe sat on the couch and nudged Hannah gently with the toe of his shoe.

"Too much of a surprise, huh?" he asked lightly.

She glanced up at him, her expression unreadable. "The trip sounds great." But there was a definite lack of enthusiasm in her voice.

"I know it's not camping and it's not the hidden by-ways of the country you want to explore, but I thought it might be fun…."

"It's a nice idea," she said, still not meeting his eyes.

She straightened her cards into a neat little stack and returned them to the deck, making sure they were all lined up.

"You okay?" he asked.

She met his eyes briefly. "We need to talk."

There was something heavy in her words.

"Okay." He stood, gesturing for her to join him in the kitchen.

She shook her head. "Later. When the kids are in bed."

He stared at her for a long moment, then nodded. It was going to be one of those kinds of talks.

The next hour crawled by. He watched Hannah out of the corner of his eye, trying to get a read on her. She'd been a little withdrawn the past couple of days. And she'd canceled dinner with him and the kids the other night. He hadn't thought anything of it at the time, but now he wondered if he should have.

We'll work it out, whatever it is.

One of the things he loved about Hannah the most was that she was such a straight shooter. If there was something wrong, she'd let him know and they'd sort it out.

He sent the kids off to brush their teeth at eight-thirty. He tucked Ruby into bed and confiscated Ben's flashlight so he couldn't read under the covers. Then he returned to the living room.

Hannah sat on the couch, her elbows on her knees, hands gripped together. She was staring at a spot on the carpet, her mouth grim. She looked like a soldier about to go into battle.

Not a great sign.

He stopped inside the doorway and she looked up at him. They stared at each other for a long moment.

"What's going on?"

"I can't go to Queensland with you," she said.

"I know I should have checked with you first—"

"It's not about that."

She took a deep breath and he realized she was shaking.

Whatever was bothering her, she was really worked up about it. He crossed the room to sit beside her.

"Hannah." He started to slide his arm around her shoulders, but she caught his hand and held it in both of hers. Her fingers were cold, her grip tight.

"I got a call from my G.P. today. I had some tests this week…" She shook her head. "Man, this is hard." She whispered the words, almost as though she was talking to herself. Her chest lifted as she took a deep, long breath. Then she looked him in the eye.

"I have breast cancer. I'm scheduled to see a surgeon on Monday."

He stared at her, barely able to comprehend what she was saying. "What…?"

Cancer. *What the hell?*

"You're too young," he said.

"Apparently not."

She winced and he realized he was squeezing her hand so tightly his knuckles had turned white.

"Jesus, Hannah," he said. He didn't know what else to say so he obeyed the impulse of his heart and dragged her into his arms. She held on for dear life, her cheek pressed against his. He could feel the fear in her trembling through her body, and he held her even tighter, trying to marshal his thoughts.

Cancer. Hannah had cancer, and she was terrified.

That one thought helped him to push his own fear and dread and shock to one side.

"You'll be okay," he said.

She huffed out a breath that was almost a laugh. "Can I have that in writing?"

"You will. They can do amazing stuff these days. And you're young."

She turned her head to kiss his cheek then eased away

from his embrace. "That's what my doctor said. But there are no guarantees, Joe."

"But you've caught it early, right?" He'd never felt a lump or anything unusual in her breasts and he figured he'd made a pretty thorough study of them.

"Yes. I think so. But they won't know anything until they've operated and seen what they're dealing with."

"You're seeing the surgeon on Monday, is that what you said? I've got a meeting with the bank, but I'll shift it so I can come with you."

Her eyes filled with tears, and she blinked rapidly until they were gone. "That's really sweet of you."

He frowned. He didn't have to be a genius to hear the unspoken *but* in her tone.

"You don't want me to come with you?"

"It's not about what I want. I don't think it would be smart."

"What do you mean? If you're worried I'll hassle the doctor or ask stupid questions, I promise to sit there quietly. Whatever you need from me."

She brushed her fingers along his jaw, her touch gentle, her eyes sad. "You're such a good man."

There was something very final in her words. He stared at her, understanding slowly dawning.

"No." He shook his head.

"I don't think we should see each other anymore," she said, confirming his guess.

"Hannah…"

She held up a hand. "Hear me out. You're a good man, so your first impulse is to stand by me. And I appreciate that, I really do. But you didn't sign on for this. I'm going to get sick, Joe. Chemo, radiation therapy… I'm probably going to lose my hair and I'm almost certainly going to lose my breast."

"I don't give a shit about any of that stuff."

"I know. But I do, and I refuse to put you through it."

"Isn't that my decision to make?"

"And what about Ruby and Ben?" she asked. "Is it their decision, too? I might die, Joe. You really want to put your kids through that?"

He flinched. "That's not going to happen."

"I appreciate the vote of confidence, but no one knows that. And I will not be the person who brings more sadness into your children's lives."

He stared at her. He couldn't believe they were even having this conversation. Just this morning he'd bought tickets for the four of them to holiday in Queensland together; now Hannah was telling him she might be dying.

"No," he said again, shaking his head.

"Once you've thought about it you'll realize I'm right. Your kids need certainty and safety and love. They don't need to watch me fight for my life, and neither do you. And it's in my power to make sure you don't have to, and that's what I'm going to do."

She stood. He stared at her.

"Where are you going?"

"Home."

"Like hell. We haven't even begun to discuss this," he said, shooting to his feet.

"How long have we known each other, Joe? A few months? Not long enough for you to have to come on this journey with me. Not nearly long enough. If we end things now, we can all walk away and get on with our lives."

"That's bullshit, Hannah, and you know it. You can't define what we have in terms of weeks and days."

"I'm being smart. This is the best thing for your kids, Joe." She turned away.

He grabbed her arm. "I get a say in this, too."

"No, you don't. This is my fight, and it's my decision. And I choose not to do this to any of us." There was absolute steel in her voice and her face. Then her expression softened and she covered his hand where it still lay on her arm. She lifted it free, turning it so his palm was up. She pressed a kiss into the center of his hand.

"For what it's worth, it's been amazing. A gift. Thanks for sharing your family with me."

He was about to demand that she stay when the low sound of Ruby's voice floated up the hallway.

"Daddy? Daddy, I had a nightmare."

Hannah gestured toward the hallway. "You'd better go to her. She needs you."

Before he could say another word, Hannah was gone, the front door clicking closed behind her. He stared at the spot where she'd stood for long seconds, a thousand thoughts and feelings churning inside him.

Hannah had cancer. And she'd just cut him loose.

"Daddy?"

He stirred himself. "I'm coming, sweetheart."

He went to Ruby's room. She was huddled in bed, her favorite bear clutched to her chest.

"What's going on?" he asked, struggling to keep his tone light.

"I had a bad dream."

"Ah. Too much cheese."

It was his standard response to nightmares and she smiled. "I knew you were going to say that, Daddy."

"Did you? When did I get so predictable?"

He talked to Ruby for a few minutes, soothing her back to drowsiness. All the while his mind was on Hannah.

Finally he left Ruby and walked to the living room and simply stood there, staring at nothing.

Hannah had cancer.

For the first time he allowed himself to feel the full impact of the news. Fear and grief twisted through him. He lowered his head, closing his eyes against the ugly enormity of it.

They'd just gotten their shit together. Ben was finally talking and laughing again. They'd started building the foundations for a new family, a new way of living. They'd barely started to enjoy one another.

He was gripped with a sudden rush of rage, so powerful he wanted to slam his fist into the wall.

She deserved better. After what her sister did to her, Hannah deserved happiness. Hell, so did he. He'd buried his wife, his kids had buried their mother. Didn't they all deserve a freaking break?

Without stopping to think, he strode out of the house. He stopped only when he'd arrived at her front door. He hammered a fist against the door, anger and fear driving him. He waited a few heartbeats, then knocked again, every muscle tense.

He had no idea what he was going to say, but their conversation wasn't over, not by a long shot. No way was she making this decision for both of them.

He was raising his hand to knock a third time when the door opened. Robyn stood there, her face very pale.

"Joe," she said.

"I need to see her."

Robyn shook her head. "I'm sorry, but she doesn't want to see you."

"I don't care. There are some things she needs to hear."

He stepped forward but Robyn didn't budge.

"I need to see her," he said again.

"You're shocked and upset."

"No shit."

Robyn eyed him steadily. "Have you ever dealt with a very sick person before, Joe? I have. My mother died from bowel cancer. Took her nearly two years to fade away to nothing."

"I'm sorry, that must have been tough. But that's not going to happen to Hannah."

"I hope not. God, I hope not. But it might. And even if it doesn't, things are going to get pretty scary. She's going to be up and down, weak and strong, high and low."

"I don't care."

Robyn nodded. "Good. Now come back tomorrow and say the same thing."

He swore under his breath. "I want to talk to her now."

"She won't talk to you. She wants to protect you."

"That's my freaking decision, not hers."

Robyn's gaze was searching. "What about your children?"

"They love her."

"And what if they lose her?"

"Hannah is not going to die."

"There aren't many times in a parent's life when you get the chance to stop your children from experiencing pain." Robyn's face was grave, her voice quiet. "Mostly it happens and you have to watch and wish you could take it away or feel it for them. But Hannah's giving you the choice, Joe. She's thought long and hard about this, and she's doing what she thinks is the right thing for your kids. The least you can do is offer her the same consideration before you make your decision."

He closed his eyes and swore again.

His gut reaction to Hannah's news was to want to wrap her in his arms and tell her the world was going to be right and move mountains to make it so. But Robyn was right—

there were no guarantees, and he had more than himself to think about.

He had children. He was their sole guide in life, their everything. No matter what he wanted to do, what his gut was telling him, he had to put his children first.

He leveled a finger at Hannah's mother. "I'll be back tomorrow."

"Good."

She closed the door between them. Joe stared at it for a few seconds before turning on his heel. Head down, he made the short walk to his house. He went straight to the cupboard in the living room where he kept his stash of whiskey and poured himself a glass. Then he took the bottle with him and went through to the kitchen. He sat down at the table, the bottle on one side, the glass on the other.

He took a mouthful of whisky and thought about Hannah. Her laugh. Her stubbornness and spirit. The way she pressed against him when he kissed her. The way she watched him sometimes when she thought he wasn't looking. How honest she was. How bold, yet at the same time so very vulnerable. The way she touched his children, the tenderness in her eyes.

He took another mouthful and thought about Ben. The guilt and grief that had come out in counseling. The heavy weight his son had been carrying. The sadness that was still inside him.

Then he thought about Ruby, with her infinite trust and craving for connection. She'd forged a bond with Hannah right from the start. How was this going to hit her? How would she cope with knowing that someone else she loved might leave her?

The glass was empty. He reached for the bottle and poured.

And then he thought about Hannah. And he thought about Ben. And he thought about Ruby.

HANNAH SNIFFED LOUDLY. Her mother passed her another handful of tissues, her third since Joe had marched away from their front door.

"This is the right thing," she said for the tenth time.

As always, her mother remained silent. Hannah blew her nose.

"He sounded angry. I knew he'd be angry, but once he thinks about it he'll know I'm right," Hannah said.

Her mother shifted on the bed beside her. "He was very angry. Scared, too, I think."

"Once he calms down and goes over it all in his head, he'll realize I'm right. This is the best thing for everybody," Hannah said.

"Is it the best thing for you?"

"I want them to be happy."

"And what if being with you makes them happy?"

"For how long?"

Her mother had no answer to that. Hannah took her hand and gave it a squeeze.

"Thank you for answering the door. I appreciate it."

"He said he'd be back tomorrow."

"Fine. I'll tell him the same thing."

"He loves you."

Hannah stared at the scrunched tissues in her lap. "He'll get over it. There are plenty of women out there who would jump at the chance to be with a great guy like him." She could barely get the words out. The mere thought of Joe with another woman made her want to punch something. So much for her self-sacrificing streak.

"You always were stubborn. It's what's going to get you

through this, you know. Nobody this stubborn dies from cancer."

"I hope you're right. Bloody hell, I hope you're right," Hannah said. She took a deep breath. "Mom, I'm so scared."

Her mom put her arms around her and pulled Hannah against her chest. She soothed a hand over Hannah's hair and pressed a kiss to her brow.

"Of course you're scared. Cancer is scary. But people beat it all the time, Hannah. And you're going to be one of them."

There was so much certainty, so much determination in her voice that Hannah couldn't help but take heart.

"If you say so."

"I do. Now, we need to make a list of questions we want to ask the surgeon on Monday. All the magazines say you have to be your own medical advocate when you have a serious illness. You have to be informed."

Her mother let Hannah go and started searching in Hannah's bedside table for a pad and pen. Hannah watched her for a moment, touched by her stern earnestness.

"Thank you, Mom."

Her mother looked up, surprised. "What for?"

"Not falling apart."

In truth, Hannah had expected her mother to crumble when she heard the news, but she'd simply stared at Hannah for a long moment before reaching out and taking both her hands. *You'll beat this* had been her first words, something Hannah would be eternally grateful for.

"Oh, there's plenty of time to fall apart later, sweetheart. Right now we've got a fight on our hands."

They talked until the small hours, until they'd both run out of things to say. Finally Hannah let her mother tuck her into bed.

She rolled onto her side and stared into the darkness. She had no tears left, nothing but emptiness. Tomorrow she would wake up and face the first day of her new reality.

SHE'D EXPECTED to toss and turn, but she slept like a log. The events of the past forty-eight hours had left her so drained, so exhausted, she didn't even have the energy for dreams. She woke feeling puffy-eyed and heavy. A flutter of dread raced through her as memory descended.

She had cancer. And Joe and his children were no longer a part of her life.

She stared at the wall and took a deep breath. If ever there was a day to stay in bed and hide from the world, it was today. She flung back the covers. Hiding from the world wasn't going to get her anywhere, and she had things to do, plans to make.

She thought about Ben and Ruby as she showered. She'd do her best to hide her illness from them, but it was inevitable that they would find out. They lived next door, after all. But hopefully by then Hannah would have had the time to create some distance between them. She'd tell Ruby she was too busy at work to finish their latest restoration project, a '56 Harley they'd bought from the scrap yard. That would keep any contact to a minimum. No more visits to The Watering Hole. No more watching the kids while Joe worked late or taking Ben to cricket practice. The kids would think she and Joe had simply broken up. They'd be hurt for a while, but a little hurt now was preferable to a lot of hurt later.

And Joe... Joe would move on, too. He might be angry with her for a while, and sad, but she knew he would eventually understand she'd done the best thing for him and his children.

She'd never thought she could love anyone so much that

she would be able to let them go when everything in her screamed for her to cling fast. But she wasn't free to love them. She had nothing to offer. It was as simple and as painful as that.

She looked in the mirror as she dried off after her shower, her gaze dropping to her breasts. Slowly she cupped them in her hands, feeling the weight of them, the shape of them, trying to imagine what it would be like to have a scar instead of rounded flesh, to be lopsided and bare.

It was impossible, but she figured the reality would come soon enough. She let her hands drop. If she was ever in a position to be worried about her vanity again, she figured she'd be one of the luckiest women in the world.

She dressed in jeans and a T-shirt and wandered out to the kitchen. Her mother was busy juicing oranges.

"Lots of fresh fruit from now on," she said. "There's a cookbook I've seen, too, about positive eating."

"That sounds good," Hannah said.

"How are you feeling?"

Hannah shrugged. "Like it's the calm before the storm."

"I can imagine."

There was a knock at the door. Hannah glanced at her mother.

"Would you mind? In case it's Joe."

"It probably is. He said he'd be back this morning."

Her mother simply looked at her. Hannah sighed. She'd always known it would take more than one conversation to convince a man as loyal and loving as Joe to protect himself.

"Okay, I'll get it," she said.

She took a deep breath, then went to open the door.

She retreated a step when she saw he wasn't alone. He was standing hand in hand with his children, Ben on his left, Ruby on his right. Ruby's eyes were puffy from tears and

Ben looked as though he'd been crying, too. Joe held her gaze steadily when she looked at him.

"I've come to give you our answer," he said. He was pale but his gaze was very direct.

"I didn't ask you for one."

"That was your first mistake."

"Joe, don't," she said. "Please. This isn't fair."

"I don't care," he said. There was a hardness to his face, a fierceness that she'd never seen there before.

"The kids and I have been talking. I told them your news," he said. Ruby sniffed and wiped her nose with the back of her hand. Hannah looked at her small, pinched face, her heart aching.

"You shouldn't have."

"They deserve to know. They love you."

Ben's eyes didn't waver from her face. Despite the fact that she'd cried buckets last night, she felt tears welling again.

"Joe, please—"

"The least you can do is hear them out," he said.

Ruby stepped forward.

Oh, God.

She couldn't believe he was putting her through this. Didn't he understand she was walking away because she loved him?

"I haven't said it to you before because I was too shy, but I want you to know that I love you," Ruby said. "And I want you to get better and I'll do whatever I can to help you. Keep my room clean and help with the cooking and go to bed on time without being asked. Anything you need."

Hannah blinked rapidly. This was too much. She glared at Joe but he stared back at her, implacable.

It was Ben's turn. He took a step forward, his hands clutched together in front of him.

"I know I was mean at the start, but I think you're ace and I really want you to come to Queensland with us because it would be cool to go on the big waterslides with you," he said, his speech so rapid the words almost ran together. He stepped back by his father's side.

She cleared her throat and opened her mouth to speak.

"Wait," Ben said suddenly. "I didn't finish properly." He blushed deeply. "I love you, too. And I don't care if you're sick."

He ducked his head bashfully. Hannah closed her eyes, but the tears spilled out anyway. She heard Joe murmur something, and when she opened her eyes again it was just him standing there. She stared at him, her chest aching with sadness.

"It doesn't change anything," she said.

"Don't you get it, Hannah? You think you can protect us but it's too late. We already love you. We're committed. You're a part of our family now, and family doesn't walk away when the going gets tough."

"I don't want to hurt you," she said, her voice barely a whisper. "Can't you understand that?"

Joe closed the distance between them. He wiped away her tears with his thumbs.

"I know, and it's one of the many reasons I love you. But you're not doing this without us, Hannah. No way. That's our choice, and we've made it freely, and we'll camp out on your doorstep if that's what it takes to make you see sense."

To her utter astonishment, Joe dropped down to one knee.

"But I'm kind of hoping it won't come to that," he said.

"No," she said, trying to pull him back to his feet. "You don't have to do this."

"I think I do. I don't want you getting any stupid ideas like this again."

He reached out and took one of her cold, trembling hands in his.

"Hannah Louise Napier, will you marry me?"

"You know my middle name," she said stupidly.

"Yes. I know a lot more than that, too. I know I love you, even though I never thought I'd feel this way or even want to feel this way again. I know I want to fight over the remote control with you and make pizzas with you and ride that Thunderbird of yours one day. I know I want to make love to you and wake up with you in my bed each and every day. I know I want to stand by your side while you fight this battle so we can grow old together."

"What if I lose?"

He didn't break eye contact for a second. "Then I'll be with you till the end. I'll take whatever chance I can get, Hannah. If the past two years have taught me anything, it's that happiness and love are too bloody precious to walk away from, no matter how fleeting they might be."

She stared into his face, taking in the clearness of his blue gaze, the proudness of his nose, the strength of his jaw.

"I love you," she said.

"I know. Say yes."

"It's crazy. We should wait until we know more."

"Until when? I love you now. I want you to be my wife now."

He was too strong. Too sure. Too compelling. And it was too close to what her heart craved. "God, I can't believe I'm even considering this."

"Is that a yes?"

"Joe…"

"Just say yes."

The word seemed to form itself on her lips all on its own. "Yes."

Joe leaned forward from his kneeling position and wrapped his arms around her waist, his head coming to rest against her belly.

"Don't ever do that to me again," he said fiercely.

She couldn't believe how brave he was, how determined. And how brave his kids were, how generous. She remembered the way they'd stepped up and said their piece and her heart swelled in her chest.

After a long moment Joe pushed himself to his feet.

"Let's go tell the kids you've come to your senses. Then we need to go buy you a ring. Ruby offered her Barbie ring, but I figured you might like to choose your own."

"You told the kids you were going to propose to me?"

"Of course. It's their family, too, you know. They have minds of their own, in case you hadn't noticed."

"I noticed."

"Thought you might have."

He slid his hand along her jaw and into her hair. "I love you, Hannah. We're going to get through this."

"I hope so."

He kissed her. "I know so."

Then he led her out into the street to find the children.

EPILOGUE

Two years later, Hannah hovered in the wings with Ruby as she waited for their cue to hit the catwalk. This was their third appearance in the annual mother-daughter fashion parade fundraiser. Last year, Ruby had insisted on shaving her hair because Hannah's chemo had left her with nothing but baby fuzz. They'd worn matching punk outfits and received a prize for being best dressed. This year they'd opted for a more conservative look, both sporting shoulder-length haircuts and strappy floral dresses.

Hannah had been lucky. The surgeon had recommended a lumpectomy to treat her tumor and performed a partial reconstruction at the same time. She had scars, and the radiation therapy had left her breast tissue sore and red for months, but she still had a breast.

The chemo had been harder in many ways, sapping her energy, sending her lurching to the bathroom morning, noon and night, making her hair fall out in handfuls. But she'd gotten through it.

Joe had rubbed her back and bought her scarves and hats to keep her head warm through winter. Ruby and Ben had played board games with her and educated her in the ways of *Spore* and *The Sims*. Her mother had come up with a million different ways to tempt her with food, even when she had next to no appetite at all. Joe's mother had made sure the house ran smoothly so Hannah and Joe could concentrate their energies where they were needed. And her sister had taken her for regular massages and brought her new niece to visit.

They'd started talking soon after Hannah's surgery, in time for her sister to attend her wedding. Hannah had decided that if she was only going to be around for a short time, she wanted her days to be as positive and full of happiness as possible. That meant forgiving and moving on and being a part of the new life her sister had brought into the world.

But it was looking more and more likely that she was going to be around for a long time. She'd seen her doctor for her regular six-month follow-up last week. Her scans were clear and she was officially in remission. She'd been tested and did not carry the breast cancer gene, which was another point in her favor.

If her luck held, she would pass the five-year mark and be officially classed as a survivor.

She was going to get there. She knew it. She already felt like a survivor.

The music changed and the stage manager pointed at Hannah and Ruby. They smiled at each other and caught each other's hands. Heads high, they started down the catwalk, strutting their stuff.

She still got nervous before doing things like this. She still hated fussing over her hair and makeup and much preferred jeans to skirts and dresses. But she enjoyed the sheer fun of it so much more now, the being alive-ness of it. Especially when she looked into the audience at the end of the runway and saw Joe standing there, arms crossed over his chest, a small, satisfied smile on his face as he watched his wife and daughter.

Their gazes locked for a long moment and Hannah imagined how the evening might unfold, how they'd go home after the fundraiser and pore over the photographs Ben was taking and tease Ruby about her growing vanity. How Joe and Hannah might wait till the kids were in bed before having a glass of wine then turning in themselves. How Joe might undress her slowly and kiss each newly exposed swath of skin. How they'd make love with tenderness and patience, or passion and urgent need. And how they might then lie in each other's arms and make plans for the future.

She smiled, and Joe smiled back, his face full of love and heat and more than a little lust.

Another good day together, with another to come tomorrow, and another after that.

It was all anyone could ask for.

* * * * *

*Celebrate 60 years of pure reading pleasure
with Harlequin®!
Just in time for the holidays,
Silhouette Special Edition® is proud to present
New York Times bestselling author
Kathleen Eagle's
ONE COWBOY, ONE CHRISTMAS*

Rodeo rider Zach Beaudry was a travelin' man—until
he broke down in middle-of-nowhere South Dakota
during a deep freeze. That's when an angel came to
his rescue….

"**D**on't die on me. Come on, Zel. You know how much I love you, girl. You're all I've got. Don't do this to me here. Not *now*."

But Zelda had quit on him, and Zach Beaudry had no one to blame but himself. He'd taken his sweet time hitting the road, and then miscalculated a shortcut. For all he knew he was a hundred miles from gas. But even if they were sitting next to a pump, the ten dollars he had in his pocket wouldn't get him out of South Dakota, which was not where he wanted to be right now. Not even his beloved pickup truck, Zelda, could get him much of anywhere on fumes. He was sitting out in the cold in the middle of nowhere. And getting colder.

He shifted the pickup into Neutral and pulled hard on the steering wheel, using the downhill slope to get her off the blacktop and into the roadside grass, where she shuddered to a standstill. He stroked the padded dash. "You'll be safe here."

But Zach would not. It was getting dark, and it was already too damn cold for his cowboy ass. Zach's battered body was a barometer, and he was feeling South Dakota, big time. He'd have given his right arm to be climbing into a hotel hot tub instead of a brutal blast of north wind. The right was his free arm anyway. Damn thing had lost altitude, touched some part of the bull and caused him a scoreless ride last time out.

It wasn't scoring him a ride this night, either. A carload of teenagers whizzed by, topping off the insult by laying on the horn as they passed him. It was at least twenty minutes before another vehicle came along. He stepped out and waved both arms this time, damn near getting himself killed. Whatever happened to *do unto others?* In places like this, decent people didn't leave each other stranded in the cold.

His face was feeling stiff, and he figured he'd better start walking before his toes went numb. He struck out for a distant yard light, the only sign of human habitation in sight. He couldn't tell how distant, but he knew he'd be hurting by the time he got there, and he was counting on some kindly old man to be answering the door. No shame among the lame.

It wasn't like Zach was fresh off the operating table—it had been a few months since his last round of repairs—but he hadn't given himself enough time. He'd lopped a couple of weeks off the near end of the doc's estimated recovery time, rigged up a brace, done some heavy-duty taping and climbed onto another bull. Hung in there for five seconds— four seconds past feeling the pop in his hip and three seconds short of the buzzer.

He could still feel the pain shooting down his leg with every step. Only this time he had to pick the damn thing up, swing it forward and drop it down again on his own.

Pride be damned, he just hoped *somebody* would be answering the door at the end of the road. The light in the front window was a good sign.

The four steps to the covered porch might as well have been four hundred, and he was looking to climb them with a lead weight chained to his left leg. His eyes were just as screwed up as his hip. Big black spots danced around with tiny red flashers, and he couldn't tell what was real and what wasn't. He stumbled over some shrubbery, steadied himself on the porch railing and peered between vertical slats.

There in the front window stood a spruce tree with a silver star affixed to the top. Zach was pretty sure the red sparks were all in his head, but the white lights twinkling by the hundreds throughout the huge tree, those were real. He wasn't too sure about the woman hanging the shiny balls. Most of her hair was caught up on her head and fastened in a curly clump, but the light captured by the escaped bits crowned her with a golden halo. Her face was a soft shadow, her body a willowy silhouette beneath a long white gown. If this was where the mind ran off to when cold started shutting down the rest of the body, then Zach's final worldly thought was, *This ain't such a bad way to go.*

If she would just turn to the window, he could die looking into the eyes of a Christmas angel.

* * * * *

Could this woman from Zach's past get the lonesome cowboy to come in from the cold...for good?
Look for
ONE COWBOY, ONE CHRISTMAS
by Kathleen Eagle
Available December 2009 from
Silhouette Special Edition®

SPECIAL EDITION

**FROM *NEW YORK TIMES* AND *USA TODAY*
BESTSELLING AUTHOR**

KATHLEEN EAGLE

ONE COWBOY,
One Christmas

When bull rider Zach Beaudry appeared
out of thin air on Ann Drexler's ranch,
she thought she was seeing a ghost of
Christmas past. And though Zach had
no memory of their night of passion years
ago, they were about to share a future
he would never forget.

*Available December 2009
wherever books are sold.*

SSE65493

Visit Silhouette Books at www.eHarlequin.com

REQUEST YOUR FREE BOOKS!

2 FREE NOVELS PLUS 2 FREE GIFTS!

HARLEQUIN®

Super Romance®

Exciting, emotional, unexpected!

YES! Please send me 2 FREE Harlequin® Superromance® novels and my 2 FREE gifts (gifts are worth about $10). After receiving them, if I don't wish to receive any more books, I can return the shipping statement marked "cancel." If I don't cancel, I will receive 6 brand-new novels every month and be billed just $4.69 per book in the U.S. or $5.24 per book in Canada. That's a savings of close to 15% off the cover price! It's quite a bargain! Shipping and handling is just 50¢ per book*. I understand that accepting the 2 free books and gifts places me under no obligation to buy anything. I can always return a shipment and cancel at any time. Even if I never buy another book from Harlequin, the two free books and gifts are mine to keep forever.

135 HDN EYLG   336 HDN EYLS

Name	(PLEASE PRINT)	

Address		Apt. #

City	State/Prov.	Zip/Postal Code

Signature (if under 18, a parent or guardian must sign)

Mail to the Harlequin Reader Service:
IN U.S.A.: P.O. Box 1867, Buffalo, NY 14240-1867
IN CANADA: P.O. Box 609, Fort Erie, Ontario L2A 5X3

Not valid to current subscribers of Harlequin Superromance books.

**Are you a current subscriber of Harlequin Superromance books
and want to receive the larger-print edition?
Call 1-800-873-8635 today!**

* Terms and prices subject to change without notice. Prices do not include applicable taxes. Sales tax applicable in N.Y. Canadian residents will be charged applicable provincial taxes and GST. Offer not valid in Quebec. This offer is limited to one order per household. All orders subject to approval. Credit or debit balances in a customer's account(s) may be offset by any other outstanding balance owed by or to the customer. Please allow 4 to 6 weeks for delivery. Offer available while quantities last.

Your Privacy: Harlequin is committed to protecting your privacy. Our Privacy Policy is available online at www.eHarlequin.com or upon request from the Reader Service. From time to time we make our lists of customers available to reputable third parties who may have a product or service of interest to you. If you would prefer we not share your name and address, please check here. ☐

HSR09R

COMING NEXT MONTH

Available December 8, 2009

#1602 A MOTHER'S SECRET • Janice Kay Johnson
The Diamond Legacy
Bad enough that Daniel Kane's mother harbored a secret about his heritage. Now
Rebecca Ballard is doing the same thing! Forget her—Daniel's son is going to know
his father. But it's a hell of a time to realize he still cares for Rebecca....

#1603 PLAN B: BOYFRIEND • Ellen Hartman
Hometown U.S.A.
Sarah Finley has always done what's expected of her and her ruddy husband leaves
anyway! God help Charlie McNulty, the only guy in her ex's firm brave enough to
help when she loses it...and pins her sights on him.

#1604 BABY UNDER THE MISTLETOE • Jamie Sobrato
A Little Secret
All eco-friendly Soleil Freeman and military guy West Morgan have in common
is that fling they had...until she discovers she's pregnant. Now these two—who
couldn't be more different—have to find a way to raise a child...together.

#1605 A SMALL-TOWN REUNION • Terry McLaughlin
Built to Last
Devlin Chandler is here to make peace with his past. And that brings him to Addie
Sutton. Though they'd once missed acting on their connection, now neither will let
that moment slip away. But when secrets are revealed, can Addie and Dev make it
last?

#1606 THEN COMES BABY • Helen Brenna
An Island to Remember
Jamis Quinn wants to be left alone. Then Natalie Steeger moves in next door, and
he's drawn to the vivacious woman. When she becomes pregnant, Jamis is forced to
face the
world again. But he's not sure he's up to it....

#1607 THE CHRISTMAS PRESENT • Tracy Wolff
Uptown lawyer Vivian Wentworth is not the defense attorney Rafael Cardoza wants
for his wrongfully accused client. But her dedication to justice surprises Rafael...
almost as much as his attraction to her.